"I do not recall invi

Her eyebrows lifted. "Do I look as if I have been invited?"

His bold blue eyes, which passed over her, convinced her he was aware of the heated flush that suddenly warmed her body beneath the folds of her dress. His gaze flicked over her, a slight smile twitched the corners of his mouth and a wicked light shone in his eyes, as though her arrival was an amusing diversion. He shook his head. "Not in the slightest."

"I always was impetuous," she retorted, holding his gaze.

"My footman informs me you have come on an urgent matter. What is it that brings you into the camp of the enemy with such urgency, Miss Deighton?"

"I have come here on a matter of great importance. As a matter of fact it cannot wait. Time is of the essence." There was not even the faintest tremor in her voice. She willed her heart to stop pounding, willed the waves of panic to recede. She could sense that he was wary, that his guard had dropped just a little, but his steady gaze told her he was not going to make this easy for her.

"I am intrigued. Of what help could I possibly be to you?"

Author Note

This book is set in Northumberland and London against the backdrop of the 1715 Jacobite rising. Poor leadership and lack of strategic direction led to the failure of Jacobite risings. *Enthralled by Her Enemy's Kiss* depicts the 1715 rising, which ended in failure, but it was not the end. This came in 1745 with the Battle of Culloden—known as the Forty-five Rebellion.

But the Battle of Culloden is a long time in the future for Francis and Jane, who belong to two families torn apart by tragedy. When Francis's brother and Jane's sister elope, Francis and Jane join forces. Beset with emotional conflicts, it's a rocky road they travel to bring their troublesome siblings home.

HELEN DICKSON

Enthralled by Her Enemy's Kiss

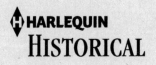

HARLEQUIN®
HISTORICAL™

Recycling programs
for this product may
not exist in your area.

ISBN-13: 978-1-335-40729-0

Enthralled by Her Enemy's Kiss

Copyright © 2021 by Helen Dickson

This edition published by arrangement with Harlequin Books S.A.

For questions and comments about the quality of this book,
please contact us at CustomerService@Harlequin.com.

Harlequin Enterprises ULC
22 Adelaide St. West, 40th Floor
Toronto, Ontario M5H 4E3, Canada
www.Harlequin.com

Printed in U.S.A.

Helen Dickson was born and still lives in South Yorkshire, UK, with her retired farm manager husband. Having moved out of the busy farmhouse where she raised their two sons, she now has more time to indulge in her favorite pastimes. She enjoys being outdoors, traveling, reading and music. An incurable romantic, she writes for pleasure. It was a love of history that drove her to writing historical fiction.

Books by Helen Dickson

Harlequin Historical

When Marrying a Duke...
The Devil Claims a Wife
The Master of Stonegrave Hall
Mishap Marriage
A Traitor's Touch
Caught in Scandal's Storm
Lucy Lane and the Lieutenant
Lord Lansbury's Christmas Wedding
Royalist on the Run
The Foundling Bride
Carrying the Gentleman's Secret
A Vow for an Heiress
The Governess's Scandalous Marriage
Reunited at the King's Court
Wedded for His Secret Child
Resisting Her Enemy Lord
A Viscount to Save Her Reputation
Enthralled by Her Enemy's Kiss

Castonbury Park

The Housemaid's Scandalous Secret

Visit the Author Profile page
at Harlequin.com for more titles.

Chapter One

1715

Having travelled from the market at Corbridge accompanied by Sam Cooper, an old family retainer, Jane was relieved to arrive at her home, Beckwith Manor, nestling among the Northumberland hills. An old Tudor manor house, it had seen better days. It was where Jane and her sister had lived in the happy chaos of their home before their mother died.

To the visitor it looked cold, strong and commanding rather than mellow and welcoming. There were gables over the Tudor windows with diamond-shaped panes cut through thick stone walls, which lit the parlour and the great chamber on the first floor. Though it was not a house to be considered grand, it had enormous charm. Jane looked at it, loving every stone of it, her eyes dwelling on the creepers growing in profusion up the house's walls, badly in need of trimming, but nevertheless she thought the house quite beautiful in its neglect. A majestic oak tree stood a little away from the house, its lofty branches reaching and spreading shade over the cobbled courtyard.

Hopefully Bessie would have a hot meal waiting and afterwards she would take a nice long bath in front of the fire in her room. Leaving Sam to unload the goods from the cart, she was crossing the yard when the door was flung open and a flustered and distraught Bessie appeared from the house.

'Oh, my dear Jane! Here you are at last.'

Concerned, Jane hurried towards her, anxiously studying the worried lines on her face. Bessie had been with the family for more years than Jane could remember. She managed the house to the best of her ability, with the minimum of daily help employed from the neighbourhood.

'Why, Bessie, what on earth is the matter? Is something wrong? Is it Lady? Has she foaled?' Lady was one of the heavy plough horses due to foal at any time.

'No, but it won't be long. Something quite dreadful has occurred,' Bessie said, clutching the front of her apron to her ample bosom as she led the way back into the house. 'It concerns your sister. How am I ever going to tell you?'

'Well, we will start by closing the door and calming down. Come, Bessie,' Jane said, taking her arm. Not until they were in the huge kitchen did she face Bessie, who was housekeeper, cook and anything else when required. When Bessie's ample body was seated, she asked, 'Now, what has happened that is so terrible? It is to do with Miriam, you said.' She sighed, going to the fire and placing the kettle on the hob. 'That girl will be the death of me, Bessie. What has she done?'

'It's dreadful,' Bessie said, clutching at the collar at her throat. 'She—she's gone off—run away with that young man from Redmires—Lord Randolph's brother.'

Jane became still. She waited a moment for what Bessie said to sink in and she could only stand there, staring at her in horror and disbelief. There must be some mistake. Miriam, her beautiful sister, would not have left without telling her. Dear God, she could not bear to lose her. She could not face a world without her sister's special blend of gentleness and loving and wisdom that calmed her own wild and impulsive nature. She sank down into a chair at the table, her colour gone, her eyes haunted. 'Run away? She wouldn't do that, Bessie—and with Andrew Randolph of all people. She is staying with Aunt Emily.'

'Yes, she was. But not any longer.'

At first Jane couldn't form a coherent thought. Not until she looked at Bessie's worried face beneath her lace cap did she recollect her scattered wits.

'She has—sent a note saying she was eloping.' Picking up what looked to be a paper with some scribbled writing on it from the table, she handed it to Jane. 'It says so there. You read it.'

Jane took it from her. Having to rely so much on Bessie over the years, she had taught her the basics of reading and writing, which had proved to be a great help to her when dealing with tradespeople. She read what was written in her sister's untidy handwriting, confirming what Bessie had told her.

'Dear God in heaven, Bessie, what on earth possessed her to do this? What a mess. I should have known something was in the air. Whenever she saw Andrew Randolph—whether it was in Corbridge or at some fête or other—I could see how they looked at one another, but I thought that was as far as it went. She knows how things stand between our families, of the hostility that still exists after all these years. I had no indication—I never suspected she would do something like this.'

'None of us did.'

'All this time they must have been seeing each other in secret and of late she has taken to visiting Aunt Emily more often. No doubt the two of them devised ways of meeting in Newcastle. Miriam writes that Aunt Emily knows nothing about it, that she thought she was returning home.'

'Yes, well, she didn't, did she?' Bessie grumbled.

Jane sighed. She would have to visit her aunt to confirm that Miriam had indeed left. Aunt Emily, her mother's widowed sister, had come to Beckwith Manor to take care of them when their mother had died. She was a woman of great sweetness and social grace and always behaved with a touching wistful modesty. With arthritic joints and suffering greatly, she had moved out of draughty old Beckwith Manor to reside in a comfortable, modest house closer to Newcastle and her friends when she was satisfied that Jane and Miriam no longer needed her. Miriam had been in her charge and she would doubtless feel responsible for her elopement. Jane had always been aware that there was a powerful will beneath Miriam's delicacy and gentleness. She was a girl who needed a strong hand to guide her, but with care.

'How could she do this, Bessie? Yes, I am shocked and disappointed. I cannot imagine what prompted her to behave so irresponsibly,' she said, trying to keep a stranglehold on her emotions. Beneath her initial anger she was deeply hurt that Miriam had done this without telling her, with no concern for how she would feel when she discovered her sister had eloped with Andrew Randolph, the son of the man their own father was accused of killing. 'How could she run off and without telling me?'

'I expect she knew how you would react—with all that unpleasant business between the Randolphs and the Deightons against them forming any kind of relationship.'

'Yes, Bessie, it's still there and it always will be.' She thought back to two days previous when she had bade her sister farewell. She had thought how happy Miriam looked, how carefree. There was a vague look in her eyes that told Jane her mind was on other things. So impatient was Jane to set about her chores that she had not paid any heed to it just then, but now she had reason to remember.

'That young man must have arranged everything. I am partly to blame.' She sighed, shaking her head despondently. 'I spend so much of my time trying to keep a roof over our heads that I failed to see what my foolish sister was up to.'

'None of us knew what was in her head when she went off to stay with your aunt. How were we to know?'

As the initial shock began to wear off, Jane's natural resilience returned and with it a fierce anger. 'I am determined that whatever it takes, Miriam must be found. She has to come home.'

'What is to be done?'

'Pursuit, Bessie. That is the only way. I must go and see Aunt Emily first thing in the morning. It's too late to travel now. I would never make it back before dark.'

Bessie shook her head. 'It's no good. She was seen getting into the post in Newcastle with the young gentleman.'

'The post? Then they must be heading for London. Oh, Bessie—how could she? And with Andrew Randolph of all people. I knew she was fond of him—flattered by the attention he showered on her whenever they met—accidentally, I always thought. Now I can see it wasn't like that. He sports a boyish expression that would turn any female heart. What seventeen-year-old would not be drawn to him? He is handsome and exciting—younger brother to Lord Francis Randolph, whose lineage is impeccable. Yes, he's the ideal man for her to become acquainted with—but he is not for her—his brother would never allow it.'

'No,' Bessie said, shaking her head. 'He wouldn't.

The Randolphs and the Deightons have been at log-gerheads for too long to allow a union of this kind.'

'You're right, of course. Since they were seen in the post together then that is all the confirmation I need. Who was it who saw them?'

'Sam's son—Michael. He arrived after you left for Corbridge. Sam asked him to be here in case the horse foaled while you were away. He was curious as to why Miriam would be in Newcastle taking the post at all.'

'I see. Then I won't go to Aunt Emily. She would work herself up into a state and it would do her no good. However, with Miriam's reputation at stake I have no choice but to go and see Lord Randolph at once. If I know where they intend going when they reach London, then I might find them before they do something foolish.' Standing up, she picked up the note and stuffed it into her pocket.

'But you can't go to Redmires alone—not after what happened.'

'That is in the past, Bessie. Besides, the way I see it, I have no choice.'

'But your father...'

'What happened hurt too many people,' Jane said, speaking more sharply than intended. 'The Randolphs are high-spirited and proud people. My father was re-sponsible for the death of Francis Randolph's father. There is no way that we can make amends. Francis Randolph is not the forgiving type.'

'Aye—proud as peacocks they are. Always high and mighty. What Miss Miriam was thinking to take up with the younger Randolph I don't know. But you can't go all the way to Redmires alone—not tonight.'

'I must. Please don't worry yourself, Bessie. I'll take Spike with me,' she said, glancing at the large hound stretched out in the doorway, looking at her with adoring, doleful eyes. 'With any luck the horse won't foal until I get back.'

Bessie got up and placed her hands upon Jane's slender young shoulders. 'When you see Lord Randolph, promise me you will watch that temper of yours. I know what you are like when roused.'

With Spike at her heels, Jane left the house to saddle her horse. She was soon riding in the direction of Redmires two miles to the north. The gentle hills were spangled with crimson and gold—the trees would soon be shedding their autumn foliage. She loved riding through the woods and over grassy spaces where fallow deer bounded. The cold waters of the beck, from which the house took its name, tumbled down in a wide sliver over the glistening rocks covered with thick green moss. It became a torrent after heavy rain. With her thoughts set on reaching Redmires, though, she took no notice of her surroundings. How she wished she had someone to share the many trials in her life.

Her mother had died when Jane was eight years old, leaving her two daughters in the care of their father. Edward Deighton, a staunch Catholic, possessed an unfailing adherence to the Jacobite cause. His brain and body had ceaselessly yearned for change since the Catholic King James II had been driven from the throne in eighty-eight and fled to France.

After his wife's death Edward became involved in a clandestine association with Lady Randolph of Redmires. Lord Randolph, upon learning of his wife's association with their neighbour, went after her when they were on one of their trysts, to bring her home. Tragically, the carriage in which he was travelling home, accompanied by Lady Randolph and Edward Deighton, left the road, killing Lord Randolph outright. Jane had never been told the details of what happened that night and it still remained shrouded in mystery. All she knew was that her father who, it was said, had been driving the carriage at the time, took full responsibility for Lord Randolph's death. The repercussions on both families had reverberated down the nine years since the tragedy and existed to this day.

The grief of losing his wife, followed by the loss of his lover and the part he had played in Lord Randolph's death, was too much for Edward to bear. He was beset by a desire to leave Northumberland, which held too many bitter memories, and concentrate on that other matter closest to his heart: to further the Jacobite cause and restore the Stuarts to the throne.

He had left for France, coming home on occasion to see his daughters, who were being cared for by his wife's sister, Emily, and to bring what money he could to sustain them. His neglect instilled in Jane a deep hurt, anger and resentment, but her entreaties for him to stay home fell on deaf ears. Where Beckwith

Manor was concerned, his fanaticism for the cause and the sale of land to support it had eroded his estate to the point where it barely existed.

Her errant father preferred the intrigues of the exiled Court of the Pretender at Saint-Germain in France, plotting to regain the thrones of England, Ireland and Scotland for the exiled Stuarts, to his own family. So, with the heavy responsibilities of the manor and her sister to take care of, urged by self-protective instincts, Jane saw little of life beyond Beckwith Manor. The result of her father's absence was that Jane had a sense of responsibility towards her home and her sister that was an intrinsic part of her. She suffered the miseries of their lowly state in the county's hierarchy, enduring the indignities, the slights and cruelties inflicted on them and other Catholic families in Northumberland. They commiserated with each other from time to time and, no matter how, deep down, Jane wished everything could have been different, she was never heard to complain.

Turning her thoughts to her mission and to Lord Francis Randolph, she recalled he was a striking-looking man with an enormous presence—a man Jane had met eighteen months ago.

They had gone to stay with Aunt Emily for a few days and, one lovely summer's day, they had travelled into nearby Newcastle to do some shopping and stroll by the river. Passing a chandler's, Jane remembered smelling the pleasant aroma of Jamaica rums, French and British brandies and cinnamon waters. They browsed the booksellers and a draper's with fancy silks and rich brocades. They purchased some trinkets before returning to the carriage. Seeing a shop selling delicious-looking sweetmeats, Jane hung back, sending Miriam and Aunt Emily on ahead, while she purchased some perfumed comfits and macaroons from the confectioner to eat on their way home.

She was passing a gateway that led into an inn yard when a horseman came clattering out over the cobblestones with such haste that, to avoid being trampled underfoot, Jane, with a cry, stepped back quickly, stumbling in the process and falling painfully to the ground, scattering her packages about her. Miriam, looking back and seeing what had happened, ran towards her in alarm.

Seeing the sudden movement out of the corner of his eye, the horseman pulled his mount to a halt and, turning in the saddle, looked back. Upon seeing Jane on the ground, he immediately dismounted and strode over to her.

Jane, feeling bruised and sore, looked up at the horseman looming over her and recognised him immediately as Lord Francis Randolph of Redmires.

Reaching out a strong brown hand, he seized her arm and helped her to her feet. Putting her weight on her left foot, she winced with pain.

'Are you hurt?' he demanded. 'I saw you trip.'

Jane stared at him incredulously, her eyes sparking with anger. 'Trip? I did not trip. Had I not thrown myself out of the way of your mount I would have

been trampled to death. You came riding out of the
inn yard as if the devil himself were after you.'

'If that is so, then I apologise. I did not see you
there.'

'Evidently,' she snapped, pulling her arm free from
his grasp and supporting herself with one hand on
the wall of the gateway while brushing away the dirt
on her skirts with the other. Gingerly she put a little
weight on her injured foot, almost crying out at the
pain that shot through it.

'Your ankle is hurt,' he said sternly. 'Here, let me
help you.'

'No—thank you, Lord Randolph,' she said quickly
as he reached out his hand, looking at Miriam who
was picking the dropped packages up off the ground.
At the mention of his name he paused and looked at
her closely, his jaw tightening.

'Good Lord!' he exclaimed, one well-defined eyebrow raised. 'If it isn't Miss Deighton.'

With his searing eyes on her, each aware of the
other's identity and what lay between them, the air
bristled with tension. Jane could see he was alert, his
consciousness as fine-honed as a sharp blade. The
black pinpoints of his eyes shot fire.

With an effort she said in the coldest and most con-
descending manner, 'That is my name. Now if you
don't mind I would appreciate it if you would stand
back and allow me to go on my way. I will manage
perfectly well with Miriam to help me. It is only a
sprain. I don't need your help.' She gave him a look
which told him she would rather die than accept his

aid, but her eyes were swimming with the silently repressed tears that the pain from her injured ankle was causing. It was evident that she would not make it to the carriage unaided. His eyes narrowed.

'I doubt that. Come—don't be difficult,' he said impatiently. 'I am in a hurry and enough time has been wasted as it is.'

Before Jane could stop him or protest, he had placed one arm firmly about her waist and the other beneath her knees, swinging her effortlessly up into his arms. Normally she would have kicked and fought at being handled in such a way, but she was too stunned at finding herself pressed so close to his chest. She could feel his warmth and the strength in his hard, lean body, which made her feel uncomfortable—and something else as well, which she could not identify.

Reaching the carriage, Lord Randolph placed her on the seat and without more ado and to Aunt Emily's horror, he shoved her skirts aside and removed her shoe, flexing her injured ankle with the professional expertise of a doctor. Jane could feel the firmness of his fingers through her stocking. As he twisted her foot to one side, she clenched the side of the carriage, almost crying out with the pain, but bit her lip in her determination not to let him know how much it hurt. At last he put her foot gently of the floor.

'You were right. There's nothing broken—just a slight sprain. When you get home get your maid to bind your ankle firmly and rest it. You'll be walking on it in a few days.'

'Why—*thank you*, Doctor,' she said with emphasis.

Ignoring her sarcastic tone Lord Randolph curled his lips into a wry smile. 'I'm not a doctor, which I am sure you are aware of, but I've had enough sprained ankles in my time and am used to dealing with such injuries when any of my horses take a tumble— although I have to say that none of my horses has quite so charming an ankle. I assure you, you will be all right—and I apologise if, because of my reckless-ness, I have ruined your visit to Newcastle.'

'Yes,' she retorted ungraciously, 'you have ruined it and it looks like I will be off my feet for days be-cause of it.'

'You are right to reproach me, Miss Deighton. If I could repair the damage, then believe me, I would.'

Jane fixed him with an unblinking gaze, but seeing that he did indeed look genuinely sorry, her manner melted towards him a little. When she next spoke her tone was kinder. 'Yes, I am sure you would. However, it was just an accident and I did not mean to reproach you quite so harshly. You said you were in a hurry. Please do not let me detain you any longer.'

He didn't. With a polite nod to Aunt Emily and Miriam, he went on his way.

Her encounter with Francis Randolph had re-mained with her since that day. In the past she had seen him from a distance and always avoided coming into contact with him. Meeting him had affected her in a way she could not have imagined. In the future she would do her best to avoid him, having no desire to come face to face with the man who held such heavy resentment for her because she was the daughter of Edward Deighton. She had seen him just once since that day. It had been in Corbridge when she was seated in the carriage, waiting for Miriam to emerge from a shop. He was in conversation with a group of gentlemen outside an official-looking building.

Seeing him again, she had been unprepared for the uncontrollable tremor that shot through her and she was unable to tear her eyes away. He seemed to radiate a compelling magnetism. Everything about him exuded a ruthless sensuality. He seemed to sense her watching him and had turned his head slowly. As their eyes met his dark brows had lifted in bland enquiry. Jane had caught her breath and, remembering how it had felt when he had raised her up and held her close to his hard chest, she felt heat scorch through her body before she hastily looked away, ashamed that he had made her treacherous heart race. She had not seen him after that and she was glad. He disconcerted her as no one else could. Yet, whenever she went into Corbridge, she kept watching for him. She couldn't seem to help it.

Forced to concentrate on the terrain as the tracks became more difficult, she breathed a sigh of relief when the house came into sight. Redmires, the ancestral home to the Randolphs for generations, was a beautiful house set in a wooded hamlet. The back of the house was loosely wedded to an old stone tower that had been built during Queen Elizabeth's reign, when noblemen, even in these remote areas of Northumberland, needed security and refuge for themselves and their animals at the time of the Border Raiders.

The Randolphs were a prosperous family. The mining of coal was anciently established in the area and belonged to a cabal of wealthy coal merchants, the Randolphs being one of them. The present Lord Randolph's father Jane remembered as being a disagreeable, forceful man—although she had only seen him from afar on occasion—and had not been well liked. His son continued in his father's ways. It was said he had a better head for business than his father and he had much smoother manners.

The house had been modernised by the late Lord Randolph. By all accounts the rooms were spacious and beautiful gardens had been laid out with fountains and statues, some brought from Italy, Jane had heard. Benefits came from this illustrious family to their tenants, too, with repairs to cottages and farmsteads in every hamlet. Tonight, grand carriages were lined up along the long gracious sweep of the drive. The tall, mullioned windows, thrusting out in square bays, were aglow with golden light. She realised, too late, Lord Randolph was entertaining. Not that it made any difference. Her mission was important and not to be put off for anything.

Dismounting, she handed the reins of her horse to a young boy, instructing Spike to stay. She had trained him so well that she knew he wouldn't move until she returned. The huge double doors stood wide open, giving her a glimpse inside the house. The sound of music could be heard—a harpsichord and a guitar. Guests were milling about, ladies in fantastic gowns and glittering jewels, gentlemen in frock coats and powdered wigs. She was suddenly reluctant to enter this place of merriment but then, angered by her own timidity, she climbed the low flight of steps and entered into a world she was not accustomed to. She felt as though she had been dropped into a beautiful jewelled box. The splendour all around her was impossible to absorb: the graceful curving staircase, the moulded ceiling.

This was worse than anything she had imagined— yet there was not time to lament about it now. She knew how unkempt she must look, with her hair all mussed up and her serviceable dark blue gown stained and creased from her day at the market.

A stony-faced footman attired in dark green livery approached her, staring at her uncertainly, his eyes taking in her attire.

'Can I be of assistance?'

'Yes. I am here to see Lord Randolph.'

'I'll see if he is free.'

She looked at him directly. 'I sincerely hope so. It is imperative that I speak to him at once.'

'Very well.' Indicating a room to one side of the doorway, he directed her to enter. 'Wait here. I'll go and find him.'

Jane stepped into the room, but she remained visible to the people in the hall. She stood on the gleaming parquet and waited, watching the brilliant, bejewelled people milling about. The air was filled with the mingled smells of perfume and hair pomade. From the depths of her envy and hopelessness she gazed at the elegant ladies as they rustled by in their fabulous gowns, then she straightened, raising her chin.

She must never forget that her own mother had been like them, a lady, a Protestant, though she was disowned by her family when she had married her Catholic father—by everyone, that was, but her beloved sister Emily, who had been devastated on her death and had shown nothing but loving kindness to Jane and Miriam. The memory came flooding back and the courage it gave her bolstered her for the meeting with Lord Randolph.

Glancing into the anteroom as they ambled past, the guests stared at her openly, exchanging wondering and puzzled glances, shrugs and raised eyebrows, but none approached. She could see shocked expressions on most faces and there were several gasps. It was too late now to efface herself—she must appear to them like a naive fool, who knew no better than to blunder into Redmires where Lord Randolph was entertaining his friends.

Born into the private establishment of privilege and exclusivity, Lord Francis Randolph had a formidable reputation with an authoritative air of breeding, command and an unconscious swagger of arrogance which spoke of generations of influence, superiority and advantage. Jane had no wish to meet him again any more than he would want to meet her. But the concern she felt for Miriam putting her in this impossible position had put her out of temper and she was in no mood to be charitable. The Randolphs had always ignored the Deightons, moved by the desire to remove all connection with a family of Papists.

Tall, virile, undeniably magnetic, Francis Randolph suddenly appeared. He was exactly as she remembered. He had an air about him that most women would find irresistible. His thick black hair drawn back to his nape gleamed in the light from the chandeliers and his eyes, even in the midst of so much darkness, were compelling and so dark a blue they might almost have been black. His nose was slightly crooked and his mouth much too wide, but these flaws only served to heighten his inordinate good looks, giving him a rakish air. He was lean, his muscular physique admirably shown off by a dark blue velvet suit cut to emphasise his broad shoulders and slender waist. His waistcoat was pearl-grey and his neckcloth of pristine white silk nestled beneath his chin.

A man like Francis Randolph would undoubtedly have a string of women, beautiful and expensive women. He had a temper, she had heard, and he wasn't at all pleased at having his evening of frivolous entertainment interrupted. He looked at her for a moment, as though debating whether or not to allow her an audience.

In that moment they both assessed the other's relative strengths and weaknesses. Those hard eyes took in every detail from her head to her toes with slow deliberation. She didn't know, now that she was here, what kind of reaction she had expected from him. She watched as his eyes hardened—the last thing she had expected was a welcome. Few people could withstand the blast of determination from Lord Randolph's eyes, but Jane did not flicker an eyelid.

'I beg your pardon for imposing myself on you like this. Thank you for seeing me, Lord Randolph. I am Jane Deighton…'

With narrowed eyes, alert and watchful, he looked into the stormy eyes of his uninvited visitor as if she were not entitled to his consideration. 'I am well aware of who you are, Miss Deighton. We have met— you remember the circumstances of our last meeting?'

'I do indeed.'

'And your recovery was quick, I trust, with no after-effects?'

'I was incapacitated for at least a week, but I got over it.'

His bold blue eyes which passed over her convinced her he was aware of the heated flush that suddenly heated her body beneath the folds of her dress. She quickly pulled herself together and raised her head in that determined way of hers, not in the slightest concerned with his arrogant, knowing smile.

'I do not recall inviting you here tonight.'

Her eyebrows lifted. 'Do I look as if I have been invited?'

His gaze flicked over her, a slight smile twitched the corners of his mouth and a wicked light shone in his eye, as though her arrival was an amusing diversion. He shook his head. 'Not in the slightest.'

'I always was impetuous,' she retorted, holding his gaze.

'My footman informs me you have come on an urgent matter. What is it that brings you into the camp of the enemy with such urgency, Miss Deighton?'

'I have come here on a matter of great importance. As a matter of fact, it cannot wait. Time is of the essence.' There was not even the faintest tremor in her voice. She willed her heart to stop pounding, willed the waves of panic to recede. She could sense that he was wary, that his guard had dropped just a little, but his steady gaze told her he was not going to make it easy for her.

'I am intrigued. Of what help could I possibly be to you?'

'I would like to speak to you—in private, if I may.' Her eyes slid to the blonde-haired woman hovering like a limpet at his side, her gown of lavender satin embroidered with delicate violet bows emphasising the full swell of her breasts above the tight bodice. There was a certain smugness stamped on her, a confidence that came from the knowledge of her own beauty and importance. Jane was cruelly aware of that golden creature and how graceless and unsophisticated she must appear by contrast. She really should have combed her hair and put on a decent dress before coming to Redmires. She suddenly wanted to slide out of sight, to remove herself from the scene.

Lord Randolph looked at her and then he stepped aside. 'Very well. I suppose I can spare you five minutes. Come into the study. We can talk there.'

She watched his face as he turned to the woman vying for his attention with what Jane thought to be desperate coquetry, which, she suspected, both bored and displeased him.

'Excuse us, Margaret. Go in to supper and I will join you shortly. This shouldn't take long,' he said, casting Jane a meaningful glance.

Margaret shot Jane a venomous look and walked away.

As Jane followed him across the hall she had a glimpse into the rooms beyond and a clear view of the people within. He opened the door next to a room where a group of men sat intently round a table where a game of cards was in progress and she had no trouble recognising several of her more affluent neighbours, neighbours who shunned them because of her father's adherence to the Stuart cause. Some of their Protestant neighbours were friendly enough, others not so friendly, who made their daily lives difficult by barring access to their land, which was a nuisance when they needed to pass through on their way to market at Corbridge or Newcastle.

Lord Randolph held the door open until she had passed through and then closed it, shutting out the sounds of merriment. The fire crackled pleasantly, filling the room with a cosy warmth and casting a rosy orange glow. An elderly man in full wig sat at a desk, his head bent over his work. He looked up when they entered and putting down his quill got up. She recognised him as Mr Berkley, Lord Randolph's steward, a kindly, good natured man. She often saw him when he rode by and, on occasion, he would come to Beckwith Manor to partake of Bessie's muffins and to pass the time of day with Sam.

'Ah—Miss Deighton,' he said with a slight inclination of his head, smiling broadly. 'It's a pleasure to see you. Excuse me. I'll leave you to your business when I've gathered up my papers.'

'It's nice to see you, Mr Berkley. I trust you and Mrs Berkley are well?'

'We're absolutely fine. I'll tell her you asked about her.'

When the door had closed behind Berkley, Lord Randolph went over to the hearth, giving a log a shove with his foot, sending sparks shooting up the chimney. Turning to face her, he stood with his legs apart, hands on hips, looking at her with a hardness in his eyes. She sensed a toughness beneath the exterior, a subtle ruthlessness in those taut cheekbones and the curve of his mouth, and felt he could be more dangerous than anyone she had ever met. Yes, he exuded an aura of power, of strength and authority, but a languid sexuality smouldered beneath the surface. She gazed at him wholly unmoved and it seemed to taunt him.

'What can I do for you, Miss Deighton? May I ask what it is that's got you all fired up. You want something from me and you must want it badly for you to seek me out like this.'

'I do. The devil drives where the devil must, Lord Randolph,' she said, feeling that the devil was certainly driving her when she had to ask this man for anything.

'State your case quickly. As you see, I have guests.'

'Yes, I do see,' Jane said icily, finding it difficult to keep her temper under control, but knowing she must if she wanted him to hear her out. He had not invited her to sit down and she knew he was deliberately keeping her on tenterhooks until she told him the reason for her visit. His manner told her he had no time to waste on pleasantries; he was busy with his own concerns. She would be better served to state her case and be on her way.

'It concerns my sister and your brother.'

He looked at her in genuine astonishment. 'Andrew?' He sighed, his expression changing to exasperation, resting his arm on the mantelpiece. 'What has he been up to?'

'He's absconded with my sister.'

'I think you will find that you are mistaken. Andrew left for the south this morning. As far as I am aware he was alone.' He spoke with sharpened authority, but his voice had wavered.

'He left with my sister.'

He lifted an eyebrow. 'And you are sure of that, are you? My brother left for Newcastle early this morning to pick up the post from Edinburgh to London.'

'I know. I told you. My sister was with him.'

'How do you know this?'

'They were seen in the post together, heading south. Your precious brother has run away with her,' she said, enunciating each word, as though she were addressing a child. 'In short, Lord Randolph, they have eloped.'

Lord Randolph faltered, beginning to see the truth behind her words. His surprise was as genuine as his annoyance. 'Eloped?' His voice sharpened. 'Good Lord! And you are certain of this?'

'Yes. Miriam was staying overnight with our aunt outside Newcastle, so I knew nothing about it until I returned from Corbridge earlier. She sent a note. Unfortunately I did not receive it until it was too late to stop her.' Taking it from her pocket, she opened it out. 'Allow me to read you the contents. She writes that she is leaving with Andrew Randolph, that they are running away. They are in love and cannot live without each other. They are to be married in London. She adds that she is very happy and for me not to worry.' She gave him the note so he could verify the contents. he scanned the missive and handed it back to her. Shoving the note back in her pocket, she faced him.

'The damned fool,' he growled, raking his hair back from his forehead.

'Now you will be in no doubt that they have run off together. Naturally I am furious—as would my father be, were he here and not—'

'In France,' he finished for her scathingly. 'I know perfectly well where your father is, Miss Deighton, and why—or maybe he is in Scotland, drumming up support to aid the Pretender in regaining the throne for the Stuarts. I know the Earl of Mar has sailed from London to Aberdeenshire for a council of war, so I think you can guarantee your father will not be far away.'

Tension filled the air between them and a dangerous hostility in the face of Francis Randolph's contempt and bitter condemnation for her father and all
the Catholics who were prepared to lose everything
in their struggle to place a Catholic king on the Eng-
lish throne. People like Francis Randolph, Jane knew,
considered the Catholics of Northumberland to be a
different species from his own, whose force of nature
threatened the law-abiding civilisation of England
and Scotland, that they conformed to no patterns of
behaviour but their own.

'If that is indeed so, I have no knowledge of it.
Because of this and that other matter which contin-
ues to fester between our families, I am sure you will
understand why there can never be any connection
between the Deightons and the Randolphs. It is clear
my sister and your brother have not considered the
consequences of their actions. They would be mon-
umental. It is imperative I find them before they do
anything foolish.'

'And what will you do?'

Her eyes hardened with intent. 'Go after them,
of course. What else should I do? She is my sister. I
will attempt to deal with the consequences of what
she and that conniving, silver-tongued scamp of a
brother of yours have done. His actions are wholly
reprehensible.'

'I agree with you absolutely.'

'I imagine a union between them would be as dis-
tasteful to you as it is to me,' she retorted. 'When I
find them and bring my sister home—and please God

she is as virtuous as she was when she left—then I will count on you to take your brother in hand and keep him away from her.'

Her words both goaded and amused him. He smiled a curious half-smile, one corner of his mouth curling up. The dark blue eyes were mocking, but there was a hardness in them now and she couldn't help but feel a curious unease. Her every instinct told her she must remain calm and aloof. She must not let him suspect the panic that had swept over her when told her sister had run off with Andrew Randolph, a panic so strong she had felt her knees must surely give way beneath her.

'I have not come here to ask for your help. I am here to ask for your co-operation. A marriage between our families is not to be considered. I know you share my concern.'

A pair of hard blue eyes regarded her dispassionately. 'I do—although all my life I have harboured the delusion that all young ladies yearn to snare wealthy husbands—and despite Andrew still living at Redmires, he is wealthy in his own right. I am amazed that you have such strong objections to my family's suitability, for our breeding is flawless and we are better connected than most.'

'I do not dispute that, Lord Randolph, that your family's credentials are impeccable, but wealth and an illustrious name does not give a man the right to do as he pleases and to do it with impunity.'

'I beg to differ. Andrew is twenty-two years old. He does not need me to hold his hand.'

'Then I, too, beg to differ, Lord Randolph. What my sister has is far too precious to squander on a man who is unworthy to receive it.'

A mildly tolerant smile touched his handsome visage, but the glint in his deep blue eyes was as hard as steel. 'You have made it quite plain that you have a low opinion of my brother, Miss Deighton.'

'I do. His constant trailing after Miriam of late like a lovesick calf has not endeared him to me in the slightest.'

'Really? This is news to me. Yes, he is what you say—a silver-tongued scamp, but easily influenced and never vicious. If it will put your mind at ease, Andrew has left Redmires to make his life in London. I didn't have the faintest idea that he knew your sister. I have other matters that concern me—but where are my manners?' he said, pushing his long frame away from the mantelpiece and moving close to her, his gaze capturing hers. 'You will have some refreshment?'

Jane gazed up at him. Those glowing eyes burned into hers, suffusing her with a growing aura or warmth she could not explain. Immediately she took a step back. 'No—thank you. I apologise for imposing, but you must understand my concern.'

'Of course I do. I, too, am concerned and your sister must be brought back. If you get to London, how will you go about locating her?'

'That is what I have come to ask you. It is difficult to see how pursuit can be made until I have precise information about where your brother has taken her. I am sure you will know his destination. I would like to have caught up with them before they reached London. It is hopeless, I know, but I refuse to let go of that slim ray of hope. If not, I must know where to look when I get to London.'

'I imagine Andrew will have taken her to our mother.'

Shocked and surprised, Jane stared at him. 'Lady Randolph? I—I am surprised. I do not imagine there will be a welcome for my sister in your mother's house.'

'Perhaps not, since your father was responsible for the death of her husband—my father. My brother is his own master, Miss Deighton. Your sister has clearly gone with him of her own accord.'

'She is just seventeen years old.'

'And I agree that the young fools have to be found before it is too late.'

'What will you do?''

'They leave me with no choice but to go after them myself. I must thank you for bringing the matter to my notice so promptly.'

'You will take me with you?'

'Certainly not. You must stay here. I will do my utmost to locate them. All you will be is a hindrance. I want neither you nor your company on the journey.'

Fire sprang to Jane's eyes. She clenched her hands tightly in the folds of her skirt and took a deliberate pace closer to him. 'Do as you like, Lord Randolph, but do you really think I will remain here while my sister is in danger? Do you think I would trust you to bring her back safely? I think not. I imagine you casting her off and forcing her to fend for herself. She has no money and will have taken very little with her for her comfort. For all we know she may have come to harm—should that be the case, then, when she is found, she will have need of me.'

'Let me assure you that I would do nothing so callous as to abandon her. You have every right to be upset and concerned about her—but you are not going with me.'

Jane's chilled contempt met him face to face, then, tossing her head, she turned from him and stalked towards the door. 'Very well. I certainly have no desire to accompany a man on a journey when he has no desire to have me along.'

'Where in God's name are you going?'

Jane felt a wave of desperation as she strove for control. 'After them. Do you think I don't know how difficult it will be? It is mad and perhaps it is impossible since I do not know where to look once I reach London—having no idea where Lady Randolph lives,' she replied, her eyes bright with anger as she turned and threw a look back at him. 'But I have to try. If you will not help me, then I must help myself, because I swear that if there is the slightest chance of finding my sister I will walk all the way to London if necessary.'

Stepping out into the hall, she closed the door behind her. Thankfully it was empty, everyone having retired to the supper room. A great wave of disappointment and anger filled her heart. She thought of the past days. Her sister, always light-hearted and gay, had been aglow and as excited as a small child with mischief in store. Looking back, she thought there had been a difference in her of late. Jane should have been suspicious then, but had chosen to ignore it. Tired of Miriam's restlessness and putting it down to her high spirits, she had sent her off to stay with Aunt Emily. A steely determination had replaced the worry and anger that had assailed her on learning of Miriam's foolishness. It was still there, locked tightly inside, but she wasn't going to let it deter her from going after her and bringing her home.

'Miss Deighton.'

Frustrated, resentful and rightly so, she paused and turned, seeing Lord Randolph's steward walking toward her, looking at her with shrewd, impassioned eyes.

'You are angry, I can see, and I cannot blame you. His Lordship can be overbearing at times and it is often unsettling to those who do not know him. He is authoritative and firm—indeed...' he chuckled '... I believe he forgets he is no longer at his place of business, but he has many tender sentiments, too.'

The subject of their conversation entered the hall and marched over to them with long strides.

'You are angry, Miss Deighton.'

'With good reason, Lord Randolph. I do not like your attitude.'

'She does not like my attitude, Berkley! Fancy that!'

'That is apparent, sir.'

'Little wonder your sister has run away.'

'She has not run away. She has eloped with your rascal of a brother.'

'It is the same thing.'

'Not to me it isn't.'

'Rascal, you say—as well as being silver-tongued and a scamp.'

'Indeed he is.'

'He is frequently cocky, I grant you, and all charm—'

'Exactly. They are always the worst,' she replied drily.

He raised his eyebrows. 'I am surprised. Tucked away at Beckwith Manor, how could you possibly know that?'

She cast him a look of icy disdain. 'It's really none of your affair. You know nothing about me. I am not here to talk about myself. I told you. I will leave for London first thing in the morning.'

'I can appreciate your concern, but you cannot embark on this mad escapade alone.'

'Yes, I can.'

'Allow me to advise you to forget this foolish notion.'

'Advice?' she gasped. 'If I wanted advice, you would be the last person I would ask.' A flush of anger had spread over her cheeks and icy fire smouldered in the depths of her eyes. 'This is my business, as well as yours. You cannot stop me going after them if I so wish.'

'Miss Deighton, you are being quite unreasonable.'

'Unreasonable? Because I am concerned about my sister?'

'Then think about the impropriety of travelling alone with me to London.'

'My reputation is the last thing I am thinking about just now.'

'Ladies don't travel alone and certainly not with a single gentleman.'

'I have little time to even think of being a lady so I wouldn't know.'

'Your father didn't help when he left you and your sister to fend for yourselves. What would he have to say about you travelling alone in a closed carriage with a Randolph all the way to London?'

'His condemnation would not be as severe as it will be should he find he has a Randolph for a son-in-law.'

'And you do not consider your virtue an important issue?'

She met his eyes head on. 'How do you know your own virtue is not in greater peril than mine, Lord Randolph?'

He laughed softly. 'Now that would be an issue. Since you have little care for your reputation, Miss Deighton, I concede. Tomorrow I leave for London— you may accompany me if you wish. I leave early, at sun-up. I will call at Beckwith Manor. I will not wait so be ready if you are to come with me.'

His manner was serious now. Jane's desolation vanished and was replaced by a tremulous sense of thankfulness. He would help her after all. She studied him more closely. The mocking, jaunty manner and audacious good looks were undoubtedly deceiving. She would have liked to tell him to go to the devil, that she wouldn't accompany him anywhere, but common sense and desperation to find her sister told her not to argue.

He followed her down the steps to her waiting horse. Spike got to his feet and wagged his tail.

'You came alone?'

'As you see,' she replied primly.

'You court danger riding alone when night is falling. The tracks back to your home are rough and not meant to be ridden in the dark.'

'And not to be undertaken by a woman, I think you mean,' Jane said, hoisting herself up into the saddle.

'You said it. I did not.'

Janes face tightened and she gave him a frigid stare from atop her horse, holding the reins tightly. 'For your information, Lord Randolph, I have ridden such tracks many times at all times of the day and night. In fact, I could ride them blindfold. I value my freedom, the freedom to do as I please—a desire which is sufficiently met when I ride out alone.'

'Be that as it may, but you should have more concern for your own safety. Have you no sense at all?'

'Apparently not and I cannot for the life of me think why you should make it your concern. Good night, Lord Randolph. I will be waiting for you tomorrow at first light.'

Chapter Two

Dusk was creeping over the hills when Jane set off back to Beckwith Manor, the autumn sun having turned to flame and apricot as it dipped low in the sky. Almost everything about her meeting with Lord Randolph seemed blurred and not quite real. Was it possible that it had really taken place? And what had he meant when he'd asked her if she was sure her father was in France? She'd had no word that he was in Scotland. During the reign of Queen Anne, the Protestants and Catholics had felt able to live in relative amity, but since the Queen's death the previous year, succeeded by King George, those who supported the return of a Stuart monarch continued to conspire to bring back to England the Catholic King James III, presently exiled in France. So far all Jacobite plots had been discovered and prevented, but it could never be certain when the next rebellion was coming, or whether it might succeed.

Jane hoped and prayed that this would not happen.

If there was indeed a rising, then it could be guaranteed that her father would be in the middle of it and she shuddered to think of the consequences to families like theirs should the rising fail. Looking at the bleak shadow lands all about her, she felt as if she were suspended in some remote space, as if everything held its breath, waiting in a climate of fear for something to come crashing down.

With her father in France and Miriam's head somewhere in the clouds, she began to realise that she was, simply, on her own. She had taken on the mantle of responsibility, making her own decisions concerning the house, the land and her family, and whether they were right or wrong she must stand by them. She ran the household with an iron hand, painfully aware of her responsibilities.

As if she had not enough to contend with, she found it hard to believe that Lord Randolph had agreed to let her accompany him to London. For the first time she considered the journey and that she would be closely confined in the coach with him. This thought caused an unfamiliar twist of her heart, an addictive mix of pleasure and discomfort. Letting her thoughts drift, she recalled how handsome he was, how it had felt when he held her to him when they had met in Newcastle. Never had she been so close to a man before. This thought brought a flush to her cheeks despite all her efforts to prevent it. She did not want to feel that way—not about him. But there was something about him that was different to any man she had known. And that something was affecting her deeply.

* * *

Back at Beckwith Manor as she prepared for the journey, trying hard not to think about Miriam's selfish and reckless behaviour and the trouble she was causing, she felt as if she were suspended in some kind of vacuum with all her thoughts and emotions turned inside out.

When her mother had died, with only Aunt Emily to watch over her during her father's frequent absences, she had been allowed to grow unfettered in the confines of Beckwith Manor. She'd had dreams of seeing beyond her own small world, but apart from market days in Corbridge or Newcastle and the occasional visit to other Catholic houses, she had ventured no further. She had, in her own way, shut her eyes and refused to look towards the future. Now it was with her and she was floundering, not knowing what to do next.

How typical it seemed of the chaos that had become her life. The painful knowledge came to her that she knew almost nothing except how to read, write and budget, sit a horse and manage the house and land. She didn't have the traditional skills of a lady, of how to oversee a fine house and entertain the neighbours. She was restless and wanted to see and experience new things. But after tonight's revelation, and seeing all those ladies in fine clothes glittering with jewels, had come a stab of devastating loneliness which she had not suffered since the night her mother had died.

Before she could settle for the night, she went to

the stables where she found Sam. The horse was expected to foal that night. There was no guarantee that she would get to bed until it was born.

Francis watched Jane Deighton ride away from Redmires, a large hound lolloping along beside her. He admired the way she handled her horse—a sleek, graceful, spirited beast, and dangerous when crossed he imagined—very little difference, it seemed, between the horse and its mistress. She was often out riding—had he not seen her himself when he, too, had taken to the hills and paused to watch her unobserved. She had no fear and seemed to have a natural rapport with the animal. She rode as if she had been born in the saddle, putting her mount at any obstacle that confronted her with a steadiness and courage that she seemed to impart to the animal itself.

A faint smile of appreciation twisted the corner of his mouth. She had taken him by surprise, coming to Redmires, and on a night when he had guests. He often entertained the local gentry and business associates. All in all, invitations to Redmires were sought after. He knew exactly why they came and it amused him to play the indulgent neighbour.

Unlike his father, who had lived for his horses, cards and women, Francis was an ardent student. Keen to learn the business that had provided his family with wealth, he had studied the coalfields of the north-east from an early age and, on the death of his father had invested heavily in many enterprises, pursuing his way to a fortune with a single-mindedness that left many of his fellow business associates gasping.

It was natural that Jane Deighton would be upset and concerned for her sister and he sensed how deeply she cared. She was an unusual female, intelligent, opinionated and full of surprises. She was also the epitome of stubborn, prideful woman. Yet for all her fire and spirit, there was no underlying viciousness. She was so very different from the sophisticated women he took to bed—experienced, sensual and knowledgeable in the ways of love, women who knew how to please him. Initially she had regarded him, not with apprehension, but carefully, warily and with reserve. She had met his stare firmly and with confidence, and he had seen a toughness and directness he had not seen in any other woman.

When she had faced him squarely and told him that she intended to go after her sister, he had seen in her face a determined nature almost as strong as his own. She had spoken with pride and a fastidious independence of spirit, he thought, and he admired her for that. When she had confronted him, her eyes were brilliant and fixed on his—strength was behind them and command so powerful that he could not take his eyes off her. It was the product of her ancestral lines equally accustomed to obedience, equally resentful of the indignity she clearly felt for having no other choice than to come to Redmires to confront him with her sister's escapade.

He remembered their meeting in Newcastle and how he had almost run her down on his horse. She had been angry with him and rightly so. When he had lifted her in his arms he had a poignant memory of how it felt to hold her, how soft she was. Her hair really was as shining and golden as he remembered. Her eyes, deeply touched with sparkles of light as they had rested on his face, really were that captivating shade of green that made him think of dew-soaked grass. Her skin was soft and creamy, her high angular cheekbones giving her eyes an attractive, feline slant which reminded him of a Siamese cat.

In contrast to these delicate features, her nose was small and pert and there was a stubborn thrust to her round chin. He had seen that she had many contradictory qualities. There was a dependence and gentleness about her, but he had seen glimpses of steely obstinacy, too.

Over the years he had noticed her on occasion—what man in his right mind would not? She was a woman whom, once seen, one was unable to forget. But because of who she was and the enmity that existed between their families, he had not approached her. He had carried anger and resentment with him since the night his father had died—that Edward Deighton was responsible he could not forget.

As for Andrew, the young fool. His younger brother drifted through life with a devil-may-care manner, totally irresponsible, and seemed to abide by no rules but his own. With his debonair good looks and broad smile, his body had thickened out of late. And matured. He was now a well-groomed young man who carried his head high. Little wonder the younger Miss Deighton had fallen for him. He was always involved in some scrape or other, but this time he had gone too far.

'So, you are to go after Andrew?' Berkley had come to stand beside him.

'It would seem he has left me with no choice.'

'Miss Deighton is a very attractive lady.'

'And way down the scale of things, Berkley. She has her father to thank for that.'

'And she has to live with the shame of it. Impoverished the family may be, my lord, but despite that tragic event which killed your father, with Edward Deighton at the reins, the Deightons' blood is as good as yours.'

'That may be, Berkley, but my father would turn in his grave if he knew what Andrew was about with the daughter of the man who seduced his wife.'

'He would, but what happened to them was between them. You are a new generation. Perhaps it's time to bury the hostilities of the past. I have often asked myself how it could come to this—death and division between friends and neighbours.'

'What happened cannot be forgotten, Berkley.'

'No, maybe not, but life goes on.' Suddenly Berkley grinned, lightening the moment. 'Still—Miss Jane Deighton is a beauty and extremely desirable and no mistake. She will make pleasant company on the journey.' Berkley laughed in the face of his employer's glower. 'Unless you order separate travelling conveyances, I'll wager that within the time it takes you to reach your destination you won't give a damn who sired her,' he taunted good humouredly before he became serious. 'Be considerate towards her. Her situation is not an enviable one. She works herself into the ground to keep food on the table. She has suffered her share of slanderous gossip and malicious revenge from her neighbours so try not to overawe the poor child. Her life cannot be comfortable.'

'I will do my best, Berkley.' Francis's voice took on a sardonic note. 'Whatever people may think of my character, it is not my intention to be cruel.'

'No, I know it isn't. I wish you luck, but by the time it takes you to locate your brother in London, I don't reckon much to your chances with so much temptation around you,' Berkley said, before going off to partake of his supper, little knowing that his words, spoken glibly, would come home to roost. Nor did he realise that for a hot-blooded male like Francis Randolph, with the legendary Randolph charm evident in every one of his lazy smiles, and whose handsome looks and blatant virility compelled the attentions of women, it would take less than that.

Francis continued to look in the direction Miss Deighton had taken, even though she was no longer in sight. As he thought about what Berkley had said, his lips broke in a wicked grin, for Jane Deighton had attributes enough to pleasure a man into eternity. She had an untamed quality running in dangerous undercurrents just beneath the surface that warned him to be wary. Pity, though, who she was, he thought with a certain degree of regret.

* * *

The heavily laden coach drawn by four bay horses, straining to be on their way, pulled up at the door of Beckwith Manor. It was accompanied by two well-armed guards, a groom and a coachman on the box. The driver jumped down and picked up the single bag waiting by the door, hoisting it atop the coach and securing it with the others.

With no sign of his passenger and impatient to be away, Francis stepped down into the yard, looking around him. Signs of neglect were everywhere. The house and buildings were sadly in need of repair. From what he had seen of the gardens they were overgrown with weeds knee high in the tangled lawn. He strode to the door, to be met by a harassed looking Bessie.

'Miss Deighton? Is she not ready?'

'Not quite, Lord Randolph,' Bessie replied, glancing across the yard to the stables. 'She's been up all night—one of the horses has foaled and there were complications. She's ready for the journey, but is taking one last look at the mother and foal.'

Cursing softly, Francis strode across the yard and into the stable. It was warm, light and peaceful. He was met by the pleasantly fecund smells of fresh straw and grain, warm animals and manure, and apples stored in the loft above. It was filled with shadows, all hazy. The lithe shadow of the stable cat slunk away. Several hens nestled in a pile of hay stacked by the door, fluffed into brown and white balls of yellow-eyed resentment at being disturbed, but were

too embedded in their nests to do more than shuf-
fle and cluck. Seeing Miss Deighton standing in the
open door to one of the stalls, he moved towards her.

On seeing him she said something to an elderly
man patting the flank of a huge plough horse, which,
by the look of it, had recently been delivered of a fine
chestnut foal. The young animal's liquid-bright eyes
looked anxiously at his surroundings as he drunkenly
staggered about until he found his way to his mother's teats. His tiny rump and sloping shoulders were
echoes of his mother's muscular perfection.

'It's a fine foal,' Francis said, taking a moment
to take in and appreciate the scene. Horses were his
abiding pleasure and seeing a newly born foal always
held him in awe.

'Yes—he's beautiful.'

'It's a wonderful thing, the birth of any animal.'

'There's always something being born, or dying,
with farmers, but the birth of an animal never ceases
to amaze me no matter how many times I witness the
event. Every time is like the first. It was touch and
go for a while, but he was delivered safely in the end.
See, he's beginning to suckle already. I am ready,
Lord Randolph,' she said, moving towards him.

'You've had a busy night.'

She paused and looked at him. 'I'm always busy.
I can't afford not to be. There's always something to
be done and not enough hands to do it. I had to take
a last look at the mother and foal to reassure myself that all is well. The horses are valuable to me. I
need them. If one gets sick or worse, then it has to be

replaced—which I cannot afford to do. But come. I'm as eager to be on our way as you are.'

'You haven't changed your mind?'

She glanced back at him. 'No. I'm sorry to disappoint you. It's a nuisance since I have much to do here, but I have no choice.'

'You have certainly got your way into accompanying me.'

'Yes, it would seem so.'

Despite their differences, Francis experienced a mixture of amusement and admiration for this young woman who had skilfully managed to manipulate him into doing something he didn't want to do. He followed in her wake, appreciatively watching her hips as they swayed with a natural, graceful provocativeness. He smiled despite himself.

'Miss Deighton, you are incorrigible.'

'Yes, others have said that before. Does it bother you?'

He grinned. 'Not a bit. In fact, I find myself looking forward to our journey together. The company will be—different. It will be interesting to see which of us will have expired before the journey's end.'

'Oh, you never know, Lord Randolph—perhaps we'll be getting on so well by the time we reach London—or wherever it is that we locate our errant siblings—that we, too, might recite our vows to a cleric.'

'I don't think so, Miss Deighton. I really don't.'

'No—neither do I. Perish the thought!'

Francis's emotions veered from vexation to mirth as he followed her, thinking Jane Deighton to be the

most provoking, insufferable female he had ever had
the misfortune to meet. She was also captivating and
alluring, with the kind of face and body that stirred
the blood. A reluctant smile of appreciation curved his
lips as his eyes caressed her trim back, leisurely enjoying watching her, focusing on the impudent sway
of her skirts. Despite their differences and the divi-
sions in their families, her sudden appearance at his
home had changed everything. She was a challenge,
a challenge he couldn't resist, and the fact that she
was determined to stand against him only spiced his
interest.

'I see your driver has taken care of my bag,' she
said, scowling when she saw the guards. 'Are they
really necessary?'

'These are dangerous times. It's necessary to guard
against footpads.'

She raised her arm to Bessie, standing anxiously
in the doorway. 'Goodbye, Bessie. It is my hope that
we will be back very soon with Miriam. Try not to
worry.'

The dog got up at the sight of his mistress and
started wagging his tail. When she approached the
coach, disappointed that his mistress was heading off
without him, he flopped down again, head between
his front paws, uttering a sharp whine when Lord
Randolph's groom assisted her inside. Francis would
bet the dog would still be there when they returned,
watching the road.

Climbing inside the spacious, well-sprung travelling coach and sitting across from her, he studied

her with renewed curiosity and she met his gaze unflinchingly.

'Make yourself comfortable, Miss Deighton. We have a long journey ahead of us. There will be times when I travel with the groom and the driver on top so you will not have to endure my company all the time.' As he caught her gaze a slow smile touched his lips. 'Besides, I fear the nearness of you will destroy all my good intentions.'

'Then I can only hope that your good intentions will continue all the way to London, Lord Randolph,' she replied archly, brushing down her skirts and picking off bits of straw from the fabric. 'Oh, dear. Having spent most of the night in the stables, I imagine I have straw sticking out of my hair.'

'Not straw, Miss Deighton. Prickles.'

'Ouch,' she said. 'I expect I deserved that.'

'You did. Since we are to travel together, Miss Deighton,' Francis said as the coach began to move away, the well-armed groom seated with the driver up front, 'there is no reason why we can't be congenial to each other and converse on matters that will not give offence to either of us.'

She fixed him with a cool, uncompromising stare. 'And what do you suggest?' she said, making herself comfortable on the cushioned seat and arranging her skirts to her satisfactions. 'That we should discuss the weather, perhaps, or the latest gossip in Corbridge or Newcastle?' she retorted, her lips twisting with sarcasm.

He gave her a hard look, his mouth tightening as he stared down at her. 'Are you always so difficult?'

'I can be impossible when something—or someone—gets on the wrong side of me,' she answered.

'He arched an eyebrow. 'Really?'

'Yes.'

'Then I suppose that is something I shall have to get used to if we are to be thrown together for the time it takes us to reach London.'

'It would be as well. I cannot think that you and I have common interests, Lord Randolph so if you don't mind I will close my eyes a while. I've been up all night waiting for the horse to foal and am sorely in need of sleep—however brief.' So saying, after making herself comfortable and resting her head against a cushion, she closed her eyes.

Leaning back, Francis stretched out his long legs, watching her from beneath hooded lids, wondering how he was going to endure the journey. He wasn't made of stone and the delectable young woman was so lovely and alluring she'd tempt any man who was alone with her for five minutes.

Miss Deighton was different to any woman he had known, a phenomenon. She was warm, giving and with thoughts that did not stray from hearth and home. She also had a touching concern for her sister. He sensed a goodness in her, something special, sensitive. There was something untapped inside her that not even she was aware of—passion buried deep. What would happen if she allowed it all to come out? In sleep she looked like a child. He was dangerously fascinated by this vulnerable side to her, he realised, and settled down to observe her sleeping profile.

Nothing made sense, for nothing could explain why he was beginning to enjoy being alone with her. Her lips were moist and slightly parted, the thick crescent of her lashes sweeping her cheeks. She wore a dark green conservative travelling dress, out of date but still elegant, and it changed her in Francis's eyes. She appeared slightly older than her twenty or so years, and the touches of cream lace at the neck, the sleekness of her golden hair beneath a small green plumed hat, all combined to give her a sophisticated beauty which, Francis thought, was more pronounced. Her manner confirmed her appearance—it, too, was cool and remote.

Something in his heart moved and softened, then something stabbed him in the centre of his chest. What the hell was wrong with him? She was the daughter of Edward Deighton, the man who was responsible for the death of his father. He had been angry and offended by her antagonistic manner when she had suddenly appeared at Redmires last night, but at the same time he thought of the impact she had made on him. She was a young woman with many contrasts. Possessed of a bright and brittle intelligence and stunningly direct, she also had a provoking sensuality and was brimming with deeply felt emotions. She had no idea how desirable she was, how captivating, and had not learned, like other ladies of his acquaintance, how to use her charms cruelly or cynically, simply for the pleasure of seeing her admiring swains dancing on a string.

After sleeping for a short while, Jane at last opened her eyes. Stretching her aching body and covering a yawn with her hand, she gazed out of the window. They travelled past fields where sheep cropped quietly. They had already crossed the River Tyne and she realised that for the first time in her life she was leaving Northumberland behind. She felt the strangeness and excitement and fear of what lay ahead. She allowed her body to relax in the swaying of the coach. Her companion, apart from loosening his neckcloth, looked exactly as he had when she had gone to sleep. She was vividly aware of the confined intimacy of the coach and was overwhelmingly conscious of him.

He had his eyes closed and whether he was awake or asleep she had no way of knowing. What she did realise was that if she was to get Miriam to come home, she needed Lord Randolph and decided to trust him. She did wonder how she was going to survive the journey with her sanity intact. There was an indomitable pride and arrogance chiselled into his handsome face, along with intelligence and hard-bitten strength. His jaw was set in a hard line, his brow furrowed as though his thoughts continued to trouble him even when he slept. It suddenly occurred to her that this elopement was as much a shock to him as it was to her.

As if sensing her scrutiny, he opened his eyes and

met her gaze. 'Ah, you're awake, I see. Do you feel refreshed?'

'A little—although I'll be better after I've had a night's sleep in a comfortable bed.' Her eyes caught sight of one of the guards riding ahead, reminding her of the perils of travelling on lonely roads. 'I hope we have no need of the services of the guards.'

'I told you there might be incidents on the way when we might need them. It is fortunate for you that I agreed to escort you.'

'Escort? I told you I did not need an escort, that I would go alone if I had an address to go to. There was no need to trouble yourself on my account.'

'Nevertheless it is more pleasant to have company when one undertakes a long journey.' His smile was lazy, masculine and supremely confident. 'This way I will make sure you come to no harm.'

The softly spoken words were murmured in a teasing undertone that held both challenge and sensuality. Jane could not help the shiver of awareness that it aroused, nor think of a rejoinder. The gentle promise in his expression, the flickering depths of his eyes, held her spellbound for the longest moment. She was conscious of the world outside passing by as the coach travelled on, of the guards riding ahead. Then Lord Randolph's gaze focused on her lips and Jane felt the oddest sensation, as if he had kissed her while his gaze caressed her mouth without touching. She swallowed nervously, aware of the ever-present tension inside her as she endured his disturbingly intimate, lazy scrutiny. Silence prevailed between them and to break the spell she averted her gaze.

After a moment and wanting to break the silence that stretched between them, taking a deep breath, she said, 'I'm sorry. I've been so concerned about Miriam that I've failed to consider how this is affecting you also. I realise this is as difficult for you as it is for me. Do you think we will catch up with them, that we'll be in time to stop them marrying?'

'Unless they have a change of heart and decide to go home then, no, I don't think we'll see them until we reach London. We are travelling the same route the post will have taken, so if they have decided to return home then we have a chance of seeing them. Andrew will know that your sister left a note telling you what they intend and will be afraid that I have been made aware of the fact and will go after them.'

'Is he usually so impulsive?'

He nodded. 'He is, but there'll be a reckoning when next we meet. I've always been too lenient with him—given him too much rein to do as he pleases. Country life bores him. He says it is too old fashioned. His interests lay with the East India Company…in trade, in commerce. With the spoils of the empire flooding into London from every corner of the earth—rich with the fruits of the trade winds—that is where he wants to be, at the centre of it. He's a good head on him for figures and what it takes to succeed. It was my hope that a new enterprise will curb his waywardness, but with this latest escapade with your sister I have my doubts.'

'Are the two of you close?'

'As close as brothers can be,' he said quietly.

Meeting his gaze, Jane saw the reflective, almost tender glimmer of light in his eyes.

'I always thought he was the lucky one.'

'Why do you say that?'

'Because he was the younger. Our parents loved us equally, but my mother always singled him out for special attention.' He smiled. 'I'm afraid she over-indulged him, spoiled him terribly, and Andrew—scamp that he was, as you correctly accused him of being, Miss Deighton—exploited her goodness.'

'I know what you mean. Exactly the same thing happened with Miriam. She, too, was spoiled by my mother and servants alike—although she was just four years old when our mother died and remembers very little about her. She can be so exasperating at times. We are different temperamentally. I like to think I have stamina and endurance—although I am accused of being wilful and cross when things aren't going as they should. Miriam is the opposite, but always engaging. She is passionate about everything and relishes any opportunity to be the centre of attention wherever she happens to be. She's like some skittish kitten who finds itself hopelessly stuck up a tree and wanting freedom.'

'Cats have a way of finding their own ways out of a tree.'

'They do. Unfortunately, for the present I would prefer her to remain stuck up that tree. At least I would know where she was.'

'The tree being Beckwith Manor.'

She sighed. 'Yes. Is that so selfish of me?'

'Not at all. It shows how much you love your sister and care for her well-being.'

'Yes, I do, which is why I want her to come home. She has stars in her eyes now—but you wait. She'll realise her mistake eventually.'

'In her letter she states that she loves Andrew.'

'Love! What is that but a delusion? Oh, your brother has turned her head all right, but it is still a delusion, the kind of trap in which innocent young girls like Miriam are caught.'

'Andrew wants to marry her, not seduce her,' Lord Randolph said harshly.

Jane bristled and averted her eyes. 'One thing I can be sure of is that Miriam will love London.'

'I imagine things have been difficult for you since your father spends most of his time in France—leaving you to run the household.'

She sighed. 'Yes—and everything else. During the summer months—and when the crops have to be harvested—I seem to spend most of my time out of doors.'

'You have a good man in Sam Cooper and his son.'

'I know that. I can always rely on them. When the harvest has to be brought in and the land got ready for planting in spring, we hire casual labour. There are plenty of willing hands who are glad of the work. I imagine the sorry plight of my family is a laughing matter to you as it is to the entire neighbourhood, but you'll hardly expect me to join in the mirth.'

He met her eyes steadily. 'I am not laughing at you. It is clear to me that you have much to contend with.'

'Anyone who has seen Beckwith Manor—which is in dire need of repair—will see that. Some men drink away their family acres, some gamble. My father gave it away to a hopeless cause.' There was a bitterness and underlying anger she could not conceal. 'For years now I have watched the Beckwith acres shrink and land sold freehold to tenant farmers.'

She fell silent, becoming lost in her musings of her home. The once noble house was badly in need of repairs, the barns leaked and the gardens were in a state of disorder and neglect. Jane hated to see the neighbours' pity and could almost feel Lord Randolph's contempt for the chaos and mess into which her father had allowed his affairs to slide. But with the spirit and the blood of her paternal grandfather in her veins, a military man who had fought relentlessly for King and Country in the civil wars that had ravaged England seventy years ago, she gritted her teeth and endured, hoping for a miracle. How could she tell someone like Lord Randolph how most days she moved blindly about her chores like an inanimate object, her mind incapable of thought beyond that of the needs of the house and others who depended on her, smiling and comforting and easing their worries.

'Do you think we'll get to them in time—before they do anything foolish? she asked, moving on from her own sorry plight.

He shook his head. 'In truth I have no idea. I would

like to think they will see sense and have a change of heart.'

'I should have seen the signs to prevent this.'

Lord Randolph didn't answer for a few seconds and when he spoke his voice was unexpectedly gentle.

'Don't be too hard on yourself. I, too, should have seen what Andrew was up to. I've been so wrapped up in business matters of late I failed. I didn't even know he was acquainted with your sister and, if I had, I would never have expected him to do something like this. I have seen your sister several times—an attractive girl. I can understand how Andrew was drawn to her—and your sister to Andrew.'

Something about his tone brought Jane up sharp. 'What are you insinuating, Lord Randolph?'

'Come now, Miss Deighton, I know of your circumstances. Your sister would naturally leap at the chance of so advantageous an alliance. What girl in her right mind would reject Andrew Randolph? She would be a fool or blind to do so.'

'How dare you say that? Miriam is neither ambitious nor self-seeking,' she said sharply.

'Forgive me. I am sure you are right. If they have decided not to go through with it and return to Northumberland, then we should meet them on the road.'

'If they do, then it may not be the end of it. The consequences for Miriam will be dire indeed if it should get out. In the eyes of everyone she has broken all the rules and will be shunned because of it. And if...' She bit her lip, unable to voice what was on her mind. For her it was a delicate issue.

'Worry not, Miss Deighton,' he said, seeming to read her thoughts. 'Despite your low opinion of my brother, he has many fine attributes, one of them being that he is a gentleman. Deflowering gently reared young ladies would violate Andrew's code of behaviour.'

Jane flushed scarlet, embarrassed that he should phrase it so bluntly. 'I am relieved to hear it.'

Francis found himself enjoying her discomfiture. 'Of course, my own code of honour is more relaxed.'

'Yes, I imagine it would be. Although you are a respected pillar of the community, Lord Randolph, you are also much talked about, with many vices I have heard.'

He laughed. 'No doubt those who gossip about me have skilfully embroidered all my faults as they would a sampler. My vices are to live well and enjoy fine horses and fine wines—and attractive ladies. You shouldn't listen to all you have heard.'

Jane fixed her level gaze on him. 'I don't. I prefer to make my own judgement about people. You are no exception.'

'And what have you concluded about me?'

Her cheeks flushed and she looked away. 'I haven't had time to make an accurate assessment of your character, but I don't think you fit the description I have heard.'

'And you, Miss Deighton? What kind of person are you?'

She smiled. 'Nothing special, Lord Randolph. Nothing special. But it is not me that should be of interest. It is Miriam and how I can stop her going through with this mad escapade.'

'You must understand that should Andrew and your sister decide to go through with it they may not find it as simple as they think—unless your sister is willing to reject her faith.'

Jane looked at him sharply. 'Reject her faith? What are you talking about? It may come as a surprise to you, Lord Randolph, but Miriam is a Protestant so that will not be an issue. My mother insisted on her marriage to my father that any offspring they produced to be brought up in her faith. It was a condition he agreed to. However, had he not and we were Catholic, then Miriam would adhere to the law of the established church and marry according to the rites of the Church of England.'

'I do not doubt it—if she is determined to marry him—and I apologise for assuming she was of your father's faith. Let us hope we get to them before they do anything foolish.'

'Those are my thoughts exactly.'

'However, seventeen is not too young to wed. Why, at seventeen many girls are already wed and christening their first infant at the parish church.'

'That is a callous thing to say.'

'Not really. It's a fact. How old are you, Miss Deighton? Nineteen? Twenty? At your age most girls are married or hanker to be lest they be left on the shelf.'

'I am twenty-one and I have no immediate desire to marry anyone.'

They fell silent. Jane had much to think about as she observed the passing scenery, not least her companion. With his arms crossed imperturbably over his chest, his legs stretched out and his eyes glowing darkly, there was something undeniably engaging about him. He made her feel alert and alive, and curiously stimulated. Concerned by her turn of thoughts, she averted her eyes to the window. Resting her head against the padded upholstery, she closed her eyes once more, thinking of the strange, easy conversation she had engaged in with her companion. Had she been too ready to judge? For the short time she had been in Francis Randolph's company, she decided that none of what she had heard of him described him or did him justice. There was a charisma about him that had nothing to do with his powerful physique or mocking smile.

There was something else, too, something behind that lazy smile, dark blue eyes and unbreachable wall of aloof strength that told her Francis Randolph had done, seen and experienced all there was to do and see, that to know him properly would be exciting and dangerous, and therein lay his appeal—an appeal that unnerved her. She told herself that he was nothing to her, just a spectacularly handsome man who happened to be helping her solve a family crisis—as soon as this business with Miriam was resolved, any association between her and Lord Randolph would cease.

Chapter Three

Nightfall was approaching when the coach halted before an inn where they would spend the night. Francis offered Jane his hand to assist her descent. His fingers, which were surprisingly gentle, closed over hers. When she stepped to the ground he released them and followed in her wake to the door.

His gaze watched the gentle sway of her skirts and the graceful movement of her body as she walked. He was unable to tear his eyes away. Her cloud of hair, which she had loosened in the coach, fell down her slender spine. The plain garb she wore was an insult to her beauty and femininity. He narrowed his eyes, mentally stripping her of her garments and redressing her, draping her lovely body in the finest of materials, imagining the gentle swell of her breasts beneath and the softness of her flesh.

The image was enough to arouse his loins uncomfortably. He closed his eyes for a moment, welcoming the dark, but the image remained to taunt him and did nothing to calm his overheated blood.

* * *

They were not the only travellers to have sought the hospitality of the inn, for the common room was almost filled to capacity. Jane was relieved that Lord Randolph managed to procure rooms and a private parlour where she could eat dinner in peace. When the meal was brought in he did not join her—he seemed to find the company of the guards and the patrons in the common room preferable to hers.

After she had eaten, reluctant to go up to her room just then, she settled herself in the corner of a high-backed settee set at an angle close to the window. Removing her shoes, she drew her feet up beneath her. As she gazed across the room in the semi-darkness into the red coals of the fire, eventually her eyelids drooped and she closed her eyes. How long she dozed she had no idea. She woke when the door opened and Lord Randolph walked across the room to stand directly in front of the fire as if he craved its warmth. He stood with both hands braced against the mantel, his head slightly bent as he looked into the glowing coals. There was a tautness about him and, while he thought himself unobserved, she kept very still. His profile was in relief and harsh, strong and arrogant—it might have been carved out of stone.

Suddenly the door opened and the innkeeper came in.

'The brandy you asked for, Lord Randolph.'

'Thank you. Place it on the table. I will pour it my-self.'

The innkeeper did as he was bade and went out. Apart from the crackling of the fire the room was silent. Jane remained where she was as Lord Randolph poured himself a generous brandy and took it to the fire. He drank deep and then, as if sensing her presence, he turned, poised, like a wild animal taken unawares. No longer able to bear the silence and the stillness, she placed her feet on the floor.

'I did not mean to disturb you. I fell asleep.'

'You should have gone up to your room.'

'Yes, I will. Have you eaten?'

He shook his head, removed his jacket and sat in a chair by the hearth, stretching his booted legs out and resting his feet on the fender. 'Sit down a moment. I have some interesting news that will concern you.'

Jane crossed to the fire and sat across from him, waiting for him to speak.

'I've been in conversation with a messenger on his way from Scotland to London. Apparently the Earl of Mar has raised the Pretender's standard at Braemar.'

'There is to be a rising?'

He nodded. 'It is highly likely. The Jacobites are gathering large numbers of men in Scotland and the north of England. Government forces in Scotland are under the command of the Duke of Argyll. Already the Government are rounding up leading Jacobites.'

'Ever since King James exited the throne, tossing the Great Seal of the Realm into the Thames on his way, it has been a time of supposition that has led to restlessness and questioning. Now the Jacobites want to place his son, another James Stuart, on the throne, the fight will go on. Is it hopeless?'

'It is not for me to say.'

'But—the French…'

'France is exhausted by years of war and, with the recent death of King Louis—it is unlikely they will play a part in supporting the cause of James Stuart.'

Jane sighed and leaned back in the chair, looking into the glowing embers of the fire. 'It has come as no surprise to me. I have been expecting something like this—otherwise what is the point of it all? My father kept to the old faith, despite the tribulations he has suffered for it. He profited by the brief return of Catholicism to England under King James II. It is no secret that my father retains the hope that the Jacobites will recapture the country and, despite his advancing years, he will be more than willing to respond to the Stuart's call to arms.'

'Then he is a fool if he believes that.'

Jane felt her hackles rise. 'He is anything but that.'

'You are his daughter. I do not blame you for coming to his defence. For myself I cannot understand the attractions of a cause that renders rich people poor.'

'Can you not? For myself I cannot raise support for either side—I leave politics and religion to others, but one cannot escape the fact that many have given their lives to the cause and I have to admire their convictions. If the rising is successful and James III is on the throne, my father will know that he has played his part. Few men will be able to claim as much.'

'That will never happen. It is plain that James III will never be installed upon the throne, yet men cast their fortunes, and their family's fortunes, into the cause.'

'That is not exactly how the Jacobites arrange their affairs,' Jane said in a censorious tone. 'To you, and people of like mind, the Jacobites are insane. You dislike my father very much, don't you, Lord Randolph?'

'I could hate him if he were worth sparing a thought and effort to.'

'My father is not a bad man. Setting aside my own personal feelings and the resentment I feel because he prefers to spend his time in France instead of at home with his family, I know he is a man of considerable intelligence and strong character. A man of that stamp is wholly committed to his beliefs, even if those beliefs go against the general rule of things. I always admired him for that. I am aware of what he is involved in, so nothing you say will surprise me.'

'He must realise that Parliament's response to this Jacobite rising is that all land of rebelling Jacobites will be confiscated in favour of the tenants who support England's government.'

Jane could not remain unaffected by this news. 'Yes, he will. But such is his loyalty to James Stuart that it will be a price he will pay. Besides, he's sold off so much of the land at Beckwith Manor that we have little left.'

'Does he ever come home?'

'Not very often—we last saw him twelve months ago—and when he returns to France he leaves behind money to tide us over. I don't know where he gets it. I've learned never to question what good fortune comes my way. Then I have to decide which of the leaking roofs to mend or which building to repair.

'But he must show loyalty to his family? If the rising fails—as it surely will—you will be made to suffer for his support of the Pretender. Does that not concern you?'

Anger flashed in her eyes. 'Of course it does. Every day, every night. In my foolishness I hoped that he would put it all behind him, that no more would he endanger himself and his family, but it was not to be. His determination to carry on with his crusade and to continue to involve himself in plots and conspiracies was often too much to be borne by my mother, who grievously endured many throughout their marriage before she died.'

'You have just cause to be angry and upset by your father's actions. If my words have frightened you, I apologise. It was not my intention to upset you.'

'You have not upset me. It's important for me to know so that I can perceive the danger and act upon it should the time arise.'

There was an intensity in her eyes that clearly conveyed the depths of her concern. 'The picture may not be so bleak. I may be wrong.'

'And I am afraid that you may be right.'

'And your sister? How will your father take her elopement?'

'Had Miriam eloped with any other man I would have let her get on with it because she would be out of it. But the hostility between our families does not allow me that relief. You have no idea of the times I have chastised her over her involvement with your brother—all the times she begged me to allow him to come to the house. In my frustration and anger I refused and I would order her not to encourage him. Unfortunately Miriam was never silent in her objections. I endured the tears and ill humours because there was no escape from them. That was when I sent her to stay with our aunt near Newcastle. What a mistake that turned out to be.' Her thoughts returned to her father. 'I am not oblivious of the dangers pressing on my father. If the rising does go against the Jacobites, if he is captured he will be shown no mercy.' She looked across at Lord Randolph, who was watching her closely. She smiled thinly. 'No doubt you would say that he is unworthy of compassion and the only mercy he can expect is a kindly executioner who will not prolong his passing.'

'The end of his life has already been ordained. It is not for me to say.'

'It might have been all very grand when King James honoured my father with a baronetcy, having pledged his loyalty and service to his King in return for land that he could pass on to his heirs, but much good it did us. We were not elevated to the realms of polite society and the title was revoked later by King William for his treasonable activities.'

'That must have come as a blow to him.'

'He didn't ask to be made a baron,' she said pointedly. 'Compared to one's beliefs, my father impressed on us that titles are meaningless. You may not agree with his religion and his unfailing loyalty to the cause, but it takes great courage to do what he does.' She was defiant in her defence of her father and the look she gave him told him so. She knew she took a risk of alienating him even more, but it was important that Francis Randolph should not be allowed to think her father was spineless, or her for that matter. She was so overwhelmed by his belligerence and holier-than-thou attitude that she felt she must claim for her father what was his due. She waited for his reaction. It was as she hoped.

'Then he is indeed fortunate in his daughter's support and forbearance and for her common sense. But he is a man who will leave his daughters all alone among his most despised enemies.

His firm reminder of the threatened repercussions and what it would mean for her and Miriam chilled Jane to the bone. His words went straight to her heart and she stared at him with all the nauseating reality of someone who has just been hit by a truth they would prefer not to hear. 'I have no illusions about my situation, but do not misjudge my father. You do not know him.'

He gave her a long assessing look. 'It might have been better had he remained in France.'

'No, it wouldn't. I can understand why he's come back,' she said softly. 'Neither time nor distance could efface his attachment to the country of his birth. He is older now and battle weary, and to end his life and have his bones consigned to the grave among strangers— far away from his native land—he could not endure. But be assured that there will be no peace in the glens of Scotland or the Catholics houses on this side of the border until a Stuart has been restored to the throne.'

'That will not happen. This is England, where to be a Protestant is more comfortable. I am not prejudiced. I am a man of the world. I believe a man should follow his own inclinations—be it in business or religion—Protestant or Catholic. But one must never forget this is a Protestant country and England will not tolerate a Catholic king or queen.'

Jane rose and looked across at him, her expression hard. 'You are right, Lord Randolph. Now excuse me. I'm going to bed.'

With a quiet dignity she turned and walked across the room. At the door she paused and looked back at him. Wetting her lips, she took a deep, steadying breath. 'I realise that all this is unpleasant and difficult for you—as it is for me. I also realise that you must despise me because of who I am.'

Rising quickly out of his chair he crossed towards her, looking down into the velvety softness of her eyes with a quiet intensity. Jane realised how perceptive this man was. She was disturbingly aware of those warm spheres delving into hers as if he were intent on searching out her innermost thoughts. Placing his hands on her shoulders, he held her at arm's length, his eyes refusing to relinquish their hold on hers. The hands on her shoulders were so powerful that Jane felt like a child in his grasp.

'Correct,' he informed her softly. 'I do not despise you. Far from it. You are upset.'

She averted her eyes, fixing them on the flames. 'It is nothing—only memories.'

Francis knew all there was to know about memories, unpleasant or otherwise, and he was sure that Miss Deighton had had more than her fair share and was often beset with dark thoughts. 'What is it that distresses you? Is it what I have told you about the rising?'

The tenderness in his tone, in his dark blue eyes, brought Jane out of her melancholy and she looked at him once more. She had been thinking of her father the last time he had come home. He hadn't stayed long and when he had ridden off she'd had no idea when she would see him again. Was he in Scotland or England? Was he safe? With so much to do she'd never been one to dwell on the past. Her father would not wish her to and she swallowed the tears that threatened. Lord Randolph was looking at her, still searching her face intently, a faint scowl between his brows, as if by sheer force of will he would drive away her unhappiness.

'I'm all right—truly,' she said, managing to smile.

His scowl relaxed. Taking her chin between his finger and thumb, he tilted her face to his. Jane felt her pulse escalate at the gesture, at his nearness. She saw how the dark strands of his hair gleamed in the firelight and felt the gentle way his thumb shifted to caress her lower lip. Suddenly recalling their circumstances, she attempted to step back to break the intimacy of the contact.

'I've known many women and ventured far and wide, but no maid has provoked my imagination to such a degree as you do. You are a temptress, Jane Deighton, dangerous and destructive in your innocence. It will be hard for me seeing you day after day, night after night, knowing you are almost within my arm's reach and not touching you as I want to.'

His voice had softened to the timbre of rough velvet and made Jane's senses jolt almost as much as the strange way he was looking at her. Suddenly her sense of security began to disintegrate and she felt a treacherous warmth seep beneath her flesh. With startling clarity she realised that something was beginning to happen between them. He was not her enemy, but what he was implying she could not allow to happen. It took all her will to summon her self-control and step back.

'Then you must be cautious, my lord, lest you forget who I am and why we are here.' Without more ado she opened the door and left him.

Early morning saw them on the much-travelled road again continuing south. The weather was fine and a low mist clung to the hollows of the hills. When Lord Randolph had told Jane of the suspected rising, she had been caught with a sense of unrest and uncertainty, for there was no doubt in her mind that it would come. She had a sense of something unpleasant closing in around her, the beginning of a frightening chain of events she had no way of stopping. A rising on the scale the Jacobites planned would bring change—failure or success, it would bring change to her life.

* * *

Lord Randolph had begun the journey seated up front with the driver and groom and did not join Jane inside until they had stopped for refreshment at noon and were on their way again. At times their talk became unfettered. The mood of conviviality between them was a relief and Jane welcomed it.

Francis shifted his position to make himself more comfortable. 'When this is over, Miss Deighton, will you ever forgive me for failing to curb my brother's waywardness? Had I taken more notice he would not be heading for London with your sister.'

His question was so unexpected that Jane searched for something to say. After a moment she shook her head, her hair rippling over her shoulders like water from a pump, and she slanted him a smile so wide it was like the sun rising over the Cheviots.

'Well,' she said, trying to sound severe despite the mirth shimmering in her eyes. 'I might forgive you for that, because I understand how it happened, but it's a hanging offence to make me sleep on such a lumpy mattress as I did last night. I can only hope the beds at the inn in York will be more agreeable.'

Francis laughed out loud at that and the unexpected charm of his white smile that followed did treacherous things to Jane's heart. She was glad to discover he had a sense of humour.

'Then I shall make sure that the accommodation suits your comforts. The further south we get the more comfortable the inns—at least that is what I have experienced. Although I do not intend to dally long at any of our stops along the way. It is imperative that we reach London before our siblings can do anything foolish.'

'I quite agree. I would have thought they were both aware of how things stand between our families and that the differences were established nine years ago.'

'And what is the relationship between our families?'

She tilted her head to one side and looked at him squarely. 'We are enemies, of course. What else?'

His eyes glowed wickedly. 'What else indeed? I do not hold your father in any esteem, I grant you—the reason being that he was responsible for the death of my own—but you—you are a different matter, Miss Deighton. You intrigue me and I have a yearning to get to know you better. For the time we are together, can we not, in common agreement, strive to be as gracious and mannerly as it is possible to be?'

'It will be more agreeable.'

'Then that is settled.'

'Yes. Do you travel to London often?'

He nodded. 'Not often, although I do come down to see my mother on occasion. Was your own mother from Northumberland?'

'Her family lived in Berwick—but they are all dead now, apart from Aunt Emily, a widow now.'

'Was it in Berwick where she met your father?'

'They met in Newcastle, when she was staying with Aunt Emily. They were attracted to each other the moment they met, but my grandparents were against a marriage between them.'

'Why was that?'

'Because my father was a Roman Catholic. But my mother was determined to have her way. My grandparents eventually gave in when my mother assured them any offspring she bore would be raised as Protestants.' Jane smiled wistfully. 'For all his faults, my father loved her deeply and he was quietly proud of the way she would stand up to him and speak her mind. He always said how stubborn she could be—that she was as hot-headed as any man and that her hot temper would make a mountain tremble.'

'Traits that have been inherited by her daughter.'

She smiled. 'I speak my mind, if that's what you mean.'

'Exactly. She must have been a rare jewel, your mother.'

Jane met his gaze, seeing his eyes were warm and smiling. 'Yes, she was. She was vibrant and lovely. She made our childhood joyous and carefree…' She faltered, remembering how it had been. 'That was before she became ill. She died when I was just eight years old. I miss her dreadfully—as I will Miriam if she does not return to Beckwith Manor. She has a free and generous spirit. There is no harm in her. Oh, there are times when she can be difficult of temper—then, when she knows she has gone too far, she becomes sweet and obedient. Her moods of warmth and generosity redeem her so that it is easy to forget what she has done before.'

'We are only a day behind them so we should arrive in London before they can do anything rash.

Maybe they already regret their impulsive decision to leave.'

'I pray that is the case. Without Miriam and my father, life will indeed be difficult.'

'It strikes me that it is all very well your father going off to France, but it is you who has borne the physical strain over the years.'

'Yes, I cannot deny it. During the early days I missed my mother terribly. She was taken years before her time. I remember her voice and sometimes her smell. When things became too much, I longed to seek her advice and reassurance while I adjusted to the shock of running the Manor. I don't know what I would have done without Bessie. It's thanks in no small part to her unstinting warmth and kindness that I was able to overcome all the obstructions placed in my way.'

'Perhaps some time away from Beckwith Manor will be good for you.'

Jane sighed. 'Perhaps,' she murmured, 'but the chores and the worries will still be there when I return.'

It was almost nightfall when they reached York and the Black Swan on Coney Street. The general air was one of comfort and respectability. It was filled with travellers, rich and poor alike, who stopped to eat and rest. There was the usual rush to serve the travellers. Lord Randolph ordered private rooms where they could eat their dinner in peace. Enquiries were made regarding Miriam and Andrew, but there was nothing. Unused to being confined for so long, Jane expressed a desire to take a walk round the town before settling down to dinner.

The sun was low on the roofs that overhung the cobbled streets. They walked towards the Minster, which Jane considered to be the most beautiful building she had seen. Lord Randolph was knowledgeable about its history and Jane listened with interest as they negotiated the intricate tangle of streets enclosed within the limestone ribbon of wall. They walked back along Pavement and before reaching the River Ouse they turned off to the Black Swan, where the appetising aroma of hot food pervaded every corner and started Jane's mouth watering.

In no time at all dinner was brought to Lord Randolph's room. Her stomach groaning for sustenance, and without wasting time, Jane began to do the food justice. They were both hungry and spoke little while they ate.

'You're obviously hungry,' Lord Randolph remarked, watching her with an amused gleam in his eyes as she tucked into the meat pie.

'I'm ravenous and this pie is so good.'

'And so it should be, considering the scandalous prices the coaching inns charge.'

'For which I thank you, although I have brought funds enough for the journey if you would work out what it is that I owe you.'

'I would not dream of taking money from you, Miss Deighton. Save what you have for the return journey should I decide to remain in London. I shall take the opportunity to meet up with some business acquaintances while I am there. It's also a while since I saw my mother.'

'I am sure she will be more than happy to see you,' Jane said, continuing to tuck into her meal while doubting her own welcome. For all her confidence she found herself wondering how Lady Randolph would react to her sudden arrival on the scene. 'I can't remember when I last ate so much. I'm usually so busy I don't know what I'm eating half the time.' She paused just long enough to take a gulp of her wine and glanced across at her companion to see that he was consuming his food more leisurely, savouring each taste fully. 'You really should eat plenty. Bessie always says you should eat a hearty meal. She also says we do not eat to satisfy our appetite. Food is strength.'

'Wise words.'

'Well, I'm enjoying the food we've been given. I need something inside me to fortify me on the journey. It's all this sitting about, not doing anything. I declare I shall be so fat by the time I return to Northumberland Bessie won't recognise me.'

When they had eaten they sat at the table and drank their wine, finding a strange kind of pleasure in each other's company the more time they spent together. Tonight Jane had asked him to tell her about

London, about the places of interest and the Court of King George.

'Never having been there, you will find it stimulating after Northumberland.'

'I imagine I shall,' Jane replied, 'but I have no intention of staying there long enough to experience it. How do you think Lady Randolph will receive me? I expect she will not be well pleased at having both daughters of Edward Deighton thrust upon her.'

He frowned across at her. 'Why would you think that? They were friends, don't forget. I found it difficult coming to terms with what happened. She was more forgiving than I. She always said that what happened was an accident.' He smiled. 'But worry not. She will not turn you out.'

'I sincerely hope not. I wouldn't know where to go.'

'Did you know of your father's closeness to my mother?'

She lowered her head, wishing he had not mentioned that. 'Not at the time. I was too young. But later—I heard the gossip. It was hard not to. I tried not to believe it, but Bessie knew.'

'The whole of Northumberland knew. After the accident, when my father died, my mother, unable to live at Redmires a moment longer, left to live in London.'

'And that was when my father threw himself even deeper into the cause and began spending most of his time in France. It was hard on me and Miriam. Having lost our mother, when Father left us it was like grieving all over again. You blamed him for what happened—I know you did—and I did not blame you, but I was angry, angry that we had been thrust into so much grief and bitterness.'

He nodded. 'I cannot deny it. I did blame him—I do—and I never want to set eyes on him again. Afterwards nothing was the same for me and Andrew, who found it hard when Mother left to live in London. In one fell swoop both our parents had been snatched from us.'

'That must have been difficult for you both. What happened affected my father to such a degree that he could not forgive himself. Do—do you really think your mother and my father loved each other?'

Francis sighed, sitting back in his chair and contemplating the red liquid in his glass. 'I don't know. She always refused to speak of it. Yet once she was away from Redmires and back in London with her friends around her, which was where she grew up, she was happy.' He looked at her. 'What is it? You're frowning. You have something on your mind.'

'I was wondering what was wrong with your father that drove her to seek affection elsewhere.'

'He wasn't an easy man to love—a force to be reckoned with. In fact, he could be downright difficult at times.'

'And, I suspect he gave Catholics no account.'

'He made no secret of it. He scorned and hated them and encouraged Andrew and me to do the same.'

'And do you? Hate Catholics?'

'No, I don't and my opinions are never influenced

by others. I make up my own mind. My father was also a strong, blunt man—some saw him as arrogant and overbearing. He was a difficult man to live up to. There was never any doubt that I would carry on his work. I loved Redmires as a boy and as a man and could not envisage living anywhere else.'

It was an emotion Jane thought he rarely permitted to show, this nostalgia for Redmires. She smiled. 'I have a feeling that you don't belong in London any more that I do. And Andrew? Does he love Redmires as you do?'

He shook his head. 'Andrew was less interested. He tried to live up to our father's expectations and failed. His heart wasn't in it. My father frightened my mother with his moods and the force of his personality. She found it almost impossible—there were arguments...'

'I'm sorry.'

'It's in the past—and as Berkley would say—better left there.' He fell silent, his eyes softening on her face. 'You know, Miss Deighton, a lovely young woman like you should be surrounded by doting swains—which could well be the case when we reach London. You may find yourself so flattered by their attentions that you may not want to return to Northumberland.'

Jane felt a blush infuse her cheeks. 'I have too much to do than waste time on doting swains and such frivolous things. I have much to do at Beckwith Manor.'

'And you will allow nothing to interfere with that.'

'No. I can't.'

'Not even love,' he murmured softly, his gaze capturing hers.

'No.'

'Are you scared of love?'

'No, of course not.'

'I don't believe you.'

'Believe what you like. It's quite true,' she retorted, feeling as if she were under attack.'

'Then if you are not afraid of love, why do you hide behind the walls of Beckwith Manor?'

'I am not hiding. I work, Lord Randolph. Circumstances have made me lay off servants both inside and outside the house. I cook, I sew, I work in the dairy and help with the harvest on the land we still possess. I also assist at lambing time when necessary—and there are a hundred other chores that require my help.'

'And I have no doubt you are efficient in all that you do. I applaud your spirit. However, I think if you didn't have all those things to occupy your time, you would be quite happy to make yourself invisible—to fade into obscurity.' He smiled at her sudden look of indignation that his words had provoked. 'I apologise if my opinion is unkind, but you must admit that it does have the ring of truth about it.'

'Whether it is true or not, I would not admit such a thing to you. I am not afraid of love—but at present I am not interested.'

'Then as a woman you are truly unique.'

Jane looked at him warily. 'Now you're mocking me.'

'I wouldn't dream of doing that. You, Miss Deighton, are far too adorable to mock.'

How could Jane be angry with him when he smiled that engaging smile and teased her in this manner? At least she hoped he was teasing. Her lips curved in a smile of her own. 'It's right what everyone says of you. You really are a complete rogue, Lord Randolph—arrogant and overbearing.'

He grinned. 'I admit it. What I need is a lovely, patient and extremely tolerant young woman to take me in hand, to make me see the error of my ways and reform me.'

'Then I wish you luck. Intolerance and impatience have always been two of my failings, but there must be a female somewhere who will fall for a silken tongue, who will be willing to expend so much energy, time and effort on such an unenviable task. The lady who was hanging on to your arm when I arrived at your house looked as if she would welcome your attentions.'

He laughed softly. 'I think you refer to Margaret Crawford, Lord Crawford's daughter, from Corbridge. Yes, she is eminently suitable, I grant you, and of excellent character. She would certainly preside over Redmires with grace and poise and has been trained to manage the demanding responsibilities of a large house.'

'But? It is evident to me that you would consider marriage to her with the same kind of dispassion and practised precision you employ when dealing with your business transactions.'

He shrugged. 'Why should you expect anything else? I am no more sentimental about marriage than anyone else. It's a contract like any other. Besides, considering my success in that area, the odds for our marriage being successful are highly favourable.'

'I think *excruciatingly boring* would be a more appropriate term to use. Marriage is not a business transaction.'

Lord Randolph was watching her with an amused gleam in his eyes. 'Her father would be delighted if I showed an interest, but she is not for me.'

'It was plain to me that she favoured your attention.'

'She does—and I will marry one day—when I think the time is right and I have met the woman I want to spend the rest of my life with.'

Jane laughed. 'Then I wish you luck in that—but I am of the opinion that the older one gets, the more selective one gets. Now, if you don't mind, I'm going to bed.'

Getting to her feet, she thought of the easy conversation she had engaged in with her companion. The light in the depths of his eyes was as enigmatic as it was challenging to Jane and, unexpectedly, she felt a quiver of excitement. The quickening in Lord Randolph's eyes told her he was aware of that response. She felt a dangerous and frightening pull of attraction towards this powerful and accomplished man. She told herself that she would resist his allure

and focus only on resolving her current crisis with
Miriam. Once done, she could bid Francis Randolph
goodbye and not look back.

Chapter Four

Francis rose from the table and followed her to the door. He wanted to hold her in his arms, but instinct told him it would be the wrong thing to do. It was as if there was a wall between her and other people, particularly people of his own class. In a strange way he felt himself humbled by her. She was all heart and fiercely loyal to those she loved—qualities he seldom saw in others. She did not give freely of herself—not her time, not her company, and most of all not her own, very private, self. He imagined she was closer to her housekeeper, Bessie, than to anyone else.

He stood over her, his heavy-lidded gaze fixed on her lips. Her dark lashes swept down over her expressive green eyes. He wanted to reach out and release her hair from its confinement and breathe in the scent of her, for his fingers to caress and feel the softness of her body. But he could not. He should not—but why not? he argued with himself. A kiss would harm no one. The prospect was infinitely appealing, even though on the morrow he would undoubtedly regret having taken things so far. On the other hand, if he was going to have regrets, he might as well have something substantial to regret.

The longer they were together the more attracted to her he was. He wondered about her allure, for it was more than her face and body that attracted him. She had a presence that warmed him and a fiery spirit that challenged him. Taking her hand, he drew her close, placing his hands on her shoulders and drawing her into his arms, a desire, potent and primitive swelling inside him, one he wanted to savour and enjoy.

'What are you doing?' she asked, suddenly alarmed and trying to pull away, but he held her firm against him. A blush stained her cheeks, partly from indignation and partly from embarrassment. 'You are quite insufferable. How dare you take liberties with me?'

Francis's mouth curved in that faint, cynical smile of his and he continued to hold her close, his hands gentle, controlled and unyielding. He recalled Berkley's words before he had embarked on this journey, that with so much temptation within his sights, by the time he reached London he wouldn't give a damn who had sired her. Berkley was right.

'I wouldn't do that. Although—I would like to kiss you. Would you like to kiss me, Jane?' He felt her body lose its resistance and relax.

'I—I...'

'For just one moment I am asking you to forget everything else. Do you not find that appealing?' he murmured, seeing her bite her lower lip as she struggled apprehensively with the decision that faced her. It plucked a deep chord within Francis. With the lightest touch he ran a fingertip along the soft line of her jaw. He felt her shiver slightly against him and her lips parted on a breathless gasp as his finger followed the softness of her cheek. When she failed to answer, he said, 'How can I persuade you? How can I help you decide? Would you object if I kissed you?'

She shook her head slowly, her eyes fastened on his lips hovering close to her own.

Her need communicated itself to Francis and he could feel her melting, ready to experience whatever lay ahead. Lowering his mouth to hers, he succumbed to the impulse that had been tormenting him and kissed her long and deep and demanding, feeling the softness of her lips. His arms went round her and tightened across her back, pressing the contours of her body to his, her breasts coming to rest against his chest. He almost lost his head when he felt her lips part and she kissed him back. He released her lips, his mouth shifting across her cheek to her ear, his tongue flicking and exploring each sensitive crevice, then trailing back to her lips and claiming them once more, ardent and persuasive, a slow erotic seduction, tender, wanting.

When he at last lifted his mouth from hers, he smiled down at her. The kiss he had given her had been spontaneous, shocking him with its sweetness, its intensity. Her expression was bemused, her melting green eyes wide, her soft pink mouth partly open. He gently cradled her chin in his hand. In the candlelight she was very lovely, with the dreamy, faraway look in her eyes and the passion his kiss had aroused softening her features.

'It is plain to me that you enjoy being kissed.' When she did not reply immediately, he grinned and murmured, 'Surely I cannot have rendered you speechless.'

'Almost,' she murmured, taking a step back. 'It certainly took my breath.'

'I would hate to disappoint.'

Jane was unaware that her golden hair was many different shades and dazzling lights. Francis's expression was unreadable, smiling, a knowing look in his eyes. She gave him a speculative look.

'Another kiss before you go?'

'One is enough. You expect too much.'

'I will be as gentle as you wish me to be, Jane.'

'What are you trying to do—seduce me?'

With a low chuckle he trailed his finger lightly down her cheek. Her face, young, vulnerable and defenceless and already turning a soft pink, was naked beneath the heavy crop of her hair.

'What do you think I'm doing right now?' he murmured.

Jane stepped backwards. 'I have a very good idea, so if you don't mind I will retire to my room and enjoy what is left of my pride.'

Francis's eyes gleamed with devilish humour, and his lips drew into a slow smile. 'Very sensible, Jane.'

'Yes, I think so. You are a scoundrel, Francis Randolph, and I am certain I am just one in a long line of women.'

Francis shook his head and laughed. He was too much of a gentleman to admit that willing bed partners had always been available to him, but that he preferred discreet, exclusive liaisons with sophisticated women. He looked into her expectant gaze. 'Suffice to say I will keep the truth of it to myself.'

'Do you always get what you want?'

'Usually,' he answered. 'Perhaps because I am arrogant and inconsiderate—or selfish.'

'Or all three,' she was quick to bite back, careful not to look at his mouth which was hovering close to her own.

'Am I bothering you, Miss Deighton?'

'You know you are. Suddenly I feel less like your travelling companion and more like a tasty morsel you are about to devour.'

He gave a satisfied chuckle. 'A very delectable morsel.' He stared down at her, seeing how the bodice of her dress clung to her, outlining the shapely peaks of breasts that were high and firm. Francis could feel himself responding once again to her closeness. Maybe it was an indefinable impression, an illusion, a trick of the light from the candles, but she seemed changed somehow. What was it? What was in her eyes and what was in the soft turn of her lips, as though she smiled at some private thought? Her soft young face was turned to his and she was gazing at him strangely, too, assessing him in some way, her gaze reflective, a glow of something in her eyes, which were soft green velvet now.

'You don't have to leave,' he said, noting that she was breathing deeply, disturbingly affected by his nearness. He fixed his gaze on her, assessing, lingering and seducing. Colour warmed her cheeks. He devoured her with his eyes. There was a fire in the blue depths, a blaze of passion and remembrance of the kiss he had given her before, and longing.

'I think I should. You really are the most exasperating man.'

'I agree, but you are a woman and I am a man— and—here we are, with no one to see us.'

Confused by the gentle warmth of his gaze and the directness of his words, Jane could not determine whether he mocked her or told the truth. She had never known a man with such persistence and single mindedness.

'And you have a silken tongue. Control your lust— and please don't do that,' she complained, brushing his hand away as he reached out to touch her cheek.

His face was in shadow, but his eyes seemed to glow, laughing at her, mocking her. With her hair tumbled about her face, she looked unbearably young and vulnerable. There was no mistaking, however, the wounded fury that flashed in her magnificent eyes or the stiffening of her spine. Taking her upper arms, he drew her to his chest. 'I told you I am a man, Miss Deighton,' he assured her, the laughter gone from his voice, 'with all the needs and desires of a man. And you, my love, are so desirable it tortures me to have you near me day after day and not be able to touch you.'

When she made no attempt to extricate herself from his hold, he lowered his mouth to hers once more. His arms went round her, his only desire to hold her, to kiss her, for her to respond so that he could savour as he had earlier the sweetness of her. When he felt her lips quiver and her mouth opened beneath his, he almost groaned aloud with the pleasure of it, as desire, primitive and potent, poured through his veins. The ardour of her response surprised him. Answering her need, he deepened the kiss, his tongue probing and thrusting as their breaths mingled, warm and as one.

She leaned into him and he kissed her with all the persuasive force at his disposal, with such possessive ease that could clear a woman's mind of all thought. His mouth slanted over hers, his hands sliding over her back, splaying against her spine to force her body into intimate, thorough contact with his rigid thighs.

Slowly senses returned. Placing the flat of her hands gently against Francis's chest, Jane pushed him away. Raising his head, Francis looked at her upturned face.

'Please don't do this. I am not so easily persuaded. When I sought you out at Redmires, you made it clear that as a woman I held no attraction for you, that being the daughter of the man you hated, I had made myself your enemy too.'

'You are right. Your father is my enemy—you are not.'

'Well—we shall have to see. But I have just kissed the man I have looked on as someone who despises my family—and with good reason—and I have reason to despise myself. My father would be disappointed in me.'

'Miss Deighton,' he said with quiet firmness. 'I don't know how things stand between you and your father, but nothing can change what has just happened.'

'Would you,' she asked, 'change it?'

'No,' he said, speaking calmly. 'I do not regret it and will not regret kissing you again. I regret causing you any distress.' She bristled at the arrogance of his statement, but Francis forged ahead. 'What passed between us just now was not against your will. I felt your response.' As if to test her honesty, he said, 'That's how it was. Do you deny it?'

She shood her head. 'No,' she whispered, the word filled with feelings and emotions Francis could not identify.

'I am relieved to hear it.'

'I am tired and have perhaps had too much wine. You have caught me unawares—in a moment of weakness. But whatever it is, this must end now. I cannot allow you to distract me from my purpose. It should not have happened,' she said, wrapping her arms about herself. 'Don't you realise that? What are you trying to do? Is it not enough that your brother has seduced my sister without you trying to seduce me? I shall always regret my behaviour just now and, if you are a gentleman, you will forget all about it.'

Despite the stubborn lift to her chin and her rebellious tone, there was a tremor of fear in her voice and when Francis heard it he became still. Since beginning the journey, Jane had shown so much indefatigable spirit that he'd actually believed nothing could shake her. Now, however, as he at looked her hovering before him, observing the faint blue smudges beneath her glorious eyes, he saw that the ordeal of her sister's elopement had affected her deeply. She was amazing, he thought—brave and determined. Perhaps if he wasn't attracted to her, drawn to her, it wouldn't have mattered that she was watching him as if he were a dangerous animal.

He let out a sigh and, quietly and without emotion, said, 'What you ask is impossible. It happened and neither of us can erase it from our minds.'

'I shall do my very best to try.'

'And I will try to restrain myself, difficult as that will be while ever we are together.' Francis gazed down at her, a slight, infuriating smile curving his firm lips. His eyes plumbed the depths of hers, reliving the experience of kissing her as he had done so often in his fantasies. He saw a spark of sensuality below the surface of her charm. It caressed him like an old acquaintance and the way it made his heart quicken and his blood run warm was worth more than coupling with any other woman.

'We kissed. You kissed me back, which tells me you enjoyed the experience.' She glowered at him as much to rebuke him for his impudent reminder of his own behaviour as to declare her own response to it.

'You allow your imagination too much liberty. Perhaps it is time you gave it a rest.'

Francis's lips twitched with humour and the twinkle in his eye slowly evolved into a rakish gleam. 'I assure you I have no intention of reining in my imagination, not when I find the subject so appealing. And do not ask me to explain my imaginings to you, for they are of a most sensual nature and not for the ears of an innocent.'

'Then you are right. It is best you keep them to yourself. I don't want a repeat of this,' she said. 'I do mean what I say. It is not proper and certainly not acceptable to me. I don't know what kind of overtures you think you are making, but I think you should stop and consider my circumstances. A kiss is only a moment of weakness. It does not break down the barriers of a bitter past. The gulf between us is immense and I could never be anything to you but a woman to be visited in secret and in shame in the dark. Too much stands between us and we have your mother's feelings to consider. There must be no outward show of intimacy between us. My position and that of my sister is precarious. To get to London and Miriam away from your brother and back home is important to me.'

Despite her words of regret, Francis was both surprised and pleased by her response to his kiss. With desire surging through him, he had to fight back the urge to take her to bed. He gazed down at her upturned face. She was wide-eyed and vulnerable, her face flushed a glorious pink, and her lips slightly parted and moist. 'That was quite a speech. Be that as it may, do I see in your warming behaviour, in your response to my kiss, some glimmer of hope for a much more pleasurable understanding between us in the future? Despite your words of regret, do not deny what you feel, because I will not believe you.'

'As to that, we shall have to see.'

'What do you think of my method of persuasion?'

Jane drew a long, steadying breath and slowly expelled it. She hesitated before answering, her eyes searching deeply into his. 'In truth, I do not trust my heart and mind to withstand the barrage of your persuasion. But when a man kisses me, I would like for him to mean it. If you are flirting with me, then you should know that I don't like being kissed for your amusement. So, Lord Randolph, I think I will put a stop to our amorous interlude and go to bed.'

'Francis.'

She stared at him. 'I'm sorry?'

'I would like you to call me Francis.'

'I do not think that would be appropriate—in fact, it would be highly irregular—but Lord Randolph is such a mouthful.'

'There you are then. You have my permission to call me Francis.'

'That is generous of you.'

He grinned down at her. 'I have my good points.'

'Yes,' she said, laughing softly. 'I suppose even *you* must have some somewhere.'

'And you will call me Francis?'

'As you are already aware that I am the unconventional type, very well—Francis.'

A tremor ran through him when she spoke his name for the first time. 'Thank you. Are you going to grant me permission in turn to use your Christian name?'

'I have a feeling that if I don't, you will use it anyway.'

'I take it that's a yes.'

She nodded. 'Now—will you let me go to bed?'

'Goodnight, Jane. Try to get a good night's sleep.'

'I will—and I trust you will do the same.'

Standing away from the door, Francis let his gaze follow her and he was puzzled by his own reaction to her. She was a curious mix of an adolescent girl, naive and yet worldly. She exuded a sensuality, the memory of which would keep him awake at night. He could still feel the lingering, warm, beguiling sweetness of her. His smouldering stare took in her retreating figure. She was so lovely, so innocent, so ripe for seduction.

He was surprised to find he was enjoying the journey with this bright-eyed enchantress and the nearer they got to London he wouldn't mind if they were delayed. Getting to know the spirited Jane Deighton had been a welcome reprieve, like a breath of fresh air in a dark room that hadn't seen the light of day for years.

But the girl was vulnerable, traumatised. He could not take advantage of such an innocent creature. He knew that what she needed right now was someone she could trust, not some ardent stranger set on seduction. The enduring ache of suppressed passion stirred his blood. His heart seemed to soften before he felt something like a stab to the chest. For a moment his resistance wavered, making him pause. It was a small warning, but a warning all the same.

Too often since they had begun the journey together he had found his thoughts straying to her and he scowled, pulling himself up sharp. He was furious with himself for having succumbed so easily and foolishly to her charm. He had let himself be mindlessly borne away on a rush of passion. What the hell was wrong with him? Was she some kind of sorceress who had cast a spell on him? He was overwhelmed by the realisation that if he didn't take care she would come to mean something to him, but there were too many problems between them for that. In that they were in accord.

Drifting between total peace and a strange, delirious joy, a feeling of disquiet was creeping over Jane as her mind came together from the nether regions of the universe where it had fled. As she made her way to her own room, she realised what she had done. The daughter of Edward Deighton, the sworn enemy of Francis Randolph, had brazenly yielded in his arms. A rush of anguish tore through her. She had let him kiss her because of deeper feelings she hardly understood and, to her shame, she thought of her father and felt like a traitor. But there was no escaping the fact that embers of desire had been fanned, embers that had licked at her greedily and almost engulfed her. But a silent objection lingered and a small, uncomfortable voice in her head said, *What if he is simply using you?* The suggestion was unwelcome and she pushed it aside. The thought that this might be so was not to be borne.

And yet, innocent of the sort of warmth and passion Francis had skilfully aroused in her, which had poured through her veins with a shattering explosion of delight, it was like nothing she could have imagined. It was like being cocooned in a warm world of sensuality. At first it had been a kiss of exquisite restraint and she had been unable to think of anything but the exciting urgency of his mouth and the warmth of his breath. Her rampaging emotions when she wondered what it would be like to love such a man disturbed her greatly and she tried pushing them away, but they were like mischievous imps playing a teasing game, flitting to and fro through her mind when she least expected it. An emotion she had never experienced before had sweetly unfolded inside her, before vibrantly bursting with a fierceness that made her tremble. She had been lost in a wild and beautiful madness that had wiped out reason and will, and she had kissed him as deeply and as erotically as he had kissed her.

That kiss had been too much and too little, arousing deep feelings she did not understand. What had happened between them had been a sudden overwhelming passion, heightened by the intensity of the knowledge that it shouldn't be happening. From the beginning he had angered her, infuriated her, yet never had she felt as alive as she did now. But then, hadn't her body betrayed her? Was she really so weak? Yes, she realised with startling clarity. Where Francis Randolph was concerned she was.

But he was not her enemy. He never had been. In fact, he made her want to get to know him better, to step beyond the hatred he carried in his heart for her father. But how was she ever to burst the festering abscess of misunderstanding when her mind ordered her to be silent? When she had pulled away from him she had longed to respond to the look in his eyes, to feel his mouth on hers once more, setting her skin tingling and her blood on fire. But the image of her father stood between them and always would. Nothing could ever erase what had happened all those years ago.

In a daze of yearning and confusion, she slipped between the sheets. Sleep eluded her as she tried to understand the turbulent, consuming emotions Francis was able to arouse in her. With the taste of his kiss still warm on her lips, his gentleness and ardour towards her had shown her something of the man beneath the worldly, harsh surface and melted her resistance. She burrowed deep beneath the covers and curled into a tight ball, trying to suffocate all the feelings struggling to the surface, but try as she might, she was unable to stop herself thinking of that kiss. She dashed away all other unpleasant thoughts—she did not want to mar one second of the moment. So lost was she in her reflections that she did not notice when sleep at last claimed her.

The kiss had changed something between them. They were conscious of each other as never before.

They had left York behind and they talked and dozed in the warmth of the coach. Peace and acceptance was established between them—an unspoken thing. Francis didn't attempt to kiss her again. The moment was gone, but the memory of it stayed with them.

As the journey took them closer to London, Francis made an effort to distance himself from Jane by travelling on top with the driver, but he could not deny himself the sight of her. He found that he was weak, for before long he was once again seated across from her.

Never had he met a woman who possessed so much freedom of spirit and courage, who was so open and direct. He knew that she would never be anything but honest and the brightness in that steady, often disconcerting, gaze proclaimed the agility of an independent mind. She had the wild, untamed quality of her Northumberland heritage running in dangerous undercurrents just below the surface that found its counterpart in his own hot-blooded, impetuous nature.

Strangely, the realisation of who she was no longer banished his pleasure. Initially he had told himself that he must never forget that the Deighton blood flowed thick and strong through her veins. That he must never forget how her father's seduction of his mother had brought about her betrayal of his own father and that Edward Deighton had been driving the carriage that had killed him. Jane's father was his enemy and he had no right to think of his daughter in any personal way. But he could not deny that from the moment he had set eyes on her in Newcastle, she had fascinated and intrigued him.

As they approached London he noted there was a sad preoccupation about her. Her hands were elegantly folded and resting on the folds of her skirt. Leaning forward, he said quietly, 'You are very quiet. Jane. It is most unusual in one who normally has so much to say. I have no wish to disturb you, but you seem apprehensive. Are you worried about reaching London?'

'Yes, I am.'

'I have felt there is something wrong for some time. Would you like to talk about it?'

She sighed, settling into the upholstery and looking across at him. 'It's silly, really, but the closer I get to London my unease on facing both Miriam and your mother increases. I find it hard to accept all that has happened. Part of me is impatient to get the business over with so that we can return to Northumberland and the other is reluctant to face Miriam's stubborn disobedience.'

'Let us hope that between us we can make both Andrew and your sister see sense.'

A little smile tugged at the corners of Jane's mouth. 'Oh, Francis. What on earth would I have done without you these past days?'

He gave her a wry smile. 'I hope you will never come to think yourself so self-contained that you cannot turn to me.'

They fell silent, their world existing within the

warm light of the coach. Francis watched Jane in admiring speculation.

Aware of his gaze, she captured his eyes. 'What is it, Francis?'

'I can truthfully say that I have not had so lovely a companion to pass the long hours of a journey,' he murmured softly.

'That is compliment indeed, Francis. It's a pity the setting is not more cosy.'

His eyes gleamed. 'And you like it less because you are here with me—alone,' he murmured, his words more of a statement than a question.

'I didn't say that and it is certainly not what I meant.'

'I'm relieved to hear it. But whatever thought is going through your mind, Jane, I must stress that, no matter what happens when we reach London, I want to be your friend, not your enemy.'

His words, spoken sincerely, brought a smile to her lips. 'It's strange how an arrangement of mutual convenience has turned to friendship. At this time when I feel that the whole world is against me, it is comforting to know that.'

Jane gazed out of the window as they approached London, craning her neck to have her first glimpse. The journey hadn't been as difficult as she imagined it would be and it was almost over now. She still felt the warmth of his kiss like some drug that crept through her, a totally new sensation that made her look back on her life as if it had been in a state of deprivation which was miraculously assuaged.

The intimacy of the kiss aside, Francis had been considerate of her needs and comfort and she had been deeply moved. They had become closer and she had begun to like him—and she wished she didn't. It was impossible not to respond to his masculinity and that warmth, try though she might to resist. Later, when they reached London, she would harden herself against him, but right now she could only consider herself lucky that he was the man he was.

He was watching her closely, a heavy lock of dark hair dipping over his brow, his eyes warm and soft, his lips ready to spread in another smile. He had never looked more endearing. She wanted to cross over to him, wanted him to hold her, to stroke her hair and banish the nervous tremors inside. As if reading her thoughts, he did smile.

Her first glimpse of the city was unforgettable. The autumn day was bright, the earlier showers having blown away, leaving the air sharp and clean. The towers and rooftops were clearly visible. London was a city Jane had never been to, but it had always seemed a place of compelling enchantment. At Beckwith Manor she and Miriam had listened avidly to travellers' tales of the happenings in London, of the men and women who made up the world of society and the court of King George. It was a place so remote it never touched their lives.

Jane found London a confusion of sound and colour. It was as if all the world was gathering in this one place. Carts and carriages of every description rumbled along the streets between crowded buildings at frightening speeds, wheels clattering over the cobbles. The pavements were congested with people going about their business and the din was incredible as hawkers cried their wares. They travelled on, making their way along fashionable streets and squares before coming to a quiet street with gracious houses.

The carriage halted outside a house of modest proportions and Francis climbed out, turning to assist Jane. He ushered her along the path to the door, reached up a shallow flight of steps that curved outward in a graceful sweep, with posts on either side which supported two large lamps. The door was opened by a friendly young female servant and they entered into a large hall. The house was spacious and, as Jane was to discover, the surrounding walled garden was an earthly paradise in miniature. A woman emerged at the top of the stairs and hurried down to greet them.

'Mother!' Francis hugged her warmly.

Jane stood back, watching the fond reunion between mother and son. Lady Randolph was a handsome woman. She carried the assurance of beauty stamped on her indelible bone structure. Jane thought her to be in her fifties. Her hair, which was arranged in a chignon, was dark brown with silver streaks. Her eyes were dark, too. Her body was closely outlined in a dove-grey dress and there was style and grace and sureness in every line of her. She had felt a great apprehension on this meeting with Francis's mother, but she need not have worried. As Jane watched her, she suddenly turned her attention to her son's companion and smiled a radiant smile of welcome. If Lady Randolph was surprised to see her, she hid it well.

'You must be Jane.' For some seconds she gazed at Jane's face in silence and then she smiled. 'How grown up you are—you and Miriam. You won't remember, but I saw you shortly after your mother...' She paused and Jane noted her eyes shone with moisture.

'No,' she said, 'I don't remember.'

'Of course you don't. I'm happy to know you, Jane, and to welcome you into my home. I have been expecting you, although not quite so soon.'

There was an air of kindliness and generosity about her and Jane liked her immediately. There was refinement to Lady Randolph, refinement and beauty, and as she was later to find out, she had a gift of friendship. It was easy to see how her father had been attracted by her.

'Please forgive my intrusion, Lady Randolph.'

'You are not intruding, my dear. Quite the opposite. Andrew and Miriam arrived yesterday—and what an enormous surprise that was.'

'Andrew is here?' Francis said, glancing around the hall, as if expecting to see his brother materialise from one of the rooms.

'He's out at present—something about seeing one of his friends, but I'm expecting him back any moment. Miriam—who I must say is a charming young woman—is in the garden,' she said to Jane. 'I cannot tell you how surprised I was when they told me of the circumstances which have brought them to London. I understand they left Newcastle without a word to anyone of what they intended—which was very naughty of them—so I imagined you would soon be hot on their heels. But I confess that I did not expect you to turn up together.'

'I was fully aware that Andrew was coming to London,' Francis said, 'but I knew nothing of Miss Deighton accompanying him—that they'd got some mad idea in their heads about eloping—until Jane arrived at Redmires to enlighten me.'

'And so you decided to join forces and come together.'

At that moment the door opened and Francis's younger brother walked in. Not as tall as Francis, he was an amiable, smiling young man with unruly brown hair and bright blue eyes. The smile on his lips vanished as soon as his eyes lighted on Francis.

'Good Lord! Francis! What are you doing here—and with Miss Deighton? I never thought—'

'What? That I would come after you?' Francis's face darkened for an instant as he strove for control. 'What the hell do you think you are playing at, Andrew? I knew you were coming to London, but you omitted to tell me you were taking Miss Deighton with you. What have you to say for yourself?'

As Francis's cold eyes flickered over him, Andrew attempted to straighten his neck linen. 'I know—I should have told you, only—' Andrew flinched before his brother's controlled rage. He was ensnared in a web of his own folly.

'You've been a fool, Andrew, a stupid, self-indulgent fool,' Francis went on furiously without giving Andrew time to reply. 'I am disappointed in you—deeply disappointed. What in God's name made you do it? You have known Miss Deighton—a well-brought-up young lady—for such a short time.'

'I have known her for months. I was drawn to her from the start and hold her in the highest esteem,' he said, doing his best to smile in an attempt to lighten the serious tones and harsh lines of his brother's face. 'Miriam wanted to come—she—'

Unable to keep silent, Jane stepped forward. 'Don't you dare try placing the blame on my sister. You knew perfectly well what you were doing when you arranged this elopement. Do you realise what damage this will have done to her reputation? You have been alone together for four days and nights. Were you serious—or are you no different from the rest of the young rakes who seduce young women and then discard them?'

Deeply offended, Andrew faced her squarely. 'If I'd had seduction in mind, Miss Deighton, I would not have brought her to my mother's house. You have it all wrong. I am no rake. I honour Miriam and I would not lay a finger on her until she is my wife.'

'Wife? Miriam is just seventeen years old. Any aspirations you might have to make her your wife you forfeited the moment you absconded with her.'

'Jane, enough,' Francis said quietly but firmly, taking her arm and drawing her to one side.

Furious, she shook her arm free. 'Enough, you say. That silly, impressionable girl, who is my sister, was so flattered by your brother's attentions that she would foolishly allow him to talk her into anything. How do we know his ardour hasn't run away with him and he's seduced her already?'

'Stop it, Jane,' Francis said sharply. 'Calm down. I will listen to what Andrew has to say while my mother shows you to your room. She will send Miriam to you and you can speak to her alone.'

Lady Randolph held out her hand to Jane. 'Yes, come, Jane. Where are my manners? You must be quite worn out after your journey—although why sitting in a coach all day should make one so, I have no idea, but it is so.'

Jane followed Lady Randolph up the wide curving staircase, aware of flowers and pale curtains and polished floors. 'What a lovely house, Lady Randolph.'

'Yes, I think so. I will show you to your room and have hot water sent up to you. It isn't a large house and we'll be a bit cramped, I'm afraid. I'm not used to having so many in the house at once. You will be sharing with Miriam. I will fetch your sister from the garden. I'm sure you will have plenty to say to her.'

'Thank you, Lady Randolph. You are very kind. I have much to say to Miriam and reproach her for.'

Lady Randolph smiled. 'Miriam is truly fortunate to have such a caring, conscientious sister.'

Lady Randolph took Jane to a pleasant room overlooking the garden. She waited by the window for her sister to be brought, gazing at the tall, crowded buildings beyond the garden, thinking that Miriam's dream of coming to London had been realised at last. She was dazzled by the rich—the fine clothes they wore and how they carried with them the air of the gay cosmopolitan world London always seemed to be. She constantly bemoaned their own situation. There had to be something more than life at Beckwith Manor, she often complained. Little wonder she had allowed Andrew Randolph to carry her off to London.

Chapter Five

Jane didn't have long to wait for her sister. Miriam entered quietly. There was a feeling of unreality in the situation against which Jane chafed. She found it impossible to accept that Miriam might become a member of the Randolph family. Her heart turned over on seeing her sister and the familiar air of fragility that drew people to her. She was fair and vibrantly pretty. Jane could also see that her sister was engulfed with guilt and remorse. She was quiet as Jane approached her, took a hesitant step forward, then halted. She twisted her hands together in a gesture of appeal.

'I did not think you would follow me, Jane.'

'I came,' Jane said stonily, 'to take you home. Did you really think I would let you run away without trying to prevent it? Did you not spare a moment's thought for me—how shocked and worried I would be when I found out what you had done?'

'Of course I did, but I knew you would try to stop me.'

'Yes, I would,' Jane said, suddenly wanting to grasp Miriam, to shake some sense into her. 'What kind of sister would I be if I didn't? Why did you do this—and with Andrew Randolph of all people? Why, Miriam? Why did you do it? Have I really been so hard on you that you couldn't talk to me?'

Miriam took a few more steps toward her. 'You were always so busy there was no talking to you,' she replied with quiet accusation. 'I know how angry you must be, Jane. I don't know how to ask for forgiveness. It's too big a thing to ask for. But if you could try... What can I say that will make sense and that you understand? Will you please try?'

'You do realise that nothing can come of this—this infatuation—because that's all it is—all it can be.'

Miriam drew herself up and anger and defiance flashed in her eyes. 'It is not infatuation. I love Andrew—and he loves me. He is everything, the whole world to me, and if to be parted from you is the price I must pay for my pride and my wilfulness, then so be it.'

Jane saw the tears that overflowed from Miriam's eyes and slid down her cheeks. Miriam was a part of her, a part of her life. She wanted to lean forward and kiss her cheek, to tell her not to worry and that everything would be all right as she had done all her life, but she could not do that. She felt the anger stir in her again—it was there all the time, the anger and the desolation. And the fear that in her anger she might lash out and destroy everything that was between them. With the absence of their father she had looked on Miriam as the most precious person in her life and she could not begin to think about being without her. She cursed this elemental, selfish force in herself, but could not deny it. But she had little time to ponder these thoughts and emotions which her sister's elopement had brought just then, nor did she want to. She forced herself to close the distance that divided them.

'I cannot do that, Miriam. You have to come back with me. Have you not thought how Father would feel—how strongly he would oppose a marriage between you and Andrew Randolph?'

'Of course I have,' she cried fiercely. 'I have done nothing else. But he isn't here. He's never here—and I doubt he would even care.'

'Yes, Miriam, he would. He was accused of killing Andrew's father. That can never be forgotten.'

'I know, but we cannot help what we feel for each other. You are twenty-one. You have been responsible for everything since Father went away. Permit me to marry Andrew and give me your blessing.'

Jane realised she was sinking beneath the weight of what was being imposed on her. Never had she known anything like it. Rage, compassion—fear. Every emotion churned and fought within her. The strongest of all was the fear.

Miriam's tears continued to fall. 'You are angry with me, Jane, and I cannot blame you. I know I must have put you to so much trouble. I am so sorry.'

Jane sighed, sitting on the bed and patting the covers beside her. 'I was worried about you, Miriam.

That note you left—it didn't tell me anything. I was at my wit's end wondering what to make of it.'

'Please don't be too angry with Andrew. I was the one who wanted to elope.'

'I am angry with him, Miriam—but it is nothing to what Francis will be.'

Miriam's eyes opened wide with alarm. 'Francis—his brother?'

'Did you not see him when you came in?'

'No. Lady Randolph brought me in from the garden the back way. What on earth is he doing here?'

Briefly Jane explained everything that had happened when she had received Miriam's note and how Francis Randolph came to be with her. 'He's none too pleased with his brother, Miriam—and you must understand why.'

'I must go to Andrew. I can't let him take all the blame.'

'Leave them for a while. Perhaps when we go downstairs Francis's anger will have abated.' Jane sighed, wondering what to do now. 'Lady Randolph is not what I expected. She's nice.'

'Yes, she is—and very kind. She was angry with Andrew for bringing me to London—I think she hoped you or his brother would come and deal with the problem we've created. But it needn't be a problem. Not when we intend to marry. Do you think there was any truth in what people said when her husband died—that she was in love with Father?'

'Perhaps. I don't know for sure. But what is to be done now, Miriam? We can't stay here—we have to get back to Northumberland. It is feared there will be a rising—Father is in Scotland and there is a warrant out for his arrest.'

Miriam's face paled. 'I didn't know.'

'Of course you didn't. How could you when your eyes were blinkered by Andrew Randolph and your mind set on eloping to get married?' She sighed, shaking her head wearily. 'I didn't know about the possible rising myself until I was halfway to London. But you must know you can't marry Andrew Randolph. Father would not allow it.'

'I've told you that Father is not here, Jane, and if he is caught then the consequences will be dire indeed—for us, too, which is all the more reason for me not to go back to Northumberland.'

'And what about me? I have to go back. Beckwith Manor doesn't run itself.'

'I know—but you are not alone, Jane. You have Sam and other workers to take care of the farm and Bessie to run the house. I want to be Andrew's wife. I cannot carry on without him. I have a right to live my own life as I choose and I choose to spend it with Andrew as his wife. This is not nonsense, Jane.'

'I believe it is infatuation.'

'No. It is love.'

'You have to return home with me. You are stronger than you know. In two or three years this will seem a small thing when you look back. Don't let it hurt so much, Miriam. If, as you say, you truly love Andrew, it will endure—later we will see—when circumstances change.'

'You would, Jane, I know,' Miriam said harshly. 'I
have not your endurance. In the meantime, what am I
supposed to do? Say I'll think about it and wait until
I'm over twenty-one? If I'm not sure of this, then I'll
never be sure of anything in my life. I know you are
concerned for my well-being, but Andrew and I have
made our plans. I—I won't give him up. I know you
think I'm young and silly and that I don't know my
own mind, but I do love him.'

Miriam's face had taken on such a look of agony
and despair that Jane softened involuntarily. 'I know
you do,' she said gently and sighed. 'I know you've
grown up, Miriam, but do you really think you're
ready to be married?'

'Yes, I do. Eloping was all my idea. I persuaded
Andrew. You mustn't think badly of him.'

'If I have misjudged him, then I am sorry. He is a
fine young man.'

Miriam looked at her, relief and hope lighting her
eyes. 'You are? Oh, Jane, I can't tell you what it means
to me to her you say that.'

'We'll talk about it later. You've always had high-
blown notions, Miriam—unfortunately, without a
dowry they are notions that can only belong to those
who could afford them. Not that we aren't well-born,
our breeding unmistakable, but Father's involvement
with the Jacobites has brought about our impover-
ishment.'

'None of that concerns Andrew.' Miriam went to
the window, Jane followed and stood by her side. 'See,
Jane. Look,' she said, taking Jane's arm and turning

her to look at the city beyond the garden. 'The whole teeming world of London waits beyond this garden. It's all so exciting—Northumberland so far away.'

'It is, Miriam, but London is not for us. Lady Randolph belongs to a fashionable society—fashionable friends and clothes. We cannot hope to enter such a world.'

'Don't be so negative, Jane. Things will change. You'll see.'

Jane wasn't convinced of that and she was even less convinced when, just before she went down to partake of the evening meal, she looked out of the window and saw Miriam and Andrew seated on a bench at the far end of the garden. They sat close together, facing each other, deep in conversation. She sighed. What was she going to do with her sister? It had become more of a problem than she had expected. She had been so certain that she would come to London and take Miriam back home with her, but it wasn't going to be like that.

Attired in the one dress she had brought with her, which had seen better days—her best summer gown, the one reserved for special occasions, not that there had been many of those in the past few years—she went downstairs.

Daylight was diminishing and candles in wall sconces and candelabra were lit in the hall. The door to the dining room was open and the table gleamed with silver and crystal. At the far end of the room was an impressive marble fireplace, above which a hung a large mirror framed in scrolled gilt. It was a house devoted entirely to the care and comfort of one woman and everything in it reflected taste and a feeling for beauty. Lady Randolph's housekeeper, a quiet, neat woman, trained to anticipate her mistress's wants, suddenly appeared in the hall and told her to go into the dining room, informing her that Lady Randolph would be down shortly.

Entering the dining room, she found Francis helping himself to some wine. He was wearing a tailored black broadcloth coat and breeches and his pale grey waistcoat was embroidered with white silk flowers. A pristine white neckcloth at his throat emphasised the darkness of his hair and the deep blue of his eyes. He was an impressive, imposing figure and her heart never ceased to do strange things when she was with him. Pouring another glass of wine, he handed it to her.

'Well?' he asked. 'How did it go with your sister?'

'Miriam is totally unrepentant,' she answered, taking a grateful gulp of her wine. 'She is adamant that she will not return to Northumberland. What am I to do? I cannot force her to return home, but she cannot remain here. She cannot impose on your mother's hospitality indefinitely. I really should have taken more notice of her in the days building up to her leaving.'

'You shouldn't blame yourself. None of this is your fault. You are not your sister's keeper, Jane. Come and sit down and try to relax.'

She let him lead her to one of the high-backed chairs set at an angle to the window. He sat in the one opposite, stretching his long muscular legs out in front of him and crossing them at the ankles.

'But I am responsible for her. With Father away from home and Miriam under age, that is exactly what I am.' Resting her head against the back of the chair, she sighed, gazing across at him. 'I'm sorry, Francis. Neither of us bargained for any of this.'

They took a moment to sip and appreciate the wine, the atmosphere relaxed between them. There was silence inhabited by the living presence of the fire. Jane found her eyes captured and held by Francis's dark blue ones. With his dark hair curling softly into his neck, the same magnetism she had seen many times was in his eyes. The room seemed to come to life with his presence, infusing it with his own energy and vigour.

'I imagine you are pleased to see your mother.'

'I am. I don't see as much of her as I would like since she came to live in London. My untimely arrival with a lovely young lady—and Andrew before me—has set the house in turmoil and certainly gives the servants something to gossip about.' He laughed softly. 'Should word get out in Northumberland that one day Andrew ran off with one Miss Deighton and the next day I was seen leaving for London with the other, it would spread through Corbridge and Newcastle like a wind through a hayfield.'

Jane was suddenly alarmed. 'I sincerely hope not. I am unconcerned about my own reputation, but where

Miriam's is concerned, she is already teetering on the edge. I was hoping we could return to Beckwith with no one any the wiser.'

'I doubt you will be able to do that. She was seen getting into the post with Andrew, don't forget. And consider what I have just said—that it will not have gone unnoticed that we two took chase together.'

Jane stared at him. 'I know. I should have thought of that at the time, but I was desperate. I suppose I should have taken the post myself.'

'I couldn't let you do that. I offered you my assistance.' His eyes glowed in the warm light coming in through the window as he gave her a lazy smile. 'I only did what any self-respecting gentleman would have done in such circumstances—and I have enjoyed having your company along the way.'

Jane's heart gave a slight leap and she met his gaze warm on her face. Andrew and Miriam entered at that moment, giving her no opportunity to reply to Francis's comment.

'Here you are, Jane,' Miriam said, crossing the room towards her sister.

'As you see, Miriam.' She stood up, placing her empty glass on an occasional table and facing her sister. 'Francis, allow me to present my sister Miriam. I am sure you will have seen her at some time or other, but you will not have been formally introduced.'

Miriam bobbed a little curtsy, her eyes shining happily and sublime in her innocence. It was as if she had done no wrong and, if she had, then all would be forgiven.

'I am pleased to meet you, Miss Deighton,' Francis said, getting to his feet. 'Although I can't pretend that I wish the circumstances were different.'

'I'm sure you do,' Miriam replied, slightly abashed. 'I—realise Andrew and I have put you to a lot of trouble.'

'Which was quite unnecessary,' Francis said, glancing at Andrew who had taken up a firm stance beside Miriam. 'Getting you back to Northumberland is our main concern.'

'And Miriam is my main concern,' Andrew said pointedly. 'We did not go through all this for her to return home.'

'I disagree. There will be no further discussion on the subject. Since you are about to start your employment with the East India Company here in London, you will remain here as planned. I will escort Jane and her sister back to Beckwith Manor.'

Andrew stepped forward. 'No, Francis. You can't do this.'

'I can and I will, Andrew. I must insist that we keep this unpleasant business between ourselves and in this you will assist us by maintaining a discreet silence. When Miss Deighton is back in the north, you will have no further contact with her. Is that understood?'

'Why, Francis? Because of who she is? I know about the past, what happened between our families, but that's where I would like it to remain. Miriam wasn't to blame any more than I was. She had no part in it and should not be made to carry the burden of it—no more than you should, Francis—or you, Miss Deighton,' he said, looking at Jane. 'Only a fool would let their feelings stand in the way of what is important.'

'Perhaps you're right, Andrew,' Francis said. 'But I meant what I said. Miss Deighton will return north with her sister.'

For a moment Jane thought Andrew was going to capitulate before the seniority and the wrath of his older brother, but he drew himself up with a determination that she couldn't help but admire.

'No, Francis. I am of an age to make up my own mind. If it can be avoided, I will not be parted from Miriam. Just give me the chance to prove my devotion to her. I'd protect her and cherish her and love her as long as she lives.'

As he took Miriam's hand in his own, Jane saw that his hand was trembling, his face set pale with deep emotion. She could not deny the sincerity of his feelings. Strangely, her heart swelled with pity. He was crushed by the wave of events that had overtaken him. There was moisture in his eyes and he blinked rapidly, leaving her in no doubt of this young man's tender feelings and deep concern for Miriam. The anger that had consumed her from the moment she had learned of the elopement evaporated, along with her belief that Andrew Randolph was anything like his brother, and nor would he be if he lived to be a hundred.

'Well,' said Lady Randolph from the doorway. 'I see you are all waiting for me. I am sure you will be hungry so let us sit up, shall we? I hope your room is to your liking, Jane.'

'Yes, thank you,' Jane replied.

'Andrew, I hope you and your brother have reached some kind of truce.'

'Francis can be quite insufferable,' Andrew grumbled, seating himself beside Miriam.

'I couldn't agree more,' said his mother, spreading a napkin over her lap. 'But I am going to ask you both to lower your swords as a favour to me—at least until after we have eaten so that we can do justice to cook's excellent meal. It wouldn't do for you both to end up with indigestion, now, would it? However, I grant Francis can be a touch overbearing at times— would you not agree, Jane, having had to put up with him all the way to London?'

'Worry not, Mother.' Francis laughed, seating himself across from Jane. 'I was the personification of a gentleman, as I am sure Jane will agree.'

Jane raised a sceptical brow, tempted to inform Lady Randolph that her beloved son was full of contradictions, but instead she said, 'Of course—but that is not to say that we were totally in agreement all the time.'

'I should hope not. That wouldn't do at all. If you disagree with what he says, then you should say so. You must forgive him, Jane,' she said, signalling to the maid to bring in the food. 'The ladies of his acquaintance are usually more accommodating. He can be quite charming when the mood takes him.'

'Most ladies do find me charming and pleasant—and some actually enjoy my company.'

'I imagine they do,' Jane said, locking eyes with him across the table. He smiled, a devilishly engaging smile, a wonderful smile. Francis Randolph exuded provocative charm, could probably charm the birds out of the trees if he had a mind to, but this particular bird wasn't prepared to take the tumble for a devastating smile and a silver tongue. 'If you are to remain here in London, then you will have the opportunity to use that charm. It would be a shame to deprive the ladies of your company if they enjoy it so much.'

Lady Randolph laughed softly, seeming to enjoy the banter between Jane Deighton and her elder son. 'I think you have the measure of Francis, my dear. Might I suggest that you do not head back north immediately? Francis was telling me that you have never been to London before. It would be a shame for you to leave without seeing it. You are very welcome to stay here for just as long as you like and I would be delighted to show you the sights—and perhaps we could go to the theatre one night.'

'That is very generous of you, Lady Randolph,' Jane said, touched by the suggestion. 'But—I—don't see how we can. We neither of us have brought sufficient clothes with us for an extended stay—and certainly nothing suitable for a visit to the theatre. I really don't think—'

'That can soon be remedied. There are trunks of gowns in the loft, doing nothing but gathering dust. You are welcome to look through them—see if anything takes your fancy. A few tucks here and there and I'm sure you could make them fit.'

There was no reason Jane could put into words even now why she should refuse, but she attempted to do just that. 'Why—that is exceedingly generous of you, Lady Randolph—but we can't possibly accept...'

'Think about it, Jane,' Francis was quick to interrupt. 'What you wear is a minor problem which can easily be overcome.'

'Of course it can,' his mother said. 'I shall see to that myself.'

'Now I am here I intend to remain in London a couple of weeks,' Francis went on. 'It will give us time to consider the situation our siblings have presented us with. When I return to Redmires, Jane, you can accompany me. That way you will not have to travel alone.'

'I won't be alone, Francis. Miriam will be with me.'

'Jane,' Miriam said, ready to argue the point once more. 'I've told you I will not be going back to Beckwith Manor.'

'I think,' Lady Randolph said, 'that we should let that particular matter rest tonight. Plenty of time to discuss what is best to be done in the morning.'

'We will not change our minds,' Andrew retorted, clearly determined to have his way.

'No,' his mother said, 'I don't expect you will.'

For the rest of the meal Jane was entertained in a manner she had not thought possible by Lady Ran-

dolph. She was as gracious and kind as she was clever
and warm. Her laughter and her charm were infectious, and Jane felt the tension she had been under
since leaving the north melt away. Talk was on the
latest London gossip and Andrew's new venture into
the exciting world of the East India Company. Lady
Randolph made no secret of the fact that she encouraged him in this and was looking forward to seeing
more of him.

Afterwards they retired to the drawing room to
drink coffee and hot chocolate. Glancing at Miriam
seated with Andrew on a sofa, Jane thought her sister
looked as if she belonged here, sipping her chocolate
daintily from a china cup, gazing at Andrew with
adoring eyes, and feeling at home in a silk gown.
Where had that come from? Jane wondered—later to
discover that Lady Randolph had given it to her—just
one out of the trunk she had mentioned. Jane suddenly
felt gauche and very much the country girl.

The evening passed in a relaxed and congenial
atmosphere. It was not late when she retired, pleasantly warmed with the wine and easy conversation,
although she had noted that Francis was noticeably
quiet. When she bade her sister goodnight in the bed
they were sharing, she made it plain that they would
discuss the matter of her returning to the north in
the morning.

Sunlight streaming in through the window filled
the bedchamber the following morning. Unaccus-
tomed to such luxury, Jane stretched in the luxurious

comfort of the bed. Strangely she moved in a glow of happiness. She might have come to London in a state of panic in pursuit of her sister, but she felt ready for everything she would see and do that came her way. At home she would have been up and doing long since before sitting down to one of Bessie's huge breakfasts. She thought there was something unreal about being here in Lady Randolph's house—the woman who had been involved in an affair with her own father—and she found it rather strange that the lady had welcomed her and Miriam into her house without any show of awkwardness.

Dressed and surprisingly hungry, Jane went downstairs with Miriam to join the rest of the household for breakfast. Miriam was her usual cheerful self, convinced that she would have her way where her beloved Andrew was concerned. Struck by the absence of Francis, Lady Randolph informed Jane that he had left early on a matter of business.

'Did he say when he would be back?' she enquired, missing his presence after being so closely confined with him on the journey.

'Perhaps later this afternoon. He's left me to take care of you so, with the weather being quite glorious today, I thought I would order the carriage and take you and Miriam on a tour of London. Does that appeal to you?'

'Why—yes, thank you, but we are putting you to an awful lot of trouble.'

'Nonsense. You have no idea how I long for company some days. It will be my pleasure. What would you like to do, Jane? Do you like music and painting and the like?'

'Yes, although I have little time for such indulgences.'

'Then we will make a point of visiting all the places of interest I think you should see—and the playhouse, occasions when we can all be present. I am sure you will enjoy the experience of learning the city by night.'

Jane spread some strawberry jam on the soft white bread, suddenly experiencing all of Miriam's restless curiosity.

The gowns Jane and Miriam selected from the trunks Lady Randolph opened up for them were spread before them in a beautiful confusion of colour and expensive materials. Jane fingered with reverence a sapphire silk she had chosen for herself and immediately set to work placing a stitch here and there. Thankfully she was useful with a needle, as was Miriam, who was delighted with the gowns and the beautiful fur-trimmed cloak she pulled out of the trunk.

After lunch the carriage was brought round and Lady Randolph ushered then inside. With Andrew seated beside her, Miriam's eyes were bright with excitement at the outing, and Jane allowed herself to fall in with her. Filled with sunlight, the air clean and clear after an early morning shower and fluffy white clouds drifting across the blue sky, London had a sparkle to it. Jane and Miriam devoured the sights and sounds of what their mother had told them was the most exciting city in the world.

The city had a lively air. The trees in the parks were changing to their autumnal glory, the flower beds vivid patches of colour. Windows of houses and shops gleamed and majestic edifices looked stately in the sunlight, a variety of spires reaching above the rooftops. A muffin man was selling cakes on the street and street sweepers dashed out to sweep away the steamy mounds the horses left behind.

With many affairs of his own to take care of here in London, Francis was away from the house until the evening meal. Jane was surprised how much she missed having him close, how her gaze would stray to the road outside the window in the hope of seeing him return. The pleasure and the intensity she had felt when they were together surprised her and the very act of trying not to think of him brought him more swiftly and powerfully to mind—how he looked, how bold his lean profile, the brooding intensity of his eyes when he didn't know he was being observed. Her treacherous mind would suddenly recall how skilfully his mouth had felt when he had kissed and caressed her lips and the exquisite pleasure he had made her feel.

Her heart suddenly swelled—with what? Admiration? Affection? Love? No, not that. It was too soon. But however hard she tried she couldn't help wanting to be with him—wanting him. Recollecting herself, she shook away such thoughts. She was being an utter fool, romanticising Francis simply because he was a handsome man, sleek and fierce and incredibly skilled in arousing her desire, and because she was weak and helplessly attracted to him.

When the evening they were to visit the theatre arrived, Jane sat before the mirror while Miriam chattered ceaselessly and a maid arranged Jane's hair, drawing it up and to the side, two fat ringlets trailing over her naked shoulder. She studied the face reflected in the oval glass. It was thoughtful and she nodded now and then at Miriam's words without hearing what she said. All she could think of was the evening ahead of her as she became part of the fashionable world of London. She had only heard stories of the elite society and was nervous about her first experience. She was wearing an off-the-shoulder gown of violet taffeta with silver lace ruffles at her bosom to disclose the tops of her breasts. It was a gown fit for any occasion. They were to attend the theatre in Covent Garden and afterwards, determined to make the most of the evening, Lady Randolph thought it would be nice to go on to supper.

Miriam went ahead of Jane, moving through the foyer of the theatre with pride and happiness by Andrew's side as she kept up a stream of vivacious chatter. Francis and Jane drew envious stares. Francis's tall lean handsomeness and Jane's beauty made them stand out as they entered the theatre. It seemed as if Lady Randolph knew nearly everyone present, for the circle of those wanting to be introduced widened around them and they were greeted warmly. Some young men pushed their way through the throng in hopes of being introduced to this new beauty to arrive on the scene. They stood and postured, finding her even more delectable close up. Their faces fell with disappointment when Francis, with some humour, took her arm and led her away. It was his way of taking care of her and Jane was delighted to see the faintest air of proprietorship there.

They all took their seats in the box Francis had reserved. Feeling her spirits rise, Jane was enthralled as she absorbed everything about her. When the first act was over, the audience spilled out of the pit and some of the people from the boxes pushed their own way into the throng in a bewildering press, laughing and talking. Having no wish to join them, when Lady Randolph left the box with Miriam and Andrew, Jane was content to remain in the box and watch the goings-on with delight. She was happy just to look as grand ladies paraded below and flitted from box to box and laughed to see them flirting with gentlemen who weren't their husbands. Francis, crisply tailored and handsome in a dark green velvet frock coat and white silk neckcloth, moved to the seat beside her to keep her company, delighted in her obvious excitement at the production.

Jane's eyes shone and her smile was quick and easy as she worked her fan with a carefree air. The way her hair was dressed revealed the exquisite set of her head and shoulders and she possessed a natural grace in the way she moved. Tonight she seemed to respond to the setting as if she had been attending the theatre all her life. She desperately wanted to know who inhabited the other boxes and listened as Francis pointed out the prominent figures from the political and social scene. Perhaps before they left she would like to be introduced to one or two. The air was warm and suffocating with the mingled smells of perfume and hair pomade and Jane worked her fan to cool her face.

'Are you enjoying the play?'

Her eyes shone delightfully as they met his. 'Oh, yes. I never imagined the theatre could be so exciting. I won't forget it, Francis, not ever.'

'You are full of surprises, Jane,' he said, chuckling softly.

'How so?'

'You look enchanting. I'm wondering how you manage to look like a woman of fashion and beauty, well used to attending the theatre, and still retain some of the freshness of the north country. Seeing you now as you swish your fan, it's an effort to recall the young woman I came upon at Beckwith Manor, having just assisted with the birth of a foal. You have used the time we have been in London to startling effect.'

Jane had been happily watching the comings and goings below her through an opera glass, storing up every detail for the time she would have to return to Northumberland. Now she turned her head and stared at Francis, snapping her fan shut. 'I have, Francis. I cannot fail to be excited and impressed by all of this and what I have seen. But I am still the same Jane. You can change the setting, but I will always be the same. Tell me where we are going when we leave the theatre.'

'I've booked a table at my favourite tavern— famous for its oysters. Do you like oysters, Jane?'

'I don't know. I've never eaten an oyster.'

Francis looked at her for a long moment with those magnificent dark blue eyes, then he smiled. 'Then look on it as a new experience. You'll love them.'

All in all, it turned out to be a wonderful and successful evening of entertainment and gastric delights. Jane swept out of the theatre on Francis's arm and was conscious of people looking her way. They dined close to Covent Garden at a restaurant popular with theatre goers and actors alike. Francis settled Jane by his side and watched as she was absorbed into the company. There were no barriers. Even in those first minutes she seemed to cross the line from north country girl into London society as if she had been born to it. She enjoyed herself and liked the oysters and drank her fair share of champagne. She studied those around her, seeing people who came from a civilised world of elegance and beauty and subtle wit, where birth and breeding and education counted for something.

The tavern echoed with good banter and friends came to their table to gossip, some taking up seats alongside them. There was a party spirit. They laughed readily over nothing and all the while Jane was conscious of Francis's close proximity, his intense gaze on her face. Lady Randolph kept up a steady stream of conversation. The company was boisterous. How strange and marvellous to have grown up and been surrounded by so large a circle of friends, without loneliness. Yet when she thought of her upbringing, she thought she did not belong in such esteemed presence.

'Your friends are impressive, Francis.'

'Yes, we are fortunate.'

'And what of me?' she enquired with a mischievous twinkle in her eyes, her defences down. She drank her wine too quickly and felt it rush to her face.

She was fishing for compliments and he eyed her speculatively. 'I believe you know what I think of you, Jane. You are not at all what I expected you to be.'

'Oh? And what was that, pray? I thought you were indifferent to me.'

'Never that. I've never been easy with words, Jane. Never good at saying the pretty things women like to hear. I suppose I take after my father—only he was worse. I suppose that was why my mother fell for your father. I'm glad to see you enjoying London.'

'How can I not? You seem to have a great deal to occupy your time, Francis.'

He nodded. 'I have connections among many concerns. While I am down here I have people to see.' A lazy smile tugged at the corner of his mouth and his eyes filled with pleasure. Rubbing his knuckles against her cheek, tenderly he asked, 'Am I to infer from your query that you would actually like having me around more?'

Jane's face turned pink. 'I can imagine the damage to your pride if I said no, but, yes, if you really want to know, I would like having you around more.'

'Just can't bear to let me out of your sight, can you?' he teased.

'Well, your mother has so much to keep her busy and Miriam and Andrew can see no one else but each other.'

'And you miss me.'

'Something like that—I've become used to having you around.'

'Then I will see what I can do to oblige.'

'Thank you. I would like that. I shall miss our banter when all this is over.'

'Then stay here in London a while longer,' he urged, suddenly conscious of a sense of desolation in her. 'I'm in no desperate hurry to return to Northumberland.'

'No, Francis.' She was startled at how difficult it was for her to form the words. The regret in his eyes was sincere.

On a sigh he sat back, but his eyes remained fastened on hers. 'Then for the time we are together I shall have to make sure you are never bored. You will forgive me if I use my powers of persuasion to get you to change your mind.'

She laughed, unaware of the tantalising picture she presented, the colour on her cheeks gloriously high, her eyes sparkling like twin orbs. 'As you like, but my own powers of persuasion are often to be reckoned with.'

Francis grinned. 'You certainly appear to have worked wonders with our friends tonight. They scarcely moved their eyes from your face throughout the play. It's amazing what effect a beautiful and brilliant woman can have on men—even those who have a wife. Were you to remain in London, before too long you would have every one of them eating out of your hand—and may well break several hearts—as you did mine when I first kissed you in York.'

'That night there was only one particular heart I would truly have liked to render into little pieces for your audacity,' she said laughing happily, touched and flattered by his remark and hoping he meant it.

Francis laughed softly, chucking her under the chin. 'I fear you are going to need to keep your wits sharp and all your courage in future dealings with me. So take heed, Jane. If you truly wish to spend more time in my company, then you might find yourself out of your depth.'

Jane's eyebrows flicked upwards. 'I have had enough time to make an accurate assessment of your character,' she said, speaking with confidence.

'You are proving to be the most charming diversion. I am willing to remain a while in London if you stay with me and it allows us to become better acquainted.'

There was an intensity in his eyes as he gave her a long, silent look. Jane was beginning to find in him a sensitivity that made him capable of perceiving her need for understanding. Was it possible that, after all the rancour of their beginning, she could believe that he cared for her—that she had come to care for him?

The play was discussed at length along with forthcoming attractions, which Jane said she would be sorry to miss, but she and Miriam intended heading back to Northumberland.

Averting her gaze from Miriam, whose eyes flashed suddenly with anger, Jane smiled at the lady she was conversing with.

Leaving the tavern, they became caught up in the boisterous revelry of the crowd milling about Covent Garden. Laughing light-heartedly, Jane dodged them and Francis's arm came protectively about her. The crowd lessened and walking was easier, but Francis still kept his arm about her until they reached the carriage.

Chapter Six

By the time they returned to the house Francis could see that Jane was more than ready to fall into bed, but he had other ideas. His mother disappeared to her room and Miriam and Andrew made themselves comfortable in the drawing room. Not to be done out of spending more time with Jane, pouring two glasses of wine and handing one to her, he escorted her to the library, where they could have some privacy.

Slowly sipping her wine, Jane casually looked at the rows of books that lined three walls of the room, trailing her fingers across the embossed spines. Leaning against the mantelpiece, Francis watched her, his eyes softening at the tantalising picture she presented in her violet taffeta gown. Her hair was drawn from her face, making it look naked, giving the appearance of fragility and wantonness, a striking contrast that touched him. The tender pink flesh of her lips was so appealing that he was tempted to savour them before they parted for the night. Francis saw, but did not remark on, the subtle changes he saw in her. There was a new radiance that shone from her face. Often he heard her laughing about small things that amused her—it was a joyous sound. There was a light-hearted easy gaiety about her which was so much at odds with the seriousness that had been present at the start of their journey.

Her eyes were the most brilliant Francis had ever seen, of a green so bright they seemed lit from within. Noticing how her gown clung to her round curves so provocatively, concealing the sweet treasures beneath, gave him a clear sense of pleasurable torture. He watched her walk towards him, her movements graceful and uncertain, like a nervous fawn. She paused in front of him. Now she was so close he could feel her warmth, smell the sweet scent of her body, all in such close proximity. The ardour that erupted in his body surprised him and sent heat searing into his loins.

He was not a man of such iron control that he could resist looking at her feminine form which she held before him day after day like a talisman. Why did this explosion of passion happen almost every time he was near her?

'This is a lovely room,' she said, sitting in a high-backed chair at an angle to the hearth. 'I imagine there are many interesting books to read.'

'My mother is an avid reader. She prides herself on her library—it is her favourite room. I am sure she wouldn't mind if you wish to read any of them.'

'I'm sure she wouldn't. She has been most kind.'

'I am relieved to know you are getting on with her. With all that is between us I do know it can't be easy for either of you.'

'It is important that we try to get along and I do like her. Although there must be times when you regret your impulsive decision to bring me to London.'

He lifted a brow and regarded her with some amusement. 'Not for one minute. You proved to be a pleasant companion.'

'You could have come by yourself—although I shudder to think how you would have dealt with my sister.'

Francis's lips curved in a half-smile as he stood with his back to the fire looking down at her. A heavy lock of dark hair dipped over his brow and the candlelight softened his angular features. 'It's strange, but despite the unconventional beginnings to our friendship, I have no regrets. You are more lovely than any of the dull creatures who preen and saunter at all the society events.'

Jane laughed. 'And you, my lord, are a flatterer.'

'It is not flattery.' Francis's face was serious but there was a smiling tenderness in his voice. 'It is the truth.'

There was a softness in his eyes when he looked at her as he took the chair opposite. Firelight gleamed on her hair and her sooty ashes cast fan-like shadows on her smooth cheeks. As he watched her now, he marvelled anew at the strange aura of innocence about her.

'Earlier you told me you would like me to spend more time with you. Were you serious?'

'Of course. I wouldn't have said it otherwise.'

'Do you have any idea how much I have wanted to hear you say that?' he said with tender solemnity.

Jane's delicately shaped eyebrows lifted in mute question. The intensity of his dark eyes seemed to hold her transfixed. 'No, Francis. In truth I had no idea.'

'Well, now you have. My hands have ached to touch you. At times the temptation almost proved too hard to resist. That unpleasantness at the beginning was no help.'

'There was bound to be a barrier between us. Remember that you first saw me as an enemy. There were numerous valid grievances between us.'

There was something in his eyes like an involuntary tenderness. 'Then we will have to rectify that, won't we?'

'We will?' Meeting the intensity of his gaze that slid to her bosom and back to her eyes, with a frisson of alarm she placed her glass on a small table at the side of her and stood up, smoothing down her skirts. 'It—it's been a long night, Francis. It's time I went to bed.'

Francis walked with her to the door, where she paused. 'Goodnight, Francis. Thank you for a wonderful evening. I've enjoyed it so much. The pleasure of it will stay with me for a long time.'

She was so lovely as she held his gaze that his one desire was to please her, but in that moment another kind of desire, potent and primitive, swelled inside him, one he wanted to savour and enjoy.

'Goodnight, Jane, but before you go I think a kiss to end the evening would be in order.'

Very slowly he dropped a kiss on her forehead, a kiss as soft as the brush of a butterfly's wing, trailing his lips, so capable and so sure of their path, to her cheek as he drew her into his arms. He felt her breath come quickly as she waited expectantly for his lips to touch hers. When they bypassed her mouth to her other cheek, she turned her head, surprising Francis by capturing his lips with her own.

At last he succumbed to the impulse that had been tormenting him all night and kissed her long and deep and undemanding, feeling the softness of her lips. His arms tightened across her back, pressing the contours of her body to his, and he almost lost his head entirely when he felt her lips open under his and she kissed him back, as if her life depended on it. The kiss was hot and bittersweet, with all the passion and tenderness of something long awaited.

After what seemed like an eternity, Francis raised his head and tenderly gazed down into her melting green eyes. The woman in his arms affected him like heady wine. Her warm, open face was unable to conceal her innocence.

'I cannot understand what it is you do to me,' she murmured. 'I seem to become a different person when I am alone with you.'

Francis's gaze caressed her upturned face, watching her eyes darken. 'And you—you are so lovely, Jane—so lovely that I ache when I look at you.'

She smiled up at him. 'And on that note I think I should go to bed. Goodnight, Francis,' she said, uttering a quiet laugh and slipping away from him.

With ease, both Jane and Miriam fitted in to the comfort of life in Lady Randolph's household like the gowns which she insisted she no longer wanted and was more than happy to provide. London was a world apart from the dull demands of Beckwith Manor. It seemed Miriam's excitement was infectious. It was all so exciting. For a short time Jane wanted to throw off the disorder of the house she had left behind, the many day-to-day difficulties, the thousand things they lacked to make life comfortable. Suddenly all the luxury that surrounded them seemed so unreal. Here Jane could escape the loneliness and struggle and banish the consciousness of fear. Lady Randolph made sure they were never bored. Finding herself alone with Francis for longer periods, and delighting in his closeness, Jane's heart began to beat faster.

There were festivities of many kinds. Musicals and more of the theatre, supper parties in hospitable drawing rooms where flowed a stream of the illustrious. Yet always on the periphery of Jane's mind was the knowledge that her father was in the north and the Jacobite rising was imminent. What form it would take she had no way of knowing, but should there be fighting, then her father could very well be in the thick of it. Reluctant as she was to involve herself, she had no wish to be so far away should he have need of her.

In a quiet, reflective mood, she was alone in the drawing room, kneeling on the floor, delving into another large trunk the servants had carried down from the attics. Beautiful gowns discarded by Lady Randolph spilled out in grand confusion on to the carpet when Francis strode in. A gown she was working on was spread over the sofa.

'You are busy, Jane.'

'As you see.' Sitting back on her heels, she shoved her hair back from her flushed face. 'Lady Randolph has presented us with yet more gowns she declares she no longer has use for,' she said, studying the array of gowns and flimsy chemises in colourful fabrics with confusion written all over her face. They lay in a bright jumble in every shade, ruffles and shining ribbons, the fabrics sprinkled with tiny seed pearls and shining beads.

'Miriam was going through them until she became distracted when Andrew returned home from a meeting with an acquaintance. My sister is endowed with an enormous vitality which exhausts me.' She sighed with frustration. 'There is one thing to be said for Miriam—she never does things by half-measures. Lady Randolph has given me a free hand and insists I choose as many as I like, even though I have insisted I have no use for fancy gowns at Beckwith Manor. I find it hard to believe she can be so generous. There are so many to choose from, all so beautiful, but I am looking for something more conservative.'

Francis leaned over to inspect the contents. 'What on earth for? Mother changes her wardrobe with each year's new fashions. My advice is to select the finest.'

Jane glanced up at him. 'And when would I have the opportunity to wear such fine gowns as these in Northumberland? I can scarcely conceive of ways to use so many.'

'There will be occasions to do so in the future. Since you appear shy of choosing the best, allow me to help you.' Leaning over, he reached into the trunk and drew out a rather fine saffron silk. 'This is a colour that will bring out the lights in your hair. Do you like the shade?'

'Why, yes—it's splendid. But too many ruffles for me.'

Holding the gown up, he inspected it closely. 'Nonsense. It will suit you admirably. You can remove the ruffles—and a few tucks here and there...'

'Francis,' Jane admonished, getting to her feet. 'It is clear to me you know how to dress a woman.'

He grinned. 'I've had my moments.'

Sitting on the sofa, he stretched his long, booted legs out in front of him, watching her as she stitched a hem on another gown his mother had insisted would suit her. His mood was pleasant and attentive.

'The house is quiet. Is my mother out?'

'Yes. She's visiting an acquaintance and Miriam and Andrew have gone for a drive in the park—with a maid in attendance, of course—which I insisted on despite my sister's objections.'

Francis chuckled. 'In my opinion I think your sister has been allowed far too much of her own way in the past.' His gaze caressed her face. 'London agrees with you, Jane. You are more relaxed than the young woman who journeyed with me from Northumberland. But you are not at home here. Am I wrong?'

'No, you are close to the truth. I cannot deny that I am enjoying this sense of ease, but I'm trying not to become too used to it lest I become soft. I'm beginning to grow restless. There is not enough occupation for my energies in the house. I'm not accustomed to sleeping after the sun has come up, to finding hot water for me to wash in when I do wake and a sumptuous breakfast on the table.'

'Make the most of it while you can.'

She lifted her head and looked at him. The light from the sun slanting in through the window added to her face's beauty and Francis felt it strike to the very soul of him.

'Life has not trained me to sit in the salons and drawing rooms of London, drinking hot chocolate and making polite conversation.'

'My mother enjoys having you here.'

'I know, but we cannot remain indefinitely.'

'Have you spoken to Miriam about going back to Northumberland?'

'I've tried, but she refuses to discuss it. Her mind is made up. She will marry Andrew come hell or high water.'

'Might I make a suggestion?'

'Of course you can.'

'Would it be such a terrible thing if they were to marry?'

Jane's eyes opened with surprise. 'I have given it much thought—but I find it hard to resign myself to it. Are you saying you wouldn't mind?'

He managed a smile. 'No, I wouldn't. One cannot fail but see the two of them are devoted to each other. Perhaps it's time to forget the past, Jane. Have you thought how unhappy Miriam will be if you force her back to Northumberland? She will resent you for it.'

Jane got to her feet and perched on the edge of a chair, facing him. 'I know that. She will hate me. But what can I do?'

'Give in, Jane—and I'm sure my mother would welcome having Miriam for a daughter-in-law.'

'I—I think she is a remarkable woman, but there are times when I am with her that I feel there is something she wants to say to me, but she always falls short when on the brink. She possesses an iron will and the speed with which her mind works astonishes me.'

'You are right. Her eyes are constantly alert to what is going on around her. But if anyone is brave enough to hold her gaze, then they would see that they still hold some of the sadness they've held since leaving Redmires. Despite the passing of time she's never fully recovered from the shock of that tragedy and whether it was the death of my father or her separation from the man she had loved—your own father, Jane—a spark has gone from her life. So you see, for reasons of her own I believe she would welcome the match between Andrew and Miriam. They love each other. Can you really tear them apart?'

Jane looked down at her hands at the same moment that Lady Randolph, having returned from her outing, crossed the hall and went quietly up the stairs. She had heard what was being discussed between her son and Jane and was deeply troubled by it.

Jane shook her head. 'No, I don't think I can separate them. But I cannot remain here much longer. It's time I went back and took up my chores. Everyone here has been so indulgent, but with a house to run and all the recent troubles in the north, I have to go back. Do you have news from the north?'

'Very little—only that many Jacobite sympathisers are rallying to the call, and that several leaders have already been arrested. There will be fighting.'

'It could mean civil war,' Jane whispered.

'It's possible. A large number of Northumberland gentry have joined the rebels. The citizens of Newcastle are resisting and have declared for King George. The Earl of Mar has succeeded in mobilising a large force of men from the Highland clans and the northeast. It might be wiser if you were to remain here in London with Miriam and distance yourself from the troubles.'

'No. If there is to be fighting, then I must think about going home. It's the uncertainty of it all, the not knowing what's actually happening. It doesn't help. I—I miss Beckwith Manor—and my father may have need of me.'

Francis sat forward, a grave intensity in his eyes.

'Jane, listen to me. To plot against the King and the government, that spirit of vengeance and hatred it stirs with Protestants and those it is directed at, makes Catholics, both militant and innocent, tremble in its wake, fearing outright war. Anyone connected with plotting against the King will be arrested. Men have lost their heads for less. Whatever offence occurs, your father will not escape suspicion.'

Francis could see that she was scarcely able to grasp the reality of it all as his words fell like hammer blows against her heart. As she stared up into his eyes a chill seemed to penetrate to her very soul.

'I am so afraid of what will happen. Dear Lord! It will ruin him. All his goods and estate will be forfeit to the Crown—and this time he will hang for sure. May the Lord save him,' she whispered.

The prayer was heartfelt and Francis looked at her closely, seeing panic in the eyes of this usually assured young woman. He had no doubt that Edward Deighton would implicate himself. Francis would not distress Jane further by saying so, but he would not give much for her father's life either. It would be a hard thing indeed to escape the full consequences if he were to be charged with rebellion and treason.

When a cotton bobbin fell from her knee and rolled across the carpet, coming to rest at Francis's feet, he reached down to retrieve it. Standing up, he crossed to her and sat beside her, watching her closely and appreciating the sweet scent of her. She had put her father's fate aside for a moment and her face was rosy pink, her eyes snapping in a bright green blaze in the light of the sun shining through the windows. He thought he had never seen such a glorious creature in his life.

Several moments passed in silence and then Francis lifted her hair and stroked the side of her neck, encouraged when she didn't pull away.

'Tell me, Jane. Do you still dream like you used to do when you were a little girl?'

'Sometimes—especially about my mother.'

'You're trembling.'

Securing the needle on the garment, she twisted her head round and looked at him, unsmiling. 'That's your fault and you can't blame me for being confused at the way things have turned out between us. In spite of everything I hold against you, you have that effect on me. You know, Francis, when I first saw you when you almost rode me down in Newcastle, because of the past—because of that night when your father died—I was determined to hate you. I tried, but for the time we have been together I have seen a different man to the one I had painted in my mind, a man who melted my resistance, and I resented that. I wanted to dislike you, but that didn't work either. And then you kissed me and I no longer knew what to think.'

'Then you are right. You are confused about me. I can see your dilemma.'

'Can you? I believe you can. You seem to have a razor-sharp perception of my deepest fears. I have never been so unsure of myself. You see, when I went to Redmires to see you, I didn't want to like you. Because of who you are I didn't want to have anything to do with you, but when you offered me your protection on our journey to London, I unwittingly made more problems for myself than I bargained for. We came together at a time when my fears were uppermost.'

'And that scares you?'

'Yes, if you must know. Yes, it does.'

Francis watched her, both touched and faintly amused by her confession and aroused by her nearness. 'Do you fear me, Jane?'

'No, not you,' she said quietly, the colour in her cheeks deepening beneath his scrutiny. 'It's what you might do to me that I'm afraid of.'

'I should have known what would happen when I agreed to let you travel south with me. You're not a woman a man can ignore. I cannot deny that I want you, Jane. I've had many women and I've enjoyed each one—but none of them meant anything to me. They were diversions. Would that you were a diversion, too. I never intended any of this to happen and I feel I must be honest with you. For a long time after that night when my father died I carried on, throwing myself into the business, trying to pick up where he had left off, trying to come to terms with my mother's distress and her absence from Redmires—and to forget her affair with your father which had brought about the horrors of that night.

'Then one day I happened to come across a young woman in Newcastle. You, Jane, and nothing was quite the same after that. I liked what I saw—in fact, I liked it so much I was astonished at myself and would find myself looking out for you. Through no fault of your own you are who you are—Edward Deighton's daughter, the man who killed my father. I can't forget that—but I believe I can learn to live with it.'

'Yes, Francis, through no fault of my own that is what I am and, despite what happened, despite his neglect of me and Miriam and the anger and hurt he has caused me over the years, I love and miss my father dearly.'

'Of course you do.'

'Sadly, I fear that because of that night, because it took away my father and suddenly left me with a house to run and Miriam to take care of, whatever I do will never afford me the freedom of others of my sex.'

'Has it been as bad as that?'

The quiet sincerity with which he broached the query stuck a chord. 'It—has been difficult.'

'Soon this will end and you will return to Northumberland and that will be that. It hasn't been a bed of roses for either of us, more like a bed of nettles—the thorns stand out on each side. But we are what we are.'

'You are right. Too much stands between us. Although it is said that nettles don't sting if you have the courage to grasp them hard.'

'Then shall we prove the point?' he said, taking her shoulders and drawing her close, his eyes locking on hers. He drew her closer still, holding her against his chest. Stunned into quiescence, she remained completely still as his lips settled on hers. Her lips were cool and surprisingly smooth. The kiss was gentle before gradually increasing pressure, becoming coaxing as he slid the tip of his tongue into the warm sweetness of her mouth. After a moment his mouth left her lips and shifted across her cheek to her ear, then trailing back to her lips and claiming them once more. His kiss became more demanding, ardent, persuasive, a slow, erotic seduction, tender, wanting. Forcing himself temporarily to relinquish her mouth, he raised his head slightly.

'Kiss me, Jane,' he demanded thickly.

Jane did exactly that, becoming lost in a beautiful madness, kissing him as deeply and erotically as he was kissing her. He groaned with pleasure, the sweetness of her response causing desire to explode inside him. When at last he lifted his mouth from hers, his breathing was harsh and rapid. Slowly she brought one of her hands from behind his neck and her finger gently traced the outline of his cheek, following its angular line down to his jaw and neck.

Disentangling herself from his arms, she pulled back and smiled. 'You really are full of surprises, Francis. I have just opened myself up to you, confessing my innermost feelings. And what do you do? You kiss me, as if it will make any difference. It won't, of course. It won't change a thing. But what of you? Tell me how everything that has happened has affected you. I ask you to be as open and honest as I have been.'

Francis sighed, resting back on the sofa. 'After what happened—when my father died, I made myself carry on. All the world thinks I've begun to accept what happened. But I haven't forgotten that night when I saw my father's broken body. I feel, sometimes, as if I haven't had a breath of clean air since then.' He straightened and, taking her chin in his hand, turned her face to his. 'I don't think I ever loved my father—he was a hard man to love—but he was still my father. Where your father was concerned, yes, I hated him for a time—perhaps because, like you, there were some things about that night that were never clarified to me. My mother was not forthcoming.'

'She must have been devastated.'

'She was deeply traumatised by what had occurred and she refused to discuss it in depth. Ever since you turned up at Redmires I began to feel that I was breathing again, as if I was finally coming out from the cloud I had been under for so long. Yes, I was angry and unforgiving for a long time—my anger and resentment directed at both your father and my mother for a time, but here, in London, I've come to my senses and I know it's coming to an end. It no longer matters who sired you. You are who you are. You're right, Jane. You don't belong here in this alien world and you're going back to Northumberland.'

Getting up and carrying the gown she had been working on, Jane crossed to the door and left him gazing after her with a look that could have been hurt, or equally could have been regret. Whatever it was, some special warmth still lived in her as she climbed the stairs, a new feeling in the aftermath of his kiss that she had tasted something that she would always hunger for.

She had no ready word to deny his statement that she would return to Northumberland because she also knew it would be easier if she went. She was falling in love with Francis and it would become a problem only if she let it, she decided, and she firmly intended to ignore those emotions his mere presence stirred so strongly. She was a mature woman and common sense told her that any relationship with him beyond their present arrangement would be a disaster.

When Jane and Miriam entered the drawing room the following afternoon, having been summoned by Francis, Lady Randolph stood in the centre of the room, Francis and Andrew by her side. On seeing Miriam, Andrew immediately went to her and drew her down on to a sofa, sitting close by her side and taking her hand in his.

'You wanted to see us?' Jane said, curious as to why they had been summoned and suspecting from the atmosphere that hung in the room that it was serious. She looked to Francis for an answer, but his expression was unreadable.

'Come and sit down, Jane,' he said. 'Apparently Mother has something she wants to say to all of us.'

'Yes—yes, that is right,' Lady Randolph said quietly. 'There is something I have to tell you—something I should have told you a long time ago. I've been putting it off, but I can do so no longer.'

Jane waited, watching her. She looked perfectly composed, but she sensed that behind that calm exterior there was turmoil.

'Your father didn't cause the carriage to leave the road that night,' she said, coming straight to the point. 'He wasn't even in it. I was driving. I'd met your father in Newcastle. William, your father, Francis, was away and came back early. He came to find me and when he did—well, it wasn't pleasant. I left with him and Edward followed on his horse. When the carriage left the road and overturned, seeing that William had suffered dreadful head injuries and was already dead, Edward stepped in and took the blame. William died because of me.'

'No, Mother,' Andrew said, clearly shocked by this. 'It was nothing more than a dreadful accident.'

'It had everything to do with me, Andrew. We would not have been there had I not gone to meet Edward, driving the carriage myself to make our meeting as clandestine as possible. Your father was in Newcastle. I didn't expect him back for several hours. He spent a great deal of his time there—with his mistress, I might add—and he always came home the worse for drink. Unfortunately he came back early that night—having had a lot to drink. When he found out I wasn't at home, already suspecting that I was having an affair with Edward, in his fury he came after me. We met him on the road as we were about to part. His arrogance had always blinded him to everything but his own feelings. I won't go into what happened next, but the scene was ugly. William tied his horse to the carriage and joined me, swearing to make Edward pay for what he had done. When the carriage left the road and slid down an embankment and he was thrown out, I could see he was dead. Afterwards I had to do what Edward told me to do and act it out as he directed.'

A slow understanding of her began to dawn on Jane. 'But if it was an accident, surely it didn't matter who was driving. He didn't have to go as far as to take the blame.'

'He wanted to protect me. He didn't want me to take the blame—to have stigma attached to my name that would cause hurt to my sons. It was a truly noble thing he did.'

'And me—and Miriam?' Jane said quietly, unable to conceal the bitterness in her voice. 'Did we not matter? Did no one think what it would do to us when it became known that our father had killed your husband? All this deceit, this subterfuge—how could Father have done that to us—and then to abandon us? And you allowed it to happen.'

All the suffering she had felt at that awful time was mirrored in Lady Randolph's eyes when she looked at Jane. 'I am sorry, Jane, truly. I have no excuse. That night has been shadowed in my memory for ever. I have been fleeing from that one night of my life I cannot forget. I have tried to live with it, trying to come to terms with my own guilt for having caused William's death. I was saddened by it, but I could do nothing. I had to get away from Redmires. What I had done was tearing me apart—and despite

the love we felt for each other, your father and I decided that it would be in everyone's best interests for
us to part. And you, Jane, and Miriam. I knew that
by my actions I had robbed you of your father. You
four, our children, are the only ones who can make
the overture of forgiveness.'

'I always suspected there was more to that night
than we were told,' Francis uttered coldly.

'I know, Francis. But what can the law do in the
face of a man who insists he is guilty? A man who
insists on taking on the blame, when there is no one
to testify to the contrary?'

Jane saw Francis take a deep breath and noticed
that the corners of his mouth had whitened. There was
a tension in him as he listened to his mother.

'You both colluded in perjury,' Francis said.

She nodded. 'Yes. Edward would have it no other
way.'

'You are saying that our father was not responsible,' Miriam said softly, holding Andrew's hand
for support.

'Yes, Miriam, that is what I'm saying.' She looked
at Jane and Miriam, a deep sadness and remorse in
her eyes. There was also guilt and shame and a terrible sadness. 'Women can't always decide which way
their lives will go. I lived in London until I went to
Redmires—the marriage was arranged by our parents. I hated Northumberland—the space—the emptiness of it all. I wanted to get away before I forgot
there were such things in the world as laughter and
being young. I traded my youth for an empty mar-

riage. When I met Edward I fell deeply in love with him. I had never loved a man before. I have not loved anyone since and never will. That kind of love only comes once.'

'And yet you parted,' Jane said softly. 'How could you do that if you loved each other?'

'The shame, the guilt—the sadness—was too much for either of us. We decided it would be for the best. I am so sorry for what it has done to you. I should not have let it happen. I made a terrible mistake when I let Edward talk me into letting him take the blame, but don't imagine for one moment that I haven't paid for it. He made me vow never to tell the truth of that night. That vow has stood the test of ten years, but I can no longer keep silent. Can you ever forgive me? You and Miriam?' She turned her face away from them. 'I can't expect you to answer that now.'

Hot tears welled in Jane's eyes. Something was breaking within her. She felt the same anger that she had felt all those years ago when her father had left them—the anger and the desolation, and the fear that in her anger she might lash out at Lady Randolph, to destroy her new-found happiness because it was due to Lady Randolph that she and Miriam had been deprived of their father.

'Jane, you understand?' Lady Randolph said, almost pleading for her understanding.

'Yes. I understand it all now.' There it all was, as vivid as ever, the memory of that night she had curled up in a chair when her father had left for France, the night she had promised to take care of Miriam and everything else. She had been twelve years old. She stood up, her only thought to get out of the room, to be by herself and to digest what Lady Randolph had disclosed. 'Please excuse me. I—I would like to be by myself.' She was unable to utter another word as she looked at Lady Randolph and felt a kind of detached pity for the remorse which still haunted her.

She did not go to her room—it was far too accessible to Miriam, and she didn't want to speak to her just then. Instead, she found her way out into the garden. Completely shaken by Lady Randolph's confession, she walked as far away from the house as she could, facing the wall where brilliant red ivy climbed in profusion. Much as she would have liked, she could go no further and all of London stretched before her, a strange and alien place, with none of the familiar things of home.

'Are you all right, Jane?'

Without turning, she nodded. She was glad it was Francis who had come and no one else. 'Yes. I…'

When she couldn't continue, he stepped over to her and, placing his hands on her shoulders, he turned her round to face him. She looked at him fully in that first moment of silence. In his face was an expression she had never seen there before—tenderness, despair, hurt—a kind of plea for understanding and for forgiveness for what had happened all those years ago.

'I'm sorry, Jane. At last we both know the truth of what happened.'

Drawing her into his arms, he held her loosely

against him. She was trembling and Francis murmured soft words, comforting her. 'You are upset. That is understandable.'

As he tried to soothe her, Jane refused to let him penetrate the barrier behind which her mind wandered, but he continued to hold her, comforting her, as one might comfort a child, and then, with a muted sob she clung to him, the tears running down her cheeks. Bending her head, she rested her face against his chest and wept, she who had shed so few tears in her life. It was a full minute before her tears were done and then there was just the misery of it all. After a while she became still. She looked up into those warm dark blue eyes. He smiled, touching her cheek.

'Do you feel better now?' he murmured.

'I think so. I didn't mean to fall apart like that. I hate women who cry. I don't usually.'

'I know, Jane. You're tough and feisty, full of spirit—which I like. Although seeing you like this makes me feel strong and protective. It makes me feel something else, too, but I must forget about that for the time being so you can relax. It was a shock for me to hear what really happened to my father, too.'

Wiping the tears from her face with the back of her hand, Jane made herself step back from him so he had to disengage his arms. 'Of course it was. You must be as surprised as I am.'

'Yes. I am shocked. I cannot believe it has been kept from us all this time—like some shameful secret. Disappointment comes in many forms, Jane, and the truth is still ugly.'

'Why—it needn't be.'

'Logically, I understand that, but a part of me will always believe that, if she had not been seeing your father, my own father would still be alive. My mother has spent endless years punishing herself. You cannot escape the fact that she was a married woman and your father seduced her.'

'He saved her from a terrible scandal. Doesn't that mean anything to you?'

'Are you telling me that I owe him a debt of gratitude?'

'No, I wouldn't go as far as that. It will take time to come to terms with what happened that night. From what I gather your mother was unhappy in her marriage to your father. Clearly there was mutual attraction between her and my father, something they couldn't resist. So much so that my father put his honour on the line to protect your mother's reputation— to make sure no shadow of blame was cast her way. One should wonder at such a love as that.'

'We neither of us know the whole truth of what happened. My father is not here to defend himself.'

'No. But I'm glad she told us—however much it hurts to know the truth. Deep down I always suspected everything was not exactly as it was told and I am glad this exonerates my father from blame. I know how close my parents were—my mother adored my father—anyone who saw them together could see that. I—I wonder how it would have been had she still been alive when he became attracted to your mother.'

'Who knows, Jane? That is something there is no answer to.'

'Do you believe what your mother said—about my father taking the blame for what happened—that he took it all, every bit of it? A sort of scapegoat for her?'

'Yes—yes, I do—and she has lived with the truth of it all this time. It was an accident. A very bad and terrible accident and we all of us have felt the repercussions of that night. She didn't mean anything bad to happen. Sometimes these things cannot be helped. Don't imagine she hasn't paid for it.'

'So has my father—and me and Miriam. But for that he may not have left for France when he did, leaving us to fend for ourselves. Although I suspect his obsession to have the Stuarts restored to the throne may have been too strong for him to resist and he would have gone to France in the end. I suddenly see how my father, seeing what had happened and totally in command, took it upon himself to do what he did. I also see the woman, your mother, whose reputation and good character he saved, has never been able to forgive herself for allowing him to do that. And so she left Northumberland and her sons to go and live in London, away from everything that had to do with that terrible event. I am aware that the tragedy of that night still circulates the taverns and drawing rooms of Northumberland. My father's supreme gesture would be lost if your mother should break. He had intended that his lover must live her life in freedom and he would follow the cause that was close to his heart in France.'

Folding her arms across her chest, she turned from Francis and saw a thin mist creeping silently across the grass, beginning to envelop the clipped shrubs and flower beds. It had a winter feeling about it, as if it might go on being winter for ever in her heart.

Francis moved closer to her, looking down into her troubled eyes. 'I'm sorry for all you have suffered because of this. We have both been affected by what happened—you more than anyone. You're a rare young woman, Jane,' he said, touching her lightly, affectionately on the cheek.

Jane flushed with appreciation at his words. He was smiling, an expression that was almost of tenderness and, also, in a strange way, almost one of recognition of something he had just discovered about himself—or of her. It was one of those rare moments that held them in thrall, when there was no need for words. Lady Randolph's voice broke the quiet moment. Jane saw Francis's expression change when he looked past her, beyond her, to his mother, who was walking towards them.

Chapter Seven

'I thought I'd come and find you. I can imagine how upset you are, Jane, at what I have told you. I am so sorry. Believe me when I say I would have spared you this. And yet it must be a relief for you to know the truth—that your father did the honourable thing.'

'Yes—of course it's a relief. I can only regret that it has taken so long for the truth to be revealed.'

'For which I apologise. I could not forgive myself, knowing what Edward must be suffering because of my actions.'

'And my father?' Francis said harshly. 'At least you and Edward Deighton survived the tragedy. He was less fortunate.'

'Lady Randolph, what was your husband like?' Jane asked in an attempt to divert the conversation from the tragedy. 'I saw him on occasion, but I cannot remember what he was like.'

'He was a big, dark-haired giant of a man. He was also arrogant and overbearing, exactly the type who

thought women were put on earth purely to serve
men. He always had a way of speaking his mind just
to see how people would react and it angered and
often upset them.' She sighed, her gaze going to the
house and beyond, as if remembering the years she
had spent at Redmires. 'I don't want to go back to
Northumberland smelling of sheep and goats and
acres of desolation—but at some time I will go back
for a visit.' She turned to Jane. 'Things at Beckwith
Manor cannot have been easy for you after your father left for France. I do realise that.'

'I've learned a few tricks about survival, Lady
Randolph. My future may be an uncharted path, but
I intend to survive what awaits me in Northumberland—whatever the cost.' She despised herself for the
quaver in her voice, the tightening in her throat that
surely was more fear than anything else.

'Do you have aspirations for the future, Jane?'

'I have never planned beyond the present.'

'I suppose I can understand your position.'

'Which is why I must leave for the north. I've
stayed in London longer than I intended. Already it
is November and the roads will become impassable
if I don't leave soon. Besides, if there is to be fighting then my father may need me.'

Lady Randolph's eyes clouded with memory. 'Yes,
I can understand that. It is good that he has you, Jane.
I cannot agree with what is happening—all this talk
of a rising and men pitching their strength against
each other on the field of battle in the name of religion

and who should be the rightful King on the throne. I pray Edward will come out of it safely.'

Jane nodded. 'Yes, those are my thoughts exactly.'

Lady Randolph sighed. 'I keep thinking of what happened, why and how I let him shoulder the blame. I've had a lot of time to think—as if I could forget. I cannot forget the misery and shame that I've carried inside me for so long. Was I sane that night? Perhaps a little mad? Nothing could excuse what I did and I have spent the time since then trying to make up for it. And when Miriam and then you came here, to this house, I welcomed you sincerely and hoped to repay—and the only way to do that is to give. I would very much like Andrew and Miriam to wed—to live here for the time being—until Andrew takes up his post with the East India Company.'

'Miriam has no dowry.'

'That does not matter. The fact that Andrew would fall in love with Miriam or she with him could not have been foreseen, but a more fortunate happening I could not have devised. It pleases me. They love each other. Let that be enough. What say you, Francis?'

'I agree.'

'I'm happy to hear that.'

That was the moment Jane gave in. What could she do when faced with such determination as this? 'Then it would be selfish of me to begrudge Miriam her chance of happiness. How soon can they be married?'

'If you agree to it, Jane,' Francis said, 'I can arrange it within two weeks.'

'So soon?'

'Yes. It will be a small affair—just a few friends.'

* * *

Miriam was overjoyed when Jane told her she could marry Andrew and she immediately began making plans for the forthcoming event. Jane hoped she was doing the right thing in allowing the wedding to go ahead. What would their father think of it? Strangely, because of what she now knew, she didn't think he would object to a union between the two families. He would know that Miriam would be in safe hands. It was to be a small affair which was to take place no longer than two weeks hence since Jane was impatient to return to Northumberland.

When the day of the wedding finally arrived after days of frenetic preparations, a radiant Miriam, beneath an enveloping cloud of lace, walked down the aisle to stand beside her beloved Andrew to recite their vows. Andrew looked at his wife with immense pride, and, in Miriam's eyes tears showed, with love.

Jane looked on with mixed feelings. As they spoke their vows they looked young and beautiful and full of innocent hopefulness and naivety. Jane envied the love they carried in their hearts for each other. She was happy for Miriam, but she would miss her terribly. Her gaze settled on Francis, standing beside Andrew in the church, his head rising above the few guests assembled, his hands clasped behind his back, his legs a little apart. Her heart warmed to him. His clean-cut profile faced the altar, his powerful shoulders moulded by his midnight-blue coat. To her at that moment he was pure perfection. Sensing her eyes on him, he turned his head and met her gaze, his dark eyes unnervingly intent.

The ceremony over, it was a proud moment for Lady Randolph as the newlyweds returned to the house. The reception Lady Randolph provided was a small affair, but splendid, and it went well. As the dining and drinking went on and seeing that Jane was preoccupied with her own thoughts—which Francis suspected were on her return to Beckwith Manor the following day—taking her hand, he led her into the hall, relieved that she raised no objection.

'It's hardly the weather for a walk in the garden, but I can't think of anywhere else that is appropriate to get you to myself. Here,' he said, taking a shawl from a chair and wrapping it about her shoulders, 'this should keep out the chill.'

Stepping outside, Jane breathed in the cool fresh air. 'How did you know I wanted to get away?'

'You seemed preoccupied. With all the attention on the bride and groom, a change of scene and a stroll in the fresh air will do you no harm.'

'It will give me a chance to clear my head—too much champagne,' she said, laughing lightly. 'It will be a long time before I get the chance to taste it again. The wedding went well, don't you think?'

'It couldn't have gone better,' Francis agreed. 'Although I think I can be forgiven if I say that your sister's maid of honour outshone the bride.'

'Miriam made a beautiful bride. She looked like an angel—your brother certainly thought so.' Looking up at him, she smiled, a wonderfully engaging smile, her cheeks pink and her eyes extremely bright. 'What do you think to my gown?' she said, releasing his arm and spinning round in her dainty shoes, her voluminous deep pink skirts spinning out to reveal her slender ankles. 'You have to admit this is an improvement on my former attire.'

Francis arched a brow and looked at her appraisingly. 'Do you really have to ask? You look ravishing, you vain creature. I can see the young lady I travelled to London with has changed her plumage.'

'It's easy for any woman to change from a sparrow into a swan with fine clothes,' Jane countered. 'Am I to understand that you approve of the transformation? Do I look less like a vagabond and a more fitting companion in my gown?'

'A very fitting companion. But it's a pity such perfection is only skin deep. I am not deceived.' He grinned with mock severity. 'Your eyes might be shining bright and your cheeks may bloom like the fairest of roses—but inside sprouts the thistle reminiscent of across the border in the north.'

Feeling too light-hearted to be intimidated, Jane smiled up at him sweetly, a look of such innocence on her face that it would melt the largest glacier, but Francis was not deceived.

'Don't play the innocent with me. I know you too well, don't forget. But I compliment you,' he murmured, his glowing dark eyes openly raking her from top to toe. 'You look adorable—ravishing, in fact.'

'And you would like to—is that not so?' Jane remarked with a playful hint of sarcasm.

Francis laughed softly down into her upturned face. 'I meant it as a compliment.'

'That's what worries me,' she said, linking her arm with his and continuing to stroll along the path.

'Your eyes are sparkling most outrageously. If I didn't know you better, I would say you were in love.'

'Who with? With you?'

'Why not?'

'Because I have far too much sense to allow myself to love a rogue like you.'

'And I have a voracious appetite. I shall try to make you change your mind.'

'You can try—but you will be wasting your time.'

His eyes gleamed determinedly. 'We shall see.'

At Francis's side and with her arm tucked in his, Jane relaxed as she walked through the dappled sunlight of the garden, her mind picturing how it would look in the splendour of spring, when the trees and flowers would burst into bloom. They strolled and talked of inconsequential things, content to find pleasure in each other's company.

When they turned to return to the house, they saw Lady Randolph walking towards them.

When she reached them she stopped and with a smile looked from one to the other. 'You know, you two would make a lovely couple.'

Francis's eyes flashed. 'Mother, you take too much upon yourself.'

'Do I? I'm sorry. It comes with age, I suppose—with little time to beat about the bush.' She looked at Jane. 'Forgive me, my dear, but I do have a habit of speaking my mind. Really, Jane, you are too good to be true—and beautiful with it. If you were to remain in London, you would very soon be all the rage. You would be an asset to any man, with or without a dowry. As for you, Francis, you are a businessman and a nobleman. You have done well since your father died and I am proud of you. Your reputation is admired. Has no young lady in the north not caught your fancy by any chance?'

'That, Mother, is my own affair.'

She laughed lightly. 'Of course it is and I would not dream of interfering. But the two of you do look good together.'

Jane cast Francis a side glance and Francis mustered a smile. 'You worry too much for my happiness, Mother, but this time you go too far. You are embarrassing Jane. Kindly leave us to arrange our personal lives.'

'Yes,' she conceded with a laugh, as she turned away to return to the guests. 'I am guilty of doing what your father would have done—always interfering. But,' she said, casting them a look over her shoulder, 'I have sown the seed. I shall now sit back and watch it grow.'

Jane watched her go, unable to fully comprehend Lady Randolph's subtle suggestion that she marry Francis! For a moment her mind had gone completely blank—now she stared at him in in confused shock.

'Did my ears deceive me? Did your mother actually suggest that we…?'

'Marry?' Francis provided. 'Yes, I believe she did. She has been waiting impatiently these last ten years for me to wed and sire children. She also has a habit of speaking her mind.'

His light-heartedness and the challenging way he was smiling at her, his blue eyes sparkling with unbridled humour, caused a spasm of resentment to wrench through Jane. Caught in a dilemma, the suggestion became a chaotic frenzy of thoughts. Her mind formed a vision of herself as Francis's wife, dressed in finery and twinkling jewels at the throat and ears. Quickly she thrust the image from her mind.

'I have a growing affection and respect for your mother and I'm beginning to realise you are right. She is forthright.'

Francis gazed at the tempestuous beauty standing merely a few feet away, her eyes flashing angry sparks, her breasts rising and falling with suppressed ire beneath the bodice of her gown. 'Are you surprised that my mother takes such an interest in my love life?'

'It's what mothers do, I suppose—and I salute her choice if she considers me suitable to marry her precious son.'

'I think you will find that she spoke in jest— although I, too, salute her choice.'

'Goodness! Next, you will be telling me that you agree with her. I've had far too much to occupy my mind and my time of late that I have given no thought to marriage. I am not inclined to marry anyone.'

'You needn't get so upset, Jane,' he teased with a devilishly wicked grin. 'I have no more inclination to subject myself to the institution of marriage than you.'

'You haven't?'

'No. Although,' he said, 'would it be such a terrible thing to be married to me?'

Jane stared at him, unable to believe he was saying these things to her, that he could be serious. A tremor went through her as his hand reached out and claimed the softness of her cheek. The eyes above her own glowed intently as his caress grew purposefully bolder. She caught her breath and stared at him in surprise as the sensations leapt through her, setting her whole body on fire.

'I told you, I have no wish to marry anyone at present.' She stepped back, forcing him to withdraw his hand.

'Things have changed, Jane. You do not have to beg your father's forgiveness for being attracted to a Randolph.' His eyes captured hers, holding them imprisoned and challenging her to deny it.

Treacherous warmth was beginning to creep into Jane's body. The meaning in his eyes was as clear as if it were written in the stars. 'I would not have to do that—considering the love he bore for your mother, I expect he would welcome the match. My father would not object to my choice of husband, as long as I am happy.'

'And here was I, trying to wheedle my way into

your good books, hoping to garner the smallest crumb of affection while you cannot wait to return to Northumberland where you will forget all about London—and me.'

His expression was of mock disappointment, which brought Jane a feeling of unease that he could jest about so serious a matter. She gave no indication of this when she spoke and kept her tone light. 'Francis, I am so sorry. Have I hurt you because I have not fallen at your feet?' she asked sweetly.

'You might say that. My pride has been mightily bruised,' he stated emphatically.

'Worry not, Francis. That will mend. You have enjoyed my company in London—admit it. You find my company pleasant—when you're not kissing me senseless, that is.'

'I am relieved that you have not taken it for granted that because I kissed you I will marry you.'

'It never entered my head. But you cannot escape the fact that you have sought to kiss me on several occasions.'

'Whenever the opportunity presented itself—and when you're not being stubborn and temperamental.'

'Temperamental! I'm never temperamental.'

'You've all the makings of being.'

'Only if you drive me to it. And you, my illustrious lord, have all the makings of a monster.'

Francis grinned most attractively. 'Never. But perhaps when you know me better and see how charming and attentive I can be, you will melt towards me.'

Jane's lips curved in a slow smile, enjoying their

light banter but aware there was a seriousness behind it which she did not care for. 'Charm is often an effective weapon, but I am not so easily won over—which I thought I had made plain on our journey down here.'

'Put me in my place, you mean?'

'If you like.'

'I thought I'd behaved in a proper manner under the difficult circumstances given to me.'

'And you will continue to be proper until the time comes for us to part.'

He chuckled, pausing to look down into her upturned face. 'Don't you ever give up? Don't tell me you didn't enjoy your journey to London with me?'

'I would say it was most illuminating—and stimulating. But whatever you have in mind where I am concerned, I will tell you now that you are wasting your time.'

Francis raised an eyebrow, amusement dancing in his dark eyes when he looked at her. 'Kindly explain yourself, Jane. What are you saying?'

'That if it is your intention to embark on a course of seduction on the return journey, I would advise you to reconsider. I have no intention of becoming a diversion—or of becoming the easy victim of a philanderer.'

Francis laughed outright, amused by her open honesty. 'I have been accused of many things, but never a philanderer. Where females are concerned, I am always serious in my intentions. I think you misunderstand me, Jane.'

Jane raised a delicate eyebrow. 'On the contrary.

I understand you very well and I would ask you not to attach any significance to our being together for so long.'

'But I do, Jane.' A silence fell between them as they walked back to the house and Francis bent his head in thought. 'However, jesting apart,' he said at length and on a more serious note. 'I have given a great deal of thought to what might await us in the north. When we reach our respective homes, Jane, It would be in your best interest if we did not meet like this.'

The gravity in his voice took Jane unawares and she glanced at him, startled. The realisation of what he was saying struck her at once. The light banter they had engaged in had gone. She thought she had always been afraid to hear those words and a foreboding of them had always been there whenever she had thought of going home. Now they were spoken and too late, the first disillusionment of love was upon her, for love him she did, with all her heart. 'What are you saying, Francis? 'For a moment her mind was in chaos, which he noted.

'Jane, don't look that way. Hear me out. This is not about me and you and where our relationship is going—that can come later when we reach the north and we've had time to assess the situation there. Should your father find himself a fugitive and seek shelter at Beckwith Manor, he will be sought by the military. Should he be taken, then the consequences will be dire indeed. Think about it, Jane. Considering my father's opinion of Catholicism and those who practise it—and the belief that I am in accord—then I will be in a far better position to offer help without arousing suspicion.'

Believing he was saying this as a way of letting her down gently—that it was an excuse for him not to see her again, that despite the kisses and soft words he was preparing the way for how things would be between them when they reached Northumberland, that everything would return to how it had been—as Jane listened to him she was unable to say the things that were in her heart. The words stayed inside her, locked there. She was too proud to speak and too fearful to offer her love and have it rejected.

He didn't know of the need inside her to beg and plead with him not to turn from her, which must be subdued. He didn't know how painful it was for her to think of being parted from him. And although he'd had the goodness to tell her he would want to offer her his protection should she need it, she wanted to see regret in his expression, in his eyes, that they would part, but she did not. She was hurt and bewildered and all she could see ahead of her was a profound loneliness.

'How excruciatingly stupid and naive you must find me. Francis, I do not expect a proposal if that's what all this is about. It never entered my head. I have far too much going on in my life just now to consider marrying anyone. But—what did you think you were doing when you kissed me? Were you simply toying with me to relieve the boredom of the journey?'

'No. I wouldn't do that. I kissed you because I

wanted to—very badly, in fact. As I recall, you raised no objections and returned my kisses with an ardour equal to my own.'

'I am ashamed of how easy I made it for you.'

'There is no apology I can offer you. No words would mean anything now. All I can say is that I would not knowingly have hurt you. Do I have to spell it out to you? You know how it is between you and the people at home. People will talk if we are seen together and make it more difficult for me to help you should the need arise.'

'And that bothers you—what people would think?'

'Not in the least. I long ago ceased to concern myself with gossip. What worries me is how it will affect you. It will not be easy for either of us if you appear too often in my company.'

Jane cast him a scathing look. 'No, you don't have to spell it out to me, Francis. No one knows the truth of what happened between our parents—and they never will. So because of my father I am held in some suspicion and it will do you no good if you are seen visiting Beckwith Manor. I do realise that and should the need arise I will resist seeking your help. The last thing I want is to endanger you in any way. So worry not. Should we meet in Corbridge or Newcastle I will walk on by.'

'Jane, don't be ridiculous. Allow me to explain. You have misunderstood me—'

'Oh, I don't think so,' she uttered brusquely. 'I think I have understood you very well. Now come along. You can escort me back to the house and we will not speak of this again.'

In the tearing, agonising hurt that enfolded her, that was the moment when a part of Jane died inside her, something that saw the last of foolish, hopeful and naive Jane Deighton who had fallen in love with him.

What Francis steadfastly refused to admit as he left her to go to the stables was that he wanted to turn back to her, to enter that house and take her in his arms, to chase away the demons and create sweet dreams. He should have explained in more detail why he believed it would be for the best to put some distance between them when they reached Northumberland.

The rebellion in the north worried him more than he cared to confess to Jane—he had no wish to cause her to worry unduly. But it was true what he had told her, that should the rising go against the Jacobites and Edward Deighton found himself a fugitive, then things could prove dire for both Jane and her father. He would be better placed to help without suspicion if it was believed his abhorrence of the Jacobites was as deep as his father's had been before him.

He hated to think Jane could believe he would put her from his mind so easily, especially when she had been so close to him for the weeks they had lived in such close proximity in his mother's house. What would happen when the rising was over and normality was restored, he had not considered. But the longer they were together she was instilling herself deeper in his heart. But until this business with the Jacobites was resolved, as difficult as it would be, there would be no more kisses between them.

What Francis didn't realise just then was that between a man's plans and deeds lies a distance that sometimes must be measured in miles. Francis would find that out on the day they arrived in York on the journey north.

It had come as an immense disappointment to have Francis say what he had to her, for him to destroy the peace they had shared in these past weeks. She would like to believe that he had spoken for solicitude for her reputation, but she thought not. She knew without it being said how seeing her on their home ground would be interpreted. What man of his standing wanted to be seen in the company of an impoverished woman whose father was a fugitive, a traitor, who had fled the country when it became known he had killed his neighbour in a carriage accident? It would doubtless involve Francis in unwanted problems.

What did she know of Francis Randolph, after all, and what kind of naive fool was she to suppose he would want to spend time with her anyway? He had other claims on his time. They had been thrown together by circumstance and they had become closer because of it. She didn't belong in London, but it had given her a short time in her life when she had felt a glorious sense of floating free, of enjoying just waking in the morning, doing this and that for pleasure, because it was another day of edging closer to Francis, and she had loved it and not felt guilty about it.

Their time together had been a pleasant interlude of fun and laughter—indeed, she had almost forgotten what that felt like. But somehow, life without Francis's proximity seemed a cold and less pleasing prospect. Being alone would be harder now that she had learned what sharing was like. How, in the short time she had known him, her dependence on him had grown—a dangerous dependence, perhaps. She closed her eyes and allowed herself the shameful indulgence of remembering how he had held her, how he had kissed her, the thrill of it. She shook her head in an attempt to dispel the memories.

During their time together she had said things to him that were too personal, unthinkable things, which in her hurt and disappointment and fear of what awaited her in Northumberland had suddenly become thinkable. She had lived through an extraordinary time and she felt as if something had been tearing inside of her and finally burst. The remnants of what she had been lay scattered around her and she wanted to draw back the words she had spoken, but it was too late. Maybe it was better if strangers who have talked too much didn't meet again.

Francis was right. She had the sense to understand that she was fighting against a tide that was flowing strongly to engulf her. To indulge in a romantic liaison would be a mistake in the middle of this crisis.

She needed a clear head, unimpeded by attachments that could never be attained in this present climate.

On the surface nothing had changed between them. There are many things to imply friendship, even where none exists. After their conversation in the garden, everything they said and did was for show. But what lingered in Jane for Francis went deep and could not be removed by mere words.

On the morning they were to leave for the north, Jane swept down the stairs, looking regal in her dark green gown, the sleeves long and the cuffs edged with fine lace. A warm woollen cloak hung from her shoulders and her hair was drawn from her face by a simple broad band of ribbon over the top of her head and allowed to hang free in heavy waves down the length of her curving spine.

Francis's gaze studied her closely and he nodded ever so slightly, happy to see she did not appear to be affected or upset by their conversation the previous day. The long-enduring ache of suppressed passion stirred his blood.

In no time at all Jane was saying goodbye to her sister. Miriam cocked her head to one side, considering Jane thoughtfully. 'What about you and Francis, Jane? You've spent a good deal of time together. It's plain to see you are beginning to get on, that you are warming to him. Did anything happen between the two of you when you travelled to London? I have often wondered so you might as well tell me.'

'Nothing happened, Miriam.'

'It *did*,' Miriam persisted forcefully. 'I know it did.'

Jane's face flamed. 'Very well. If you must know he—he—he kissed me,' she confessed quietly.

Miriam's eyes widened with amazement. 'Kissed you? Goodness! And didn't you like being kissed by him?'

'No—yes—oh, Miriam, I don't know.

'I knew it. I've watched you these past weeks and I think you have feelings for him.'

Jane flushed and lowered her eyes. She would have liked to dispel Miriam's speculation that she had an interest in Francis—or that he had any in her—but she could not hide her true feelings from Miriam's sharp eyes. 'I—I feel that I can be close to him—but—it cannot happen. I am impatient to return to Beckwith Manor, Miriam. There will be much to do after being away so long.'

'You must think of yourself, Jane. Francis cares for you—I can see that.' She sighed, hugging Jane close. 'I'm going to miss you so much. Be happy for me.'

Jane studied her expression sadly. Her face was stern with determination and at the same time radiant in a way Jane had never seen it before. Just thinking of Andrew could transform her. Every day Miriam had been in her life. Jane loathed the thought of her leaving, yet she had to respect the judgement of this. She saw in her sister's widened eyes the light of incredulous joy, then the shimmer of tears. Her own eyes misted over and she squeezed Miriam's hand tight. 'I love you, Miriam.'

'I know you do.' She smiled and touched her sister's face.

It was one of the most beautiful things Jane had ever seen in her life. 'You have something that is very rare, Miriam—rare and wonderful. May it continue always.'

Jane would never forget her time in London, and when she closed her eyes she lived again the things she had done—the walks in the park, the simple pleasures. The city throbbed with an intensity that pervaded her heart and her flesh and quickened her pulse. Never before had she felt so young, so alive, with others who matched her mood. She had almost begun to feel human in the company of Francis's family. There had been things to share, so much to talk and laugh about and make the most of the kind of frivolous relaxation she had never known. She had never been so free or unfettered and Northumberland had seemed a long, long way away. Now she was returning to her home so much had changed from when she had left, so much was different and could never be the same again. She had broken through the small world she inhabited, had seen things she had never thought she would see and had been stirred to a depth she couldn't comprehend.

That time had come to an end. It suddenly dawned on her that she'd be leaving Francis soon and the realisation pierced her with unexpected poignancy. All things considered, she realised with an awful ache in her heart, he'd treated her with more gallantry than she'd expected. They would both have memories of the closeness they had shared and, if it were no more than a memory, then they would let it be so. But she could not deny that she had lived with some wild hope that some day they could be together. But that's all it was, a wild hope, a wish—a desperate wanting. Nothing could come of it. They could never be together. Things like that didn't happen to her. But she would continue to dream and go on wanting.

The journey north was uneventful until they reached York. Jane passed away the hours reading a book Lady Randolph had given her on leaving, telling her it would offer respite from the tediousness of the journey. Francis frequently sought relief from this on top of the coach with the driver. There was no opportunity for the kind of intimacy that had been present on their journey south.

The further they travelled, the more Francis became concerned about the situation in the north. He had gathered information at the places they stopped for refreshment and to change the horses on the way. As he'd predicted, the news was grim. At the same time as a battle was being fought at Sheriffmuir over the border in Scotland, there were risings in the north and west of England, which added to the sense that the Hanovarian regime was in trouble.

The government was quick to respond and the army hurried north to deal with the troublesome Jacobites. The battle at Sheriffmuir was inconclusive with both sides declaring victory. However, the Earl of Mar's failure to secure a decisive victory and take control of central Scotland meant defeat for the uprising. This was further secured by the surrender of the Jacobite army in Preston in Lancashire. Over a thousand prisoners were being taken to London to stand trial.

Knowing how worried Jane would be, Francis kept what he had learned to himself. Unfortunately, by the time they reached York, the situation in the north had become the main topic of conversation. The Black Swan was almost filled to capacity with travellers. A fire blazed in the hearth and an aroma of cooked food rose in the air. After speaking to the innkeeper and securing two rooms for the night, they settled at a table in the corner where they were served with drink and food. It was impossible not to hear the conversation of several of the patrons drinking at the bar, of the battles fought and lost and Jacobite prisoners being marched to London and others being sought throughout the length and breadth of the north.

Francis watched Jane closely. Her attention was divided between her food and listening to the conversation going on around her. Her appetite seemed to leave her. She was locked in silence, her face frozen in stillness and deathly white. It held a look of undisguised pain such as he had never seen there before. When Jane rose and excused herself a short time later, Francis rose, too.'

'Jane, my room is next to yours if you should need me.'

'Thank you,' she said, without looking at him.

* * *

Jane experienced a terrible fear for the safety of her father. With the failure of the battles, if he had not been taken prisoner then he would be a fugitive. It was as though she knew of the tragedy that was waiting, with little knowledge of what the ending would be, and that wore on her nerves. She was confused and thoroughly terrified of the outcome of all this. Suffering a sense of helplessness in the face of terrible events, sleep, chased by a thousand images of battles and blood and her father running away, eluded her.

Feeling the need to talk to Francis she slipped out of bed. With her heart pounding, she crossed to the door and stepped on to the landing. Sounds of people still about drifted up to her, indicating that the hour could not be all that late. Francis's room was next door. Knocking lightly, she prayed he had come to bed and was not down in the common room drinking with the driver and the guards. She breathed a sigh of relief when it opened.

'Francis! I— I— Can I talk to you?'

He opened the door wider for her to enter. After sharing a few late-hour brandies with the coach driver and the two guards, he hadn't been in his room long. 'You should be in bed, Jane.'

She turned and looked at him, guessing that he had been expecting her. 'I couldn't sleep.'

'I am not so insensitive that I don't know what you must be going through. You heard what they were talking about, didn't you?'

'How could I not? I am so worried—so afraid.' She sighed deeply and her expression was uncertain, as if she were suddenly too confused to grasp the pace of events that flowed past her. There was an intensity in her lovely eyes that clearly conveyed the depths of her concern—in fact, such was her concern that she seemed oblivious of the fact that she was attired in nothing but her nightdress, her wonderful wealth of hair tumbling about her shoulders.

'I can't stop thinking about what might have happened to my father. If he is caught, he will be branded a traitor and will be led straight to the gallows.' Unable to bear the thought of him dying, she swallowed down the lump that suddenly appeared in her throat. 'This is terrible,' she said, beginning to pace back and forth. 'All this was happening while I was in London. I should not have left Northumberland to go chasing after Miriam. He might need me. God willing, he will have escaped the battle unscathed and will be on his way back to France. May the Lord save him,' she whispered.

Her prayer was heartfelt and Francis looked at her closely, seeing panic in the eyes of this usually assured young woman. 'You have just cause to be upset. What you heard is the reality of the situation. I will not paint a pretty picture—but then again it may not be as bleak as you think. What you heard may have been an exaggeration of the facts.'

Francis's voice was surprisingly gentle and the unfamiliar sound caused an embarrassed flush to sweep Jane's cheeks. He was looking down at her and for a moment she fancied there was a strange expression in his face she had not seen before. She searched his eyes, groping for reassurance. There was none he could give.

'I am afraid they may be right. I can't stop thinking about what I heard. Did you know about Sheriffmuir, Francis?'

'I did. I hoped to see you safely back in Northumberland before you found out,' he confessed. 'It pains me to know that I failed you.'

Jane stared at him in disbelief. '*Failed* me? How can you say that? Without you I would not have reached London. I am in awe of what you and your mother have done for me. You were not to know which direction the rising would take. There was nothing you could do.'

'Yes, there was. I should have done my utmost to persuade you to remain in London a while longer.'

Jane would have protested, but he pressed his fingers gently against her mouth to still her arguments. She blinked at the sudden wetness in her eyes as he leaned down to press his lips to her brow. When he reached out and drew her close, she did not object. At that moment his closeness was what she needed, what she craved for most. She found her head against his chest, a warm, familiar place against her cheek to nestle. She did not weep because tears were of no use. But she could not speak. All she wanted to do was to hold on to Francis, for his protective arms to encircle her, to feel his strength and his gentleness.

He stroked her hair. His mere presence gave her a sense of security and safety. She nestled closer and turned her face into his chest. It was as if she wanted to hide herself in his embrace.

Releasing his hold, Francis turned her face up to his and stroked the hair from her face. 'You are a remarkable woman, Jane. I don't believe any woman I have ever met is your equal,' he said, his tone soft and unlike the Francis Randolph she thought she knew. 'You are also very lovely and you don't deserve any of this.'

Jane tilted her head and stared into his fathomless dark blue gaze while his soft voice caressed her. 'No, perhaps not, but it is as it is and there is nothing I can do to escape it.'

Standing close to him, she brushed his face with her fingers. His skin was warm to her touch. Her fingers moved to his lips and in a swift movement he caught her hand and gently pressed a kiss on each finger before placing his hands on her upper arms and pulling her back into his embrace. With her bright head pressed into the curve of his shoulder, she sighed.

'Please don't make me leave.'

'Then you must stay, if that is what you want.'

Her voice trembled and she looked at him. 'Then I will stay.' He stood there, silent, frowning, the frown digging a deep groove above the bridge of his nose. The air between them was charged with a new kind of tension and anticipation. Those deep blue eyes studied her, darkening to almost black. Jane knew what he was thinking and it frightened her a little as she looked directly into his eyes. There was an intensified look in them, hard and dark and burning with hope. Her silence said more than words. The decision was hers, she knew that, and she knew she should leave now, while there was still time. But she didn't want to leave.

When he took her in his arms once more she felt the strength in them and the warmth of his masculine body. Slowly the real reason that had brought her to his room began to recede, but she made no effort to free herself from that tight circle of arms and Francis didn't seem to have any intention of letting her go while she was content to remain there. She could feel the hard muscles of his chest and smell his maleness. A tautness began in her breast, a delicious ache that was like a languorous, honeyed warmth. Tilting her head back, she gazed up at him. His face was poised above hers, close, looking deep into her eyes, his warm breath caressing her face.

It seemed a lifetime passed as they gazed at each other. In that lifetime each lived through a range of deep, tender emotions new to them both, exquisite emotions that neither of them could put into words. As though in slow motion, unable to resist the temptation Jane's mouth offered, slowly Francis's moved inexorably closer. His gaze was gentle and compelling when, in a sweet, mesmeric sensation, his mouth found hers. Jane melted into him. The kiss was long and lingeringly slow.

When he released her Jane's eyes went in the direction of the bed. Francis smiled and she made no effort to resist when he went and drew back the covers.

Chapter Eight

'Don't fret, Jane. You can share my bed tonight.' His eyes did a quick sweep of her nightdress and he laughed softly. 'I'm glad to see you have come prepared. You have my word that if all you want to do is sleep, then you will be quite safe.'

Jane couldn't even manage a discomfited blush as he lifted her up and placed her between the sheets. Submissively, with a grateful sigh, she turned on to her side and curled into a ball, closing her eyes.

'I know I will, she murmured. 'We will make no promises, no commitments. We will just see where it leads us. Anything is possible.'

'Yes. Anything is possible. Now rest yourself.'

Whatever protest Jane might have made was lost in an overwhelming sense of relief and safety and comfort and welcoming warmth that soon settled within her as he covered her. After that she knew nothing more, not even when he smoothed the hair from forehead and pressed a soft kiss to her cheek before climbing into bed beside her. Later he took her in his encompassing arms, careful not to penetrate the barrier of her sleep. But as the night wore on she moved closer, instinctively sensing his body beside her, his strength and protection.

She continued to sleep and so did he, content to just to hold her, until she shifted a little and her leg crossed over his to make herself more comfortable. His arms tightened instantly. The unconsciously possessive gesture seemed to penetrate her mind and she nestled closer to him, her cheek against his chest. Slowly an awareness of where she was began to dawn on her and she opened her eyes.

'Francis!' she gasped, struggling to sit up. 'What must you think of me? When I came to your room I—I didn't mean for any of this to happen. It's just that I couldn't bear to be by myself.'

With a sense of tenderness surging through him, Francis tipped her chin up and said with quiet gravity, 'Then I'm glad I was next door so you could come to me.' Lifting his hand, he brushed the tousled hair off her cheeks, slowly combing his fingers through it and watching it spill over her shoulders. He smiled. 'I've been fantasising about how it would feel to do that ever since I met you. You have lovely hair, Jane.'

Jane felt a warmth begin to seep through her entire body at his words and lay back down beside him. She became languid and relaxed with sensuality and sensations like tight buds opened and exploded into flowers of splendour, growing stronger and sweeter. As if Francis sensed the way her body melted into

him, he lowered his head and captured her lips with
his. She felt the hardness of his body pressed close to
her own and a melting softness flowed through her
veins, evoking feelings she had never experienced
before or thought herself capable of feeling.

'Do you wish to leave, Jane? Do not feel that you
have to stay.'

The intensity of feeling between them was evident, but not easily understood. What she did know
was that now, with Northumberland not far away and
separation from him imminent, this might be the last
time they could be together like this. Gathering together all her strength, she thrust away her fears, her
anguish and all thoughts of farewell.

She shook her head. 'I don't want to leave—not
yet.'

Those blue eyes studying her darkened to almost
black. She did not lower her eyes. Her silence, her
level gaze, said more than words. She knew that she
should go while there was still time, while there was
still a choice—but she could not do that. Her senses
and emotions and her physical desire were immense.
Francis had come to mean everything to her, yet the
dangers he posed towards her continued to ache inside her. A small insidious voice whispered a caution,
reminding her that any liaison with Francis would
bring her nothing but heartbreak, but another voice
was whispering something else, telling her not to let
the moment pass, to catch it and hold on to it. In that
instant she did not want to fight against destiny. She
wanted to take down the ruthless barriers she had

erected around herself and for a few hours just be a woman who desired a man. In a future that looked so bleakly empty, she had to have some memories.

Francis's eyes filled with tenderness and Jane knew he was feeling as she did. With the faltering limits of his will sorely strained, she knew well enough what her scantily clad form was doing to him. His boldness knew no bounds as he spread his hand over the curve of her breast, pressed her hips tightly against his loins and sought her lips. It was a long moment before the wild beating of her heart slowed and her reeling senses returned to something resembling normal. She knew that his desires had increased and his power to master them had weakened.

It was a knowledge confirmed when, lifting his head briefly from the lips which he'd been crushing under his own, he whispered softly. 'A man cannot control how his body responds to a beautiful woman. Being with you arouses longings I've struggled hard to suppress ever since we embarked on this journey. I'm a man, Jane, subject to all the feelings and flaws of my gender. I enjoy having you near me. You're soft and alluring and you graced my mother's home like an elegant, fragrant flower that bestirs the senses. I do desire you as a woman and yet I would never force you or knowingly hurt you.'

Through a haze of desire—unbidden, unexpected— she heard his murmured words. As she half opened her eyes, an incredible warmth enveloped her heart as she searched his eyes and found a strange sincerity there. Raising her hand and gently touching his cheeks, she murmured, 'I understand, Francis. Truly I do and this is what I want.' A soft, quivering sigh passed her lips. 'I thought you wanted us to part. Does this mean that you have changed your mind?'

'I believe it does.' Warmed and intrigued by her response, he drew a ragged breath. 'It's a mountainous task for me to hold you and remain tender and patient when my hunger for you has brought me to the brink of starvation.' As if to prove this, unable to curb his impatience for her, he got out and peeled off his breeches and shirt and then got back into bed. Without waiting to be prompted, Jane pulled her nightdress over her head in one swift movement.

For a moment Francis was stunned at the frank sensuality of the gesture, but then he reached for her and drew her back into his arms. Gently cupping the soft, scented roundness of her breasts within his hands, he lowered his head and caressed them with his mouth, pressing wanton kisses over their warmth. Jane's head fell back as the fires raged in the depths of her body. Francis raised himself above her and slid warm hands over the rest of her naked form. As if in a trance, she lay beyond thought, beyond awareness, unmoving beneath the touch of his hands. A pulsing heat began to throb in her loins, spreading outwards, reaching upwards until she thrust out her breasts to luxuriate in the hot, flicking strokes.

He had held the most precious, wonderful scantily clad woman in his arms—in his bed—and not made love to her. Now, he couldn't believe she had turned to him, wanting him, as much as he wanted her. Since their first meeting he had never ceased to be amazed and fascinated by the enticing blend of innocence and boldness he had seen in Jane. He lost himself in the beauty of her, in the perfection of her body which gleamed in the golden candlelight, his gaze and his caresses worshipping it with the purest of expression.

She wriggled against him, in the course of which she heightened a multitude of sensations that had already been stimulated in him when he had kissed her. Her trembling innocence was incredibly erotic—he longed to bring her to ecstasy. Her body clutched his, her long slim legs wrapping themselves around him along with her twining white arms. Her glorious hair fell sensuously about them both. Her mouth welcomed his, soft and deliciously sweet.

The hot blood had surged through him with swift and fiery intensity at the very instant his lips made contact with hers, making him achingly aware of his ravaging desire. A moment later the ravenous flames still pulsed with excruciating vigour through his loins. With every fibre of his being, he was acutely aware of the elusive fragrance of Jane filling his head, that same fragrance which he breathed with intoxicating pleasure every time he was near her.

Taking charge, he rolled her on to her back and his weight was on top of her, penetrating her, placing his mouth over hers when she gasped and stiffened her body, taking a moment to give her time to welcome him with deep pleasure. Her yielding woman's body was eager to submit itself to the languid, stretching, searching joy of his hands and lips. When she moaned it was with a deep, inner joy. It seemed to Francis that she became aware of a driving need to appease a burgeoning, insatiable hunger as her world reached out of control and a ravishing, rapturous splendour burst upon her, as they were joined as one, fused by the heat of their loins.

It was only when his shuddering release was over and his breath was coming in ragged gasps, his rock-hard body glistening with sweat, that he even remembered why he had harboured any reservations of forming an intimate relationship with Jane. In the wonderful lethargy of after-love, that deep, warm tide of contentment akin to sleep, his thoughts were scattered and fleeting, yet centred around the woman beneath him. When he felt her stir, he rolled away, taking her with him and holding her close, feeling her heart beating against his chest.

He breathed deeply of the perfumed heat of her body, satiated after the deep fulfilment of their love-making. He kissed the silken top of her golden head where she lay in the fold of his arm and snuggled against him, her arm draped across his waist, her body still glowing and throbbing from his caressing hands. At first he was almost afraid of the pure perfection of her naked body, but his need for her overcame his fear. He was amazed and delighted that she had returned his passion with equal fervour.

It was incredible the way she could torment and satisfy his senses at the same time. Even now, exhausted from the gratifying climax, he wasn't immune to her tantalising attractions. Her lips were parted sightly and her breath rippled across his skin.

'How do you feel, Jane?'

Drowsily she opened her eyes. 'Happy,' she whispered, languid and sated. 'And needed. I never thought it could be like this. I simply didn't know. I—I thought it was something a woman owed to her husband. A duty. It didn't feel like that.'

Jane's reaction surprised him. He had been prepared for tears, recriminations, condemnation of herself, of him. But not for calm acceptance, wonder and joy.

'It's strange,' she went on, but I thought I'd feel shame—I don't. I feel like I've been set free—but free of what I have no idea. When I sought you out I did not expect to end up in your bed.'

'Do you mind?'

Tilting her head back she met his gaze. 'Not in the least. Your bed is much more comfortable than mine.'

He chuckled softly, bending his head and giving her a long, leisurely kiss that set her pulses racing. 'Is that all that attracted you to my bed?' He sighed, smoothing a heavy lock of hair from her face. 'Do you realise how lovely you look when you're still half-asleep?'

'Do I? I find that hard to believe—or that someone would say those words to me.'

Francis gazed into her glowing eyes and he saw the kind of gentle beauty and unquenchable spirit that could be the undoing of any man. His heart constricted with an emotion so intense that it made him ache. 'You also have a beautiful smile.'

Again they loved. This time their lovemaking had an intensity neither of them understood. It was as if each time might be the last. Jane was aware of how much pleasure her body was capable of giving and how much pleasure Francis was capable of giving her, and they spent the late hours discovering each other—unashamed, greedy and besotted until, at last, they slept.

When Francis moved beside her, Jane started awake and blinked her eyes open, trying to focus her vision. Then she remembered. 'I must go before the inn wakes up. If I am seen on the landing in my nightgown, it would raise an eyebrow or two,' she murmured thickly through her drowsiness. Scrambling on to the edge of the bed, she reached for her nightgown, pulling it over her head. As she leaned over the bed to say her goodbye, Francis reached up, drawing her head down to his.

'Francis, I—I—must...'

He stopped her words with a kiss, kissing her long and deep and honestly, with all the longing and tenderness and desire he really felt. He was glad she wasn't shocked or embarrassed on becoming joined to him in the most intimate way imaginable. Then he remembered he had told her they would part when they reached Northumberland. It was amazing, he thought, that he should want to reassure her. When he released her she stepped back.

He searched her face and, seeing the soft flush on her cheeks, said quietly, his gaze filled with tenderness, 'I imagine this means that you won't be seeing the last of me when we reach Northumberland. You misunderstood me when I told you that we should put some distance between us when we reached home.'

'I did?'

'I'm afraid so. I told you that should the rebellion go against the Jacobites and your father finds himself a fugitive, I will be in a better position to help you both without suspicion if we are not together. What I didn't say and what I should have, I realise, is that I had no intention of letting you go. You have become too precious to me for me to do that. Do you understand what I am saying, Jane?'

She nodded. 'Yes,' she whispered. 'It would appear I foolishly mistook your intent. How very noble of you, Francis, but there is something I wish to say to you before I leave.'

'Oh?'

'I do not expect anything from you. This night has been special to me—has meant something special. I wanted you to make love to me and the last thing I want is for you to feel obligated to me in any way. I have no idea what awaits me at home. If my father has indeed been caught up in the rising, then he may have made it back to France—or he may be a fugitive. Until I know for certain, nothing can be decided. If he is indeed a fugitive, with Miriam gone and the threat of Beckwith Manor being confiscated, if it's possible for my father to get out of the country, then

I might well go with him.' Without giving Francis time to reply, she left him.

Francis lay awake a long time after she had gone, finding it hard to believe she had been with him and that it was not a figment of his imagination. Before tonight, every time he had thought of her and how it had felt when he had kissed her, his whole body had tingled with memory. It was as though by the simple fact of having her with him his life had changed. Now he tried to analyse this new feeling, moving warm and soft within his heart. And then suddenly he knew, knew what it was. It was love. Could this last? he wondered. With other women he had felt nothing like what he was feeling now. Just then he could not stretch his imagination to remember how it had been. He could only remember the boredom, the emptiness, the meaningless loves—if he could ever call them that.

But this was Jane—this newfound wonder. Sleep continued to elude him as his mind now became occupied with how he was to keep this woman who had come to mean so much to him in his life.

Jane didn't see Francis at breakfast. He was outside supervising the preparation of the next part of their journey. Jane's stomach fluttered at the memory of what had occurred when she had gone to his room. When she had eaten she went out into the yard, where carriages and horses were being got ready to go on their way. She saw Francis standing with their coach driver, watching as the horses were fastened to their coach. His masterful face was set in taut, unreadable lines. So many conflicting sensations were flitting about within her, exciting and dangerous emotions that were bewildering.

Memories of the night that had held a thousand exceptional and unexpected pleasures came rushing back and a rosy hue mantled her cheeks when she remembered the incredibly wanton things they had done. She had always imagined her first time would bring bewilderment. She had seen animals mate and had always thought it was something that would be done hastily. But it wasn't like that. Francis had made it different and she had felt the surrender of something strange yet familiar. She could have stopped it any time, but she had wanted him so much, for him to drive the loneliness from her soul.

Her body still tingled with their lovemaking, which they had given and taken in equal measure. There wasn't an inch of her that he hadn't touched or tasted as he had aroused her body with such skilful tenderness and shattered every barrier of her reserve. He also had the ability to tease, to cajole, to delight her senses in ways she could not have imagined. He had created feelings inside her she was a stranger to, yearnings she wanted to satisfy, and only Francis could do that. No longer could she maintain her indifference towards him or ignore the strange forces at work that had drawn them together. What had he done to her? What had happened to her? Was she wanton for wanting him to make love to her again?

She had told him that if her father could escape

from England then she would go with him, even though she couldn't bear to think of breaking away from Francis when they reached her home. But separate they must. Tears formed in her eyes, blurring her vision. She could not marry him—not that he would ever ask her—and nor could they pursue their present course. But after what they had done, she would be unworthy of any other man, since she had sinned both in the flesh and in the mind. For even as she felt guilt seize her, she knew she would go to Francis again and again, that no warning voice in the back of her mind could stop her.

Jane saw him look her way. When their eyes met a seductive smile curved his lips and he walked to where she stood.

'How are you this morning, Jane? Did you sleep well?'

The flush on her cheeks deepened and her eyes shone. 'You might well ask,' she murmured.

'I missed you when you left,' he said in a low voice.

'Did you?'

'I enjoyed your company. Did you think of me afterwards?'

The intensity of his gaze ploughed through her composure. 'Yes,' she confessed, unable to deny it.

'All night?'

'Maybe—but I will not pander to your ego. It's already overinflated.'

He grinned, watching as she climbed into the coach, eager for them to proceed towards Durham.

* * *

Having left Durham behind, they were just hours away from Beckwith Manor. Jane was now too tired and absorbed with what might await her. Francis caught her mood and they were silent the further north they travelled. With Miriam's leaving, Jane felt an extra burden placed on her. Every day her sister had been there. The sense of hurt and loss was more keenly felt now that they had parted. Never had she felt so alone. The pace of the coach seemed slower and Jane felt an impatience rise in her. She felt the fatigue of the long journey wash over her, the strain of it all. All she wanted at that moment was a hot bath and to go to bed.

Dusk had fallen over the windswept moor, the glorious pink and purple heather which clothed the rolling hills in autumn having turned brown. On the edge of open woodland a cluster of fallow deer lifted their heads and watched, undisturbed, as the coach rolled by. Jane smiled when a golden plover rose and went soaring into the sky. She breathed the cooler air inside the coach, filling her lungs with its sweetness, exhilarated to be back where she belonged.

Francis did not see the plover or feel what made Jane's spirits soar. His mind was mulling over what he knew of the situation in Northumberland, having made a point of questioning everyone he came into contact with when they stopped. His mood had darkened and his expression was grim. Although he looked calm and in control, his mind was in a continual turmoil of conflict. He had learned that the rebellion in England and over the border in Scotland was finished. An atmosphere of crisis already prevailed by the time they got to Northumberland, with the authorities searching houses for information of those involved in the rising,

It was dark and the coach rumbled on as they turned on to the drive to Beckwith Manor. The tall elms in long lines on either side, having shed their leaves, gave Jane a comforting feel. The coach halted before the door. A large shaggy shape rose from the yard. Giving a joyful whine and a yelp and an excited wag of his tail, Spike almost knocked his mistress over in his delight to see her back home. Jane fussed over him, then, ordering him to lie down, she opened the door.

She wondered why she was suddenly so conscious of the neglect and shabbiness of Beckwith Manor. It had been her home for ever, loved and familiar. As she entered, she saw it now as a stranger might see it and thought of the peeling paintwork, the crumbling walls and the buckets in the attics to catch the water from the leaking roof. A strange silence lay over the house. Jane looked beyond Bessie to the shadowed, silent rooms and wide staircase beyond the hall. An eeriness hung in the air she had never felt before. It was an awareness of something fearsome and threatening trying to communicate itself to her.

Bessie hovered in the hall, casting wary glances at Lord Randolph.

'How are things here, Bessie?'

'Much the same as when you left.' She looked at the carriage and the waiting guards. 'Miss Miriam? Is she not with you?'

'No, Bessie. Miriam married Andrew Randolph and is to remain in London. We decided it was for the best.' Jane knew what she was thinking. Bessie shook her head in disbelief, for a misalliance such as this—a Deighton married to a Randolph—would surely come to grief. 'Is there news of Father?'

Bessie opened her mouth and seemed to think for a moment, before snapping it shut and shaking her head.

Panic seized Jane momentarily. Something was wrong. She could sense, feel it in the air. She knew Bessie wouldn't speak in front of Francis. She turned to him, walking with him to the door, trying hard to appear calm and composed.

Pausing in the doorway, he looked down at her. 'I worry about you, Jane. You could do with some extra protection.'

'You think I am in danger?'

'It is possible.'

'I'll be all right. Don't worry about me.'

'I would have contempt for myself if I did not.'

He seemed sincere. Jane could see it in his eyes. He did want her to remain safe, she believed that.

'I—I will be all right, Francis. You should go. You must be eager to get to Redmires.'

Francis looked from Jane to the watching Bessie and back again. 'If you're sure.'

'Yes—thank you.'

Jane watched him open the door and then he was gone. Tears of frustration and weakness brimmed in her eyes, which she dashed away. Despair that Francis was leaving her and not knowing anything about her father was a bitter pill to take and she swallowed it down. Now was not the time for hysterics. She waited until the coach had pulled out of the yard and the door was closed before turning to Bessie.

'Bessie? How are things really?'

'Not good.'

'Father?'

'He's here. I didn't like to say in front of Lord Randolph—knowing he's a King's man. He escaped the battle at Sherrifmuir and managed to elude his pursuers—although how he made it here I don't know. No one else knows he's here.'

Jane's heart stopped as she stared at Bessie. 'Where is he?'

'In the priest hole in the library.'

'I must go to him.'

'He's wounded—he took a sword wound in his side. He was conscious, his mind lucid, but the wound is nasty and deep. I pray it doesn't become infected. I've dressed it as best I can. Try to be strong for his sake. You were the first person he asked for.'

Before Jane could see her father they heard the jangle of harness outside the house, followed by the sound of men dismounting. They waited until they heard the ring of booted feet on the stone flags as whoever it was strode to the door. With a worried look at Jane, Bessie went to let them in. A shiver of apprehension and fear scurried up Jane's spine as she watched three soldiers in the uniform of the King's army stride in. She noted the swaggering confidence of the man in front. He halted, staring at the two women. An unpleasant feeling akin to revulsion slithered through her, creeping up her spine. She could not believe this was happening.

Jane and Bessie stood side by side, taking strength from each other, their eyes fixed on the intruders. The air was charged the way it was before a storm. How dare they come strutting into her home? The face of the soldier in front was hard and uncompromising. His eyes, cold and derisive, settled on Jane with a bold stare. If he hoped to see a flicker of emotion pass across her face, he was disappointed. A cold hand clutched at Jane's heart, but, remembering who she was, she behaved like Edward Deighton's daughter with as much dignity as she could muster. She would not give this man the satisfaction of seeing her disturbed. She stood still while he raked his gaze scathingly over her.

'What can I do for you, sir?' Jane said. 'I don't imagine this is a social call.' A faint, contemptuous smile touched his lips and Jane felt the malevolence in him.

'You are Jane Deighton, daughter of Edward Deighton|'

'I am.'

'I am Captain Walton. I'm not here to pay my respects. I'm sorry to disturb you, although you must know why we are here. We're looking for fleeing Jacobites—those who fled the field after Sherrifmuir.'

'Jacobites?'

'I came to tell you that Edward Deighton, your father, a notorious Jacobite as well you know, is on the loose and was seen heading south. A full-scale search has been ordered. It's important that we apprehend him. Have you seen him?'

'There are no Jacobites in this house.'

'What? Not even you, his daughter?'

'I am not of the Catholic faith and if I were it would not necessarily make me a Jacobite. The *last* time I saw my father was twelve months ago.' His eyes narrowed, assessing her, no doubt wondering if her emphasis had been deliberate. 'Are you telling me my father is dangerous?'

'Any desperate man is dangerous,' he replied coldly. 'We have reason to believe he was wounded, how badly I cannot say, but he won't get far. Where would a wounded man go if not to his family?'

'Then I pray he still lives.'

'And I pray your prayers are answered.' He stepped forward and looked down into her eyes, speaking with deliberate menace. 'When Edward Deighton is caught he will be interrogated. Hopefully he will give up the names of his associates. If you are harbouring him in this house, I demand you give him up.' His eyes scanned the hallway, as if expecting Edward Deighton to materialise from the oak panelling.

'There are no fugitives in this house,' Bessie told him firmly.

'I would hardly expect you to hand them over if they were,' he uttered coldly. 'I am tempted to search the house myself—but I have to be elsewhere.'

'Then don't let me hinder you. Should you locate my father, will you be kind enough to inform me?'

His eyes impaled her and an ugly smile twisted his handsome face. 'I will make a point of it. Be sure we'll be back. I trust you will think twice before you grant succour to any rebels who might find their way to this house. The consequences are dire to anyone found harbouring traitors.'

Jane met his gaze defiantly and did not move, did not speak, lest her fear show. She noted the sword he was fingering, almost lovingly, as if he wanted to unsheathe it to run someone through.

Thwarted in his attempt to discover the fugitive, he gave a cursory bow and turned on his heel, the two troopers following him. Bessie shut the door behind them. Jane felt an iron band tighten suddenly around her head and there was a taste of ashes in her mouth. As she attempted to check her mounting fury, her hands, hidden in her skirts, clenched so hard that her nails bit into the tender palms.

Bessie looked to Jane and read the concern and fear on her face she felt for her father. Not until they heard the soldiers ride away and the bolts slide home did they go to the library. With a pull on a small lever behind a shelf, a partition in the wall of books swung open to expose a reasonable-sized chamber. Secret places such as this were no novelty in a house built in such a period of history and would have been used many times. The Deighton family had always been Catholic and heard Mass, had been prepared to defend the old faith—the true faith—and give shelter and succour to any hunted man who fled and defied Protestantism.

What Jane saw when her father emerged from the gloom was a tall gaunt man whose expression was pained, as if he suffered from his wound or remembered too much. He seemed much older than he had looked when she last saw him a year ago, but his shoulders were still broad if somewhat stooped. There was much grey in his drawn-back hair and the downward lines around his mouth had deepened, but his dark eyes were alert.

Seeing Jane, he folded his arms about her, as if seeking strength.

'Thank God you're here, Jane. Bessie tells me you have been to London.'

'Yes—I will tell you about it shortly. Come and sit near the fire. Soldiers have been to the house, searching for you. Should they come back—and I am sure they will—they will search it. It is known you fled the battle at Sheriffmuir and that you were wounded.'

He raised his head. 'I expected them to come, but not so soon.' As he sat close to the fire, his expression was of frustration and near-despair, defiance against the fates which had turned against him and delivered this unspeakable blow of failure.

Bessie brought food and poured a brandy, forcing it into his hand.

'Does your wound pain you much?' Jane asked, seeing his shirt beneath his leather jerkin was stained with dried blood.

'Not too much just now.'

'I will get you some clean clothes. Why do you do it, Father?' She sat across from him, wondering what was to be done, how she was going to keep him safe. There was an unspoken threat all around them. She must prevail over the uncertain future, must continue to show strength in word, deed and action. 'I am deeply concerned about what is happening.' Impatient to have her say and brave whatever her father told her, she let the words came tumbling out in a rush. She spoke of her fears both for him and the future and what it would all mean to her, more so now Miriam was no longer there to give her support. At first he looked so shocked she thought he had taken ill, but the shock was short lived. After traversing varying degrees of complexity and horror, his expression became grim, his manner telling her with certainty that what she feared was true and that the unthinkable was about to happen and he would be arrested.

'I am sorry, Jane. I know how difficult this is for you.'

Her eyes lit with anger. 'I cannot forget the misfortunes that fell upon our family because of Jacobites and your treasonable activities. The circumstances have blighted my whole life. Just this once be frank with me. I know you are being sought and I am deeply concerned as to the nature and seriousness of it. Considering your past record for insurrection you can hardly blame me. I know that much of what you do is for the good of your faith, but can't you spare a thought for me? Must you persist in embroiling yourself in plotting and scheming? Must you always solve things so dramatically—so violently? Will you never trust to reason?'

Jane could see he would not answer her questions as she wanted him to. He had learned to keep his thoughts to himself over the years. To speak them aloud could lead to disaster, which was why, in this instance, he would keep his own counsel and wait for events to unfold. He had always spoken to her of truth and honesty, and of the respect one could earn if one always abided by this, but at that moment he was unable to stand by the doctrine he preached to others. He shook his head slowly, avoiding her gaze.

'No, Jane. I cannot. I am still fiercely loyal to the cause to which I have dedicated my life.'

'Which we were made to share.' The Jacobite situation was something Jane had been made aware of from an early age and oft were the times when she quietly resented the Pretender across the water because it took her father away from them and he was in constant danger.

His eyes filled with remorse at the suffering his actions had brought to Jane. 'Life has not robbed me of ambition, Jane, but age is beginning to distance me from the young hotheads of this new age. I'm not one for fighting. I realised in battle that I was no longer up to it. I came to gather support for the cause. But I fear it is too late now.'

'That is as I thought,' she said quietly. 'Then it is damning indeed, Father.'

'Where is Miriam? Why is she not here?'

Jane sighed, wondering how he would take what she had to tell him.

He was surprised and more than a little shocked to learn of Miriam's elopement with Andrew Randolph, but he accepted it calmly. When she told him what Lady Randolph had told her concerning the tragic accident that had killed her husband and that she had claimed responsibility, for a long time he was silent. After a while he nodded slightly.

'It was my doing, Jane—the whole thing. Yes, she was driving the carriage that night. I didn't want her to take the blame, but I can see why she told you. She has punished herself for long enough. The one thing she desired above all else was for her sons to be content in their lives. She couldn't bear what their father's sudden death would do to them.'

'And what of me—and Miriam?' she retorted bitterly. 'Did it not concern you how it would affect us?'

'Of course it did. I tortured myself over it. But you were very young, Jane. How could I tell a child something of such magnitude? You had your Aunt Emily and Bessie. I knew you would be taken care of.'

'Yes—they did that, but nothing could eradicate the stain on this house because of your actions that night.'

* * *

Jane, her nerves on edge, had been too afraid to sleep. She had lain, stupefied and numb, with a sensation of pain and fear, of helplessness. Was there no one she could turn to? She knew then the loneliness, the feeling of being cut off from the world.

It was in the silence of the dark hours when Jane strained her ears to listen, wondering what had disturbed her. Hearing the sound of iron-shod hooves striking the cobbles, the sound heralding the approach of visitors, immediately she was wide awake and out of bed. Pulling back the heavy curtains, she peered anxiously out of the window, seeing the dark shapes of two riders. Fear of the unknown seized her and, grabbing her robe, she wrapped it round her, dashing out of the room and down the stairs. The silence of the house was shattered by urgent banging on the door. Expecting the return of soldiers, she was relieved to see it was Francis followed by Mr Berkley, both wearing wide-brimmed hats and shrouded in dark cloaks.

Chapter Nine

Striding into the hall, Francis looked at Jane. Those hard blue eyes took in every detail with slow deliberation. As a loyal supporter of King George, he had convinced himself that distancing himself from Jane at this time would leave him free to be of help should she need it without attracting suspicion to himself. As he studied her, the unguarded misery on her face tugged at his heart. He noted that her eyes were tense, which told him she was under great strain.

If she was surprised to see him there, she didn't show it. He expected defiance, hauteur, but there was neither. He met a pair of velvety green eyes filled with sadness and raw vulnerability. Her potent stare struck him like a punch in the gut. She moved towards him, her eyes broodingly sad.

'I'm surprised to see you, Francis. You must forgive my state of undress, but it's a strange time for you to come calling.'

'I was worried about you.'

'Really? There was no need.'

'What did you expect? The whole of Northumberland is in turmoil following the battle at Sherrifmuir, with government soldiers searching out fugitives in many Catholic houses. If your father fled the battle, then it is certain they will come here.'

'They have already been—shortly after you left. I'm surprised you didn't see them.'

'No, I didn't. Do you know what has happened to your father?'

She nodded. 'He is here.'

'Then thank the Lord I came.'

'You didn't have to.'

'Do you imagine I could stand by and see you taken? Do I let you hang yourself in your efforts to protect your father?'

'My decisions have been made, Francis. What you must know is that I must do all I can to save my father's life, even if it means bringing down the wrath of the Crown on my own head.'

'You know the penalty of aiding and abetting rebels.'

'I do, but as a decent Christian and daughter I must care for his life. I will shelter and assist him.'

'Then I am here to be of help. It's an appalling state of affairs. How are you coping?'

'As well as I can. What else can I do? You will not betray him, will you, Francis?'

'Of course not and it pains me that you should think I would.'

Sighing with great weariness, Jane bent her head,

putting the back of her hand to her eyes for a moment. 'It's all such a dreadful mess.' She tried hard not to let her worry for her father show and she had succeeded to a certain extent, but she was storing up a terrible burden of emotion.

Francis's eyes were suddenly warm with concern. She looked tired and worn out and, behind her calm exterior, he sensed she endured a nauseating turmoil of distress. Romantic illusions aside, she should never have had such responsibilities foisted on her at such a tender age. It was not the work for gently bred young ladies of character and he hated to contemplate what she had seen and done in the process. He stood and looked at her, his face carefully blank, while all the time he wanted to reach out and take her in his arms, to kiss and soothe her and tell her he was going to make everything all right, and yet, remembering the deep division that stood between them, how could he?

'Take me to your father now, Jane.' When she didn't reply he cursed softly. 'Tell me. You have to trust me.' His voice was low, urgent and compelling. 'He can't remain here. We have to move him.'

'But—what can I do?' she cried frantically. 'Where can he go where it will be safe?'

'Redmires. I will take him to Redmires.'

She stared at him with astonishment. 'Redmires? What are you saying? To do that you would be implicating yourself.'

'I am not a Jacobite, Jane. No one will expect to find fugitives hiding in my house.'

'But—the servants. They talk.'

'I'll call on Berkley's assistance. We'll take him to the tower. It's been neglected for long enough and is in dire need of attention, but he should be safe enough there. Let me see him.'

Edward Deighton was sitting by the hearth in the library, close to the hiding place. Should the soldiers return he would have time to slip inside. His head was lowered. It came up when Francis entered, his body tense, alert. On seeing Francis, he got to his feet, clutching his injured side and clenching his teeth when a wrenching pain shot through him.

Francis calmly studied him in silence. The firelight threw a yellow flicker upwards, carving the older man's face from the shadows behind. Francis had to admit that he was an impressive-looking figure—tall with a good breadth about the shoulders—and he'd have a fair reach with a sword.

'I'm Francis Randolph. You remember me?'

'I do—though I have not seen you for many years.'

'I have come to take you somewhere safe. While ever you are here Jane is in danger. Did you not think of remaining north of the border with Mar?'

'I could have, but I didn't reckon anything to my survival. It was not the time for heroics. I was wounded and of no further use in battle.' He looked to where Jane stood beside Francis. 'I have few virtues, Jane, and my faults are many. I beg your forgiveness for the hurt I have caused you, but no dispute or failure will turn me from my loyalty to James Stuart. I intend to leave at the earliest opportunity and no one will be any the wiser.'

Francis nodded slightly. He could see regret in Deighton's eyes quite clearly. The man was genuinely worried that he had endangered his daughter's life by coming here.

'Does your injury pain you?'

He nodded. 'It could have been worse. It will soon heal, thanks to Bessie's ministering.' He smiled weakly. 'She always was good at making things better.'

'At this present time anyone who fled the battlefield at Sheriffmuir is being hunted. There are soldiers and informers all over Northumberland. It isn't safe for you to remain here. You will be better in hiding for the present—but not here. The soldiers will be back and next time they will search the house.'

'When should I leave?'

'On the instant.' He saw doubt cloud Edward Deighton's eyes. 'Trust me. You must let me judge for you. It is best for you to go—and for Jane. While ever you remain here you are placing her in danger.'

'I could try to make it to Newcastle and take ship for the Low Countries.'

'If you care to hide in ditches and trust your luck in Newcastle, where hostility to Jacobites is rife, then by all means go, but I swear you will fare worse upon the open road than you are likely to do if you consent to my help.'

'And where do you suggest I should go?'

'There is somewhere where they will not think of searching.'

'Where?'

'The tower at Redmires.' Seeing Deighton's surprise, he went on. 'I am a highly trusted member of the community—and it is not forgotten that my father despised all Catholics. They will not suspect me of hiding a fugitive.'

'May I ask why you are willing to place yourself in danger?'

Francis smiled grimly. 'Since my brother married your daughter, we are family and families protect each other—regardless of their religion.'

'Have you news of what happened at Preston?'

'The Jacobites surrendered. A large number of prisoners are being taken to London.'

Edward's face didn't change for a moment, then the words fell into place. 'May God show them mercy,' he said softly, deeply affected by this news, 'for the King will not. What a mockery it all seems now. We came to England with our hopes high, convinced that God was on our side—only to be met with failure.'

'The struggle between the Earl of Mar and the Duke of Argyll's forces goes on over the border in Scotland.'

'And James Stuart?'

'As far as I am aware he has not yet set foot in Scotland.'

Edward sighed, shaking his head wearily. 'I fought for King James and my own ideals at Sheriffmuir. No matter what happens now, I do not regret having done so, and while I am free and there is breath in my body I shall continue to fight until he sits on the throne of England.'

Francis was struck by the man's fervour. His strength of purpose was evident in the set of his unshaven face and he could see in his eyes how proud he was to have stood firm by his convictions, to have fought for what he believed was right. Nothing could divert him from his cause. Francis was almost overwhelmed by an unexpected feeling of admiration, which replaced some of the resentment he had long harboured for him, and with the admiration came guilt and something else he could not ignore, for the loyalty, determination and courage of Edward Deighton made him feel ashamed.

Francis looked across at Jane. 'We'll leave together. Berkley will remain with you. The house may be being watched. Two men were seen entering. Two men will be seen leaving. Berkley will make his way back to Redmires later.'

'Thank you, Francis. I appreciate what you are doing for me.'

A slight hesitation in Francis's step showed the words had been heard. He turned and glanced back. 'I've just returned from London after spending time with my mother. She told me what happened when my father was killed. She also told me she had been driving the carriage that night. So if I am helping you now, call it the tribute of a repentant conscience.'

They left the library and went into the hall, where Berkley was waiting. Francis turned to Edward Deighton. 'I will leave you to have a word with

Berkley. Don his cloak and hat, which you will pull well down over your face. I would like to speak with Jane before we leave.'

Taking Jane's arm, he led her to the door, stepping outside and drawing her into the shadows. He wasn't as insensitive and heartless as not to realise how she must be feeling on parting from her father so soon, nor was he oblivious to her hidden fears. The events since he had left her had clearly affected her deeply. 'I know how worried you must be, Jane, but I assure you he will be well taken care of.'

'Yes—I am sure you're right, but I can't help it.'

'Of course you can't. That is understandable, but it's as well he's not here should the soldiers return.' Placing his finger beneath her chin, he tipped her face to his. 'I doubt they will harm you, Jane. They would have to find your father first and they won't do that. Be brave.' He touched her cheek and she covered his hand with hers. Just to touch her caused heat to seep through his clothes, desire already tightening his loins—and *that* with just a touch of her hand. He didn't understand why she had such a volatile effect on him, but he understood that he wanted her. He wanted her in every way it was possible for a man to want a woman—by his side, in his bed, warm and willing in his arms.

'I hate to leave you to face this alone. The neighbourhood is likely to be crawling with soldiers and I expect Beckwith Manor will be seized eventually. But promise me that if you are in trouble, you will come to me—or find some way to send me word. I would come at once.'

'Thank you, yes. If my father is safe somewhere, then nothing else can matter—although the last thing I want to do is place you in danger.'

'Don't worry about me. I'm more than a match for the local militia.' Lowering his head, he placed his lips on hers. The kiss was brief, but Francis hoped he had reassured her.

Jane felt helpless and sick with anxiety as she watched her father ride away with Francis. They were shrouded in long black cloaks, their hats pulled down to conceal their faces. Even though Francis had assured her that her father would be safe in the tower, she had fear in her heart that he would be found.

Mr Berkley came to stand beside her. 'Your father will be quite safe. Try not to worry.'

'Will he, Mr Berkley? Can you be sure of that?'

'Aye—as sure as I can be.'

Two hours after Francis had left Beckwith Manor, Mr Berkley borrowed a horse and returned to Redmires.

With the soldiers searching houses for hidden fugitives and others involved in the rising, an atmosphere of crisis prevailed. True to their word, the soldiers returned to Beckwith Manor to search the house. Such was Jane's anxiety and strain while she waited that it was almost a relief when she heard the soldiers galloping into the yard. Without waiting to be admitted, they strode into the hall.

'Your father has not been found,' Captain Walton bellowed out. 'I have the authority to search Beckwith Manor from top to bottom. I trust you will be sensible and raise no objections.'

'It would do me no good if I did. Feel free to search where you like—the house and stables and the grounds—anywhere you wish. I do not have the power to stop you. You will not find him. He is hardly likely to come to a house he knows you will search.'

'Rest assured, if he is here we will find him.' He turned to the men who had followed him inside. 'Carry on,' he said, 'and leave no board unturned.'

Jane watched them disperse to different rooms in the house, their muddy boots trampling the floors. It seemed to her that she stopped breathing as she listened to the relentless tramping of enemy feet. Her stomach knotted with fear, although she didn't know why it should. They wouldn't find her father or any other Jacobites in hiding. She thanked God that Francis had taken her father to safety. She stood and listened. Beckwith Manor had never before resounded to so many strident voices and boots hammering on the floor.

Childish laughter and chatter had infiltrated the fabric of the ancient walls when she and Miriam had been young, but this? This sounded like an alien invasion as hangings and paintings were stripped from the walls and she heard the splintering of wood as panelling was ripped away. Cupboards and presses were flung open, the contents spilling out on to the floor. Books were swept from the shelves in the library and furniture turned over as they tore the house apart in wanton destruction. They searched from the cellars upwards, and when this was done they went to the stables and searched there. It seemed to go on and on.

When the search was over and had proved futile, they returned to the hall. An angry frown creased the captain's brow. He was clearly disappointed that Edward Deighton continued to elude him. He looked at her with a hard, intent gaze.

'Well,' said Jane, 'are you satisfied now?'

'No. We found a hiding place in the library. There is evidence of it being occupied recently. Who was it, Miss Deighton? Your father and, if so, where is he now?'

Jane paled and said nothing. Why had she not thought to remove the evidence of her father's presence?

'Is he still here—in this house? How many other hiding places are there where a man can hide? Think, Miss Deighton. Think what this will mean for you. Admit it. He was here. Where is he?' Captain Walton persisted angrily.

Jane raised her head and looked at him with contempt. There was a streak of cruelty in him as ingrained as his pride. 'I have told you. He is not here.'

'I trust you will consider your actions before you grant succour to any rebels who might find their way to Beckwith Manor. The consequences are dire for anyone found harbouring traitors.'

His face darkened as his eyes passed from Jane to Bessie, who had come into the hall and taken a seat beside the hearth, where they lingered before returned to Jane. 'Edward Deighton will be found. We *will* find him.'

Jane met his gaze defiantly and did not move, did not speak until she had composed her thoughts, lest she let her fear show. 'I sincerely hope not.'

Captain Walton looked at her hard before sliding his gaze around the hall. 'We shall see. This is a large house. I am not persuaded that he is not here.' A deadly smile twisted his features and his voice became dangerously soft. 'Should he continue to elude us, then I will be tempted to return to smoke him out.'

On that note he turned on his heel and strode to the door, his entourage of soldiers following. The house was quiet once more. Bessie came to stand beside her.

'Thank goodness they've gone. I hope they don't come back—but it's going to be hard work putting the house back to rights.'

Jane let out a huge sigh of relief. 'Yes, Bessie, they've gone. As for the house—that is the least of my worries just now. If, as I have been told, my father's property and estate are to be forfeit—or if the soldiers return and burn it to the ground—then it won't matter how much damage has been done.'

After several days and no news from Redmires, Jane was unable to stand not knowing what was happening, saddled up her horse and started on her journey, shutting Spike in the barn so he did not follow her. She knew the location of the guard that Captain Walton had left to watch the house, so she travelled by a different route, keeping away from the main thoroughfare.

The hour was late and dusk had fallen. After some time without seeing a soul, an odd, disconnected shape appeared like a ghostly apparition out of the dark. It was the ancient tower-like structure attached to Redmires, just one of many which dotted the Northumberland landscape. This particular tower house had been built by Francis's ancestors. It was a strong structure, almost derelict, but Francis had assured her that it would provide her father with much-needed refuge until the dangers of arrest had passed.

On reaching the house, she was met by Mr Berkley, who swiftly went to inform Francis of her arrival. He appeared immediately, drawing her away from the curious eyes of the servants into his study, where he closed the door and took her hands in his.

'You have taken me by surprise, Jane. The hour is late. I did not expect you to come here.

'Forgive me, Francis, but I had to. Not having heard anything from you, I had to satisfy my need to know how my father fares.'

'Your father? And here I was thinking you have come to see me.'

Glancing at him now, she saw the trace of an amused smile curve his lips and there was a hunger there that had nothing to do with her father. It triggered a quickness in her heartbeat, one she strived hard to hide. Having discovered a sensuality within herself that she had been ignorant of before Francis had awakened it, Jane found it difficult to keep her thoughts well aligned to that which a virtuous young woman might ponder. Her sudden propensity for wayward thoughts became even more apparent when she was with him. His very presence evoked an unfamiliar tumult within her, making her fearful of what he might discern if he looked into her flushed face.

'You are well able to take care of yourself, Francis. At this present time my father is not—so please exercise some degree of control.'

Unmoved by her gentle chiding, he laughed softly. 'Whenever I find myself in your presence, Jane, I find I have to strive to do that. I apologise for not contacting you, but I was afraid we were being watched. Your father is comfortable and safe—which is what matters. How are things at Beckwith Manor?'

'Not good. The soldiers returned and searched the house—it has been ransacked, with floorboards ripped up and panels ripped from the walls. It will take some putting right.'

Francis gripped her shoulders in alarm. 'The devil they did! Did they harm you, Jane?'

She shook her head. 'No, but Captain Walton—a truly nasty individual—has threatened to return and burn the house if he is not found. I hope you do not come under suspicion, Francis.'

'I doubt they will come here to search the house, but we must see about getting your father away.'

'They have left a guard to watch the house. Fortunately I know where he is positioned and managed to leave without him seeing me. Can I see my father? Will you take me to him?'

'Yes, of course. Come with me.'

They left the house and made their way to the tower. The basement had been used for stock and the entrance to the upper storeys was on the first storey up a flight of stone steps, desperately in need of repair. Jane followed Francis, waiting as he rapped four times on the door. In no time at all a bar could be heard sliding back and the heavy timbered door swung open.

Francis drew her inside and closed the door, sliding back the bar. 'I apologise for the sorry state of the place. It's dismal, I know, but it should serve its purpose. I doubt anyone will think of looking here— more so since it belongs to the Randolphs. As you see we have tried to make it as comfortable as possible,' he said, indicating a pallet with a straw mattress. 'Berkley takes care of him'

'He does,' Edward said. 'He is very attentive— dressing my wound and bringing food and drink and seeing to my comforts. He also spends time with me—and he plays a mean game of chess.' He indicated an overturned box which acted as a table, on which remnants of food littered the surface and a chess set. 'He has also provided me with books to read—so you see, Jane, I have no time for boredom to set in. Thankfully it is warm enough and I have plenty of blankets so there's no need of a fire—the smoke could attract attention.'

'And the servants?' she asked, turning to Francis. 'They don't suspect anything?'

'No. We are careful, but if they did suspect, they value their positions too much to say anything.'

With the light from a single candle, Jane's eyes did a broad sweep of their surroundings, able to make out tattered shreds of hangings on the walls encrusted with years of mould. A couple of small windows were set high in the walls and mildewed rushes were strewn on the floor. Despite what her father had told her to reassure her, she imagined the hours dragged by with tedium.

Jane sat with him for a while. When Mr Berkley came bearing her father's supper, she left him then and returned to the house with Francis. She would have ridden back to Beckwith Manor, but he insisted she stay a while. There was a matter he wanted to discuss with her. The house was quiet, the servants occupied elsewhere. In the study where a fire glowed warmly in the hearth, Francis poured them both a Madeira and they sat across from each other before the fire.

'What is it you want to speak to me about, Francis?'

'I think it is time we reached a clear understanding about what is happening between us.'

As if his need had communicated itself to Jane and

wondering if she had misread what he was saying, she shook her head in confusion. 'I—I'm sorry, Francis, but—I don't understand… We—we are friends…'

His eyes searched hers and almost hesitantly he enquired, 'We are more than that, surely.'

She looked at him, holding her breath. His face was expressionless, except for his eyes searching hers. She felt those eyes, felt them as a physical force, probing deep within her. Gathering together all her strength, she thrust away her fears concerning her father and her anguish and all thoughts of what was happening in Northumberland. 'I give you leave to think anything that you might,' she murmured softly. 'But, yes, we are more than that.'

Francis swirled the amber liquid in his glass, raising it to his lips and drinking deep before placing the empty glass in the hearth. 'I am deeply concerned about you, Jane—more than you realise and more so since Beckwith Manor was searched.'

'Captain Walton has made it clear that I will be arrested for giving succour to my father if he is found at Beckwith Manor. I cannot deny that I am worried. I don't think he believed me when I told him I wasn't hiding my father—I do fear someone will torch the house, or some other disaster will befall me.' She was unable to mask the fear which must show clearly on her face. Everything could be taken away from her in a single stroke and she could hardly bring herself to imagine the devastation it would cause.

'Then you are right to be afraid.'

'Anyone would think my father is the only fugitive

being sought—when nearly the whole of Northumberland came forward to support the rising. Where are they now?'

'In hiding, I expect, or over the border with Mar. Beckwith Manor is not the only house to have been sacked. Walton has acquired a certain reputation in the area. To further his career he intends to round up as many fugitives as he can. He has blackened the character of those who took up arms, prejudicing any potential sympathiser by making sure their traitorous activities both now and in the past are spread in every scandalous detail.'

'And are people listening?'

'Those who hold the Catholics in disfavour and are angry that the Jacobites tried to take control are.'

'And what do you think, Francis? Are you prejudiced towards Catholics?'

'As a logical man, I am a great believer in individual liberty. I respect the rights of others to have faith in whatever they choose, as long as they do no harm to others.'

With a sigh Jane shook her head. Now more than ever she began to feel the strictures of her situation. 'I wish others were of the same opinion. None of what the soldiers are doing surprises me. I have lived long enough to have a fairly cynical view of human nature and to know how directly public opinion expresses itself. My father was not alone in what has happened—there are Catholics all over Northumberland who took part in the rising. My own fate does not bear thinking about if my father is caught. I know the consequences—but I'd prefer not to have to dwell on that aspect of the matter.'

'No,' Francis agreed, 'neither do I. Whatever happens, Jane, be assured that I will do what I can. My influence is strong in Newcastle and beyond.'

'Thank you, Francis. That means a great deal to me. There are many Catholic sympathisers who are too afraid to appear to openly befriend Father. I have to consider what to do now. If I can get him away, I will go with him to France.'

A flash of annoyance crossed Francis's features. 'What is this foolishness? Why are you so hell-bent on going with him?'

Jane's jaw set mutinously and Francis could see the light of battle in her eyes when they met his in wilful defiance. 'It is not foolishness. Where else can I go? Do not forget that my home will no longer be accessible to me. Besides, I cannot bear to think of the bleakness of a future without both my sister and my father. His wound has weakened him. He might have need of me.'

With blazing eyes Francis leaned forward slightly, fully vexed. She had a propensity to spar with him and render him exasperated to the point of madness by remarks that could pierce his armour like the sharpest blade. 'With him holed up at Redmires it's out of the question at present, so like it or not you will have to face it out. You are welcome to come and stay at Redmires with me and brave the curious—to put up with my hospitality. But let there be no mistake, Jane. Because of everything that transpired in

London and the way I have come to feel about you, I now feel a certain obligation to your father to make sure you are safe—and I intend to do exactly that.'

Jane's green eyes flashed with fiery sparks as she got to her feet. 'I believe you. But that does not give you the right to appoint yourself as my protector—or perhaps I should say my keeper,' she flared with heavy sarcasm.

Francis's eyes hardened. 'Whatever title you attach to me, Jane, you will remain with me until I consider the time is right to move your father. If going with him is what you want, then I will not stand in your way. It is your God-given right.'

'If he has to go—either by choice or because he cannot remain in England—I shall have to alternative but to go with him.'

Francis regarded her with serious intent. He felt a hollow sensation in the pit of his stomach. 'Jane, listen to me. There is no reason why you have to go. He has taken care of himself for years now, he is not so badly wounded that he cannot continue to do so.'

Jane stared at him. She wanted to shout he was one of the reasons why she had to go. She loved Francis with all the beauty and blinding passion in her young heart. She wanted nothing more than to let desire have its way and surrender herself to the silent demand in his eyes, to forget the vow she had made to herself not to become entrapped by him. But if she intended going to France to look after her father, then she must not weaken.

'My mind is made up.'

As she was about to draw away, unexpectedly Francis stood up and took her hand, placing it against his chest. 'I have time to change your mind.'

'No, Francis.'

'I know I don't have the right, but what if I said that I cannot live without you?'

His words pierced Jane's heart. The gravity on his face alarmed her. 'I would know that would not be true,' she answered quietly.

Placing his hands on her shoulders, Francis drew her close. 'And what if I said I did not want you to go for no other reason than I want you to stay with me? That I want you to stay for purely selfish reasons? That I cannot bear the thought of never seeing you again.'

Jane was unable to believe he was saying these things to her. 'I would still go,' she whispered, her lips trembling, unable to resist his eyes as they probed the depths of her being and her heart streamed into his. She stepped aside to pass him by, but he moved quickly to stand behind her, his firm hands coming to rest on her waist as he turned her back to him.

Unable to restrain himself a moment longer, he put his arms around her and drew her against his hard chest. Jane's breath dragged in her throat and the scent of him, of leather and the outdoors, filled her senses. Before she knew what was happening, his lips took possession of hers with such accomplished persuasion that she felt a stir of pleasure sigh through her as her body responded to his kiss. Unresisting, she closed her eyes, aware of nothing in the world but the hard rack of Francis's chest as she was crushed against it, feeling the tense muscles under his leather jerkin as his arms locked about her. His lips tantalised and teased, deliberately touching, caressing, as light as thistledown, stirring her passion.

By slow degrees his mouth parted more to pluck the sweetness from her own, sipping, savouring and sampling until Jane felt intoxicated, roused by an answering response so that his tongue became a fluttering firebrand as his mouth consumed hers with a hunger that would not be appeased. With a strangled gasp she pulled back, dragging her lips from his and turning her head aside, but he forced it back with his hand, his arm curled about her waist, refusing to let her go.'

'No, Francis. Please don't do this,' she entreated, unaware of the heat of her body reaching out to him and that the regret in her lovely eyes was sincere. 'Let me go.'

'Nay, not yet,' he murmured. 'I have waited too long for this moment.'

'I think I remember a time at the beginning of our acquaintance when I told you not to try to seduce me.'

'And I remember telling you that you might be persuaded—and you were—in York. Don't resist me now, Jane,' he breathed, his gaze fastening on her lips. 'What's the matter? Are you afraid that the feelings and emotions you experienced that night might be resurrected?' he asked quietly, the softness of his voice weaving a strange spell around her.

Staring at him in dazed confusion, Jane watched

his finely moulded lips hovering just above hers. He stood before her, tall and powerful, his face austere. 'Yes,' she murmured, 'yes, I am.'

She half turned from him, a gnawing disquiet descending on her. She was disturbed by his presence. She did not know how much longer she could tolerate being near him. The memory of that night would be with her always. She remembered how he had looked when she was about to leave him after they had made love, how her eyes had covertly caressed his manly form, and it shocked her unduly when she had found herself closely eyeing the sheets that had settled softly over his loins. The torpid fullness led her mind swiftly astray to visions of his long, nude body glistening with droplets of sweat after he had made love to her.

The kindling warmth that swept through her in ever-strengthening surges affected her until she became ambiguous about her own reserve. Whenever she was with him, his presence was a constant reminder of what she had done, what they had done together, when she had failed to hold her passions in check, carelessly forgetting the future.

Prey to a desire stronger than reason, Francis fixed her with burning eyes. 'Since, in your desperation, you are considering putting yourself at risk by leaving England, I'd like to offer a solution to the problem. There is a way you can remain here, where you can live out the rest of your life in safety.'

Jane tilted her head to one side, her dark eyes suspicious. He was watching her intently. She met his gaze, which was warmer now. 'How can I do that?'

'Forget your father for the moment. I am not usually a man of hasty decision when it concerns a lasting relationship, but I am asking you to marry me. Let me bring you to Redmires as my wife.'

Jane stared rigidly at him in disbelief, momentarily lost for words. He looked so cool, so dispassionate, and completely self-assured. She wondered what had prompted him to offer such a drastic solution to her problem and was not feeling particularly complimented by his offer.

'Your wife!' she replied, surprised. 'But—I told you in York that you must not feel under any obligation to me. I gave myself to you freely. I didn't expect anything from you then and I don't now.'

'Think about it before you make any hasty decisions about going to France. For you, marriage to me would be advantageous indeed.'

'It would? How?'

'Your home in all probability will be taken from you. Your life may be in danger. You need protection and somewhere to live that is safe. I can defend you. Under my protection there isn't a man in Northumberland who would dare threaten you.'

Jane stared at him, rendered silent. At length she said tightly, 'Thank you for your concern, but I'd rather not inconvenience you further. I can live without your protection. And you? How will marriage to me benefit you? What will you get out of it? I have nothing to give.' Jane was so humiliated by his reference to her plight that it took a moment for what he said next to register.

'You, Jane. I get you.' Taking her face between his hands, he looked deep into her glorious eyes. His expression held no laughter when he searched the hidden depths with his own and when he spoke his voice was husky. 'Little fool. My attraction to you is both powerful and undeniable. I have wanted you from the moment I met you—despite doing my damnedest to deny it.'

Jane was unable to believe he was saying these things to her. Francis wasn't just any man. To her he had become something very special and he did things to her emotions and her body she did not understand. Her confusion came from the haunting sense of pleasure that he gave her, the fact that every time his visage appeared in her mind's eye her heart beat with a sweet wildness that stirred her very soul. What spell had he cast upon her that she should desire him so? That made her want to cling to him, for him to give her that which she yearned?

She had never felt so fully a woman as when she was with him and she was amazed that no shame or guilt rose to condemn her for the kisses they had shared. Could she bear it if he were to disappear from her life completely? Could she really delude herself into believing that she could turn her back on him and walk away?

'I apologise if the manner of my proposal seemed cold and callous, Jane, but you are a difficult woman to win over. I would be deeply saddened to see you leave, separated by a chasm of misunderstandings and anger. Does the thought of being my wife bring you such misery?'

Jane was shocked by his unexpected gentleness and completely at a loss as to how to answer. She wanted nothing more than to throw herself into his arms, to declare her love and be done with all the shilly-shallying between them, for him to take away the fear of poverty and insecurity, but she had already made up her mind to go to France. 'No, the idea doesn't make me miserable. Not at all.'

'Then I think we should discuss why you reacted to my proposal so angrily. Perhaps then we will be able to resolve the issue.'

'We will?'

'I want to take your pain away, to see you happy— the way you were in London. Do you really believe that you are so undesirable that I would take you for my wife simply to protect you? You know very little about me if you think mere words can quench what I feel for you.'

'I don't know what to think. I want you to want me for who I am.'

'Will it change how you feel if I tell you that it is not mere lust that torments me, but a desire to have you with me every moment, to feel your softness close to me and to claim you as my own.'

Jane stared at him in speechless wonder. His words were effective in bringing to mind a similar awareness of her own desires. But she must try to put them from her mind. 'Francis,' she said, resignation and determination in her eyes. 'I have made my decision. When my father leaves I will go with him. I have to go. I have a duty to care for him.'

He gave a bitter laugh. 'Yes, of course. It is your duty.'

Jane sensed the bitterness in his tone. Abruptly she took his hands in her own. 'Francis, why do you say it like that? You know very well how things stand and that I must go with him. I have no choice in the matter.' She didn't want to think of that day when she would be parted from him. She stood still, feeling her heart break, her vision blurring.

Francis smiled then and looked down at her with great tenderness. Drawing his hands from her grasp, he cupped her face. 'I intend to do my utmost to arrange for his departure. He won't be moved from the tower until it is safe for him to do so. I will have the time between now and then to see you, Jane—to try to get you to change your mind. There is one thing I want you to promise me.'

'Oh?'

'It must be faced. There is a chance that you may find yourself with child. If that proves to be the case, I want you to promise me that you will remain here and be my wife.'

For a moment she was unable to speak for the tears blocking her throat. She swallowed them down, knowing she had to be strong. 'With so much happening, I—I had not thought that I might be with child—but—but, yes, Francis. If I am with child I will marry you—but first I will go with my father and return to you when he is settled and I have made sure he is taken care of. Would you agree to that?'

'No—but if that is how it has to be, then I will have to let you go.'

'Thank you. And now I should be getting back. Bessie tends to worry when I'm away for long periods.'

'Jane, I want you to stay here where I know you will be safe. It would be for the best.'

She knew he was saying it to convince himself as much as her. 'I know. But I will not abandon my home. I will not let anyone drive me out.'

'Then I'll ride back with you. It's not safe for you to be riding alone after dark.'

They rode to Beckwith Manor without incident, seeing no sign of the guard. Francis didn't turn back until he had seen her disappear inside the house.

Closing the door on the outside world, Jane crossed the hall and perched on the edge of the chair by the hearth, staring into the dying embers of the fire. She quietly reviewed the past weeks she had come to know Francis, dissecting each moment they had shared with meticulous deliberation in an attempt to put some semblance of order to her emotions. It was no use hiding from the fact that they had been drawn to each other from the beginning.

Francis had the ability to delve into her nature and, she thought on a warm tide of feelings, he could also tease and delight her senses in a way she had never experienced before. He had created yearnings inside her that only he could satisfy. He had made it plain that he wanted her as a man wants a woman. But she had crushed the yearnings felt by them both, and now, in this weakening of her will, her longings would not be still and she wanted to discover the mystery of this man who had succeeded in bringing her to a state of submission. How could she even think of breaking away from him and leaving him for ever?

Chapter Ten

It was an hour before midnight when Sam came out of the stables. For some reason the horses were uneasy and he'd gone to make sure there was nothing to worry about.

As he always did before going to bed above the stables, he took a last walk round the house to check no windows had been left open to tempt anyone who took it in mind to burgle the place.

He was crossing the cobbled yard when he thought he saw a movement at one of the ground-floor windows. Thinking it must be either Miss Jane or Bessie, he continued on his walk.

After completing a circuit of the house and seeing nothing amiss, he returned to his rooms above the stables, oblivious to the shadowy figure standing motionless at a window inside the house, watching him.

The fire started a short time later.

Jane woke to a strange feeling of dread. She sat up, smelling smoke. Getting out of bed, she flung her robe about her shoulders and ran to the door, seeing smoke drifting underneath. With panic rising inside her, going on to the landing she shouted Bessie's name, relieved there was no one else in the house to think about. She could hear the roar of the flames and, glancing out of the window, saw clouds of sparks and bits of burning matter blowing past, borne on the wind. Flames could be seen coming from the lower rooms and the stairs would soon catch hold. She knew they were in danger of being trapped if they didn't get out immediately.

Bessie, her greying hair escaping her nightcap and thrusting her arms into her robe, came hurrying towards her in alarm. 'We must get out at once,' she gasped, grasping Jane's hand and pulling her towards the stairs. 'There isn't time to get dressed. Hurry. It will spread quickly if the wind doesn't ease off.'

Covering their mouths as best they could, together they just managed to make it down the stairs before flames began licking at the dry timbers. Already the rooms were an inferno, the fire quickly consuming the wooden floors and beams. At one point Bessie stumbled and almost fell, but Jane, her vision blurred, had hold of her and forced her towards the door at the same moment that Sam burst in.

'Sam,' Jane cried. 'We're all right. We must get out at once. What are you doing?' she asked when he made a move to the stairs. 'You can't go up there.'

His voice was urgent. 'There's someone up there. I've got to see who it is—to get them out before it's too late.'

'There isn't anyone up there, Sam. We're the only ones in the house.'

'No,' he shouted above the noise of the fire. 'I saw someone in the house earlier, but thought it was you or Bessie so I thought no more of it. When I came out and saw the fire I looked at the upstairs windows and I saw someone—a man—I'm sure he was in uniform.'

Jane immediately turned and looked up the stairs. The fire had taken hold of the dry timbers and were blazing fiercely, consuming everything it its path. 'But you can't go up there. You'll never get back down,' she said, coughing into her hand and wiping her streaming eyes. 'The stairs are likely to go at any minute.' As if to prove her point, the stairs began to collapse. She backed to the door, grasping Sam's arm and taking him with her. At the same moment she looked up. Her heart almost stopped when she saw a hulking form. Wiping her stinging eyes, she focused on the figure, taking note of the uniform he wore.

Without stopping to wonder what he was doing in the house, she called, 'Captain Walton. You have to get out.'

She could see his face was red with rage and the heat from the fire and that his eyes held an irrational light. The orange flames were spreading quickly and black smoke was curling along the walls. He made a move as if to try to make it down what remained of the stairs, just as a beam burned in half and fell, striking him on the head and setting his clothes alight. He fell forwards, tumbling headlong down to the hall, where he lay sprawled in a grotesque fashion. Coughing and gasping for breath, Sam ran towards him, grasping his leg and dragging him to the door and out into the yard. Unable to stand the intense heat any longer and in danger of being roasted alive, Jane dashed after him, gulping in the cool night air.

Jane and Bessie looked at the fire, feeling its heat and moving further back towards the stables. Great tongues of fire were licking out of the shattered windows. The fire was out of control and soon the whole house was alight. The noise was ferocious, like an animal in torment, the flames reaching high into the sky. Drawn by the fire, people were beginning to appear from neighbouring farms and hamlets. Even though there was nothing they could do, they stayed to watch as it burned. With mixed emotions the three of them stood in silence and watched the inferno. The roof seemed to heave upwards before imploding, as if it were some living creature caught up in howling agony. It was a fearful sight, with the flames reaching up into the sky with a howl like the wind. Unhampered now, the flames shot higher and roared in greedy delight.

Returning from the tower after playing a long game of chess with Edward Deighton, it was Berkley that woke Francis, having seen the flames coming from the direction of Beckwith Manor in the night sky. Francis came awake with a start, alert and all his senses focused. With an urgency he dressed quickly and joined Berkley, who had saddled the horses and was waiting outside the house. They were soon galloping in the direction of the fire which was becoming brighter the closer they got. All he could think of was Jane and the full horror of what might have happened to her crushed down on him with appalling gravity. He prayed, with a desperation born of fear, that she was unharmed.

On arriving at Beckwith Manor, the night sky was full of blazing wood and glowing ash. Francis threw himself off his horse, his eyes searching for Jane. And then he saw her. In her night attire, her feet bare, she stood like a beautiful pale frozen statue, her hair all shades of shining gold, staring at the burning ruin that had been her home. Immediately he was striding towards her, having to dodge the airborne burning debris falling all around him. Everyone in the yard gaped at Lord Randolph, but Francis didn't notice the stares. Turning her head, Jane gazed uncertainly towards him, her hand lifting to her heart and a gasp rising in her throat.

Without any thought other than she was safe, he took hold of her and pulled her into his arms, wrapping them around her with stunning force. His hand cradled her tear-streaked face against his chest, shielding her from the curious as he bent his head and whispered hoarsely, 'Thank God you're all right. I thought I'd lost you.' There was overwhelming relief in his voice. Her breathing ragged, she slid her hands around his neck, her face buried against his chest, holding him fiercely to her. She was too overcome with smoke and emotion to speak.

With his arm about her shoulders, Francis led her away. Seeing Bessie standing with Sam, he went to her.

'Are you harmed, Bessie—and you, Sam?'

'No, Lord Randolph. We got out in time,' Bessie replied.

'How in God's name did this happen?'

'We think it was set deliberately.'

'Did you see anyone?'

'I did,' Sam said, 'earlier when I went to check on the house before seeking my bed. There was someone in the house, but I thought it was either Miss Jane or Bessie.'

'Clearly you did see someone. Who? Who was it?'

'We need look no further than Captain Walton,' Jane told him.

'You are sure?'

'Yes.'

Francis's arms tightened about her. He felt the tension running through him snap like a broken wire. He'd been strung up like a puppet since he'd left Redmires. He should have kept a better watch over her. He should have taken it more seriously that the house might be torched and that Jane was not safe.

'He was in the house when we were leaving,' Jane whispered. 'He—he was trapped upstairs. Why he didn't get out after starting the fire I cannot say. He didn't make it, Francis. He—he's over there.'

Francis followed her gaze, seeing Captain Walton's charred body.

'The fire took hold fast in the wind. It's too far gone to do anything. There's nothing anyone can do. Captain Walton threatened something like this. I should have known that he would not meekly go away and leave me alone—not until he found my father.'

Seeing Jane's lovely face, pale with shock, and dark, fear-filled eyes, red and moist with the smoke, Francis felt the anger swell suddenly in his chest, a huge, solid thing, pushing hard enough to burst it. His arm was still around her. He could feel her heart beating against him and a small shudder ran through her. Unconsciously she stepped closer to him, seeming to take comfort from his nearness. He looked towards the fire, his thick hair tousled and flecked with bits of charred debris.

'How did you know to come here?' Jane asked.

'The fire could be seen from Redmires—it fills the night sky for miles around. I knew with a blaze of that magnitude it could only be Beckwith Manor.'

Jane looked past him to the burning house. He had the feeling that she was looking far beyond him, through him, but then the focus of her gaze came back and she looked directly at him. 'There's no saving anything. I have nothing left. I have lost everything. Soon there will be nothing more the fire can consume. I didn't even have time to get dressed.'

'We'll sort all that out tomorrow, Jane.' Realising that she was still shaking from the shock of the fire, Francis felt he had to get her away. 'You are in shock, Jane, and cold.'

'I'm all right—a little shaken, but I am fine,' she answered firmly.

Unconvinced, Francis turned to Sam. 'Could you

prepare the carriage and have her taken to Redmires—
and Bessie. You will both be taken care of. Berkley
will go with you and make sure you are settled in. I'll
stay here and see what can be done. The fire won't
burn itself out tonight—it will likely be smouldering
for days. I'll be along later.

'Where's Spike?' Jane asked, looking frantically
around the yard.

'He's in the stable with the horses. The animals are
all uneasy but unharmed. They'll soon settle down.'

Francis lifted Jane up into the carriage, where she
settled herself beside Bessie.

'All I had was here, in this house,' she said softly,
looking back at the burning building, 'and now it's
gone and I have nothing with which to replace it, only
memories. It will make it easier when the time comes
for me to go to France.'

Without another word the carriage started forward,
Berkley riding along side. Deeply concerned, Fran-
cis watched it leave before turning to have Captain
Walton's body removed.

Hearing the sound of a horse's hooves on the gravel
drive, Jane stirred her exhausted body beneath the
warm covers of the bed at Redmires. Throwing them
back, she went to the window in time to see Francis hand his horse to a groom and disappear into the
house. Slipping her feet into a pair of soft slippers
provided by the maid who had assisted her when she
arrived here, and thrusting her arms into a clean robe,
she left the room and hurried down the stairs.

One of the servants directed her to the study, where Francis stood by the window, watching the sun rise, hazy rays of watery amber light spreading across the garden while clouds of thin mist rolled over the hills and moors beyond.

He stood with his back to her, so she took a moment to look at him. Parts of his hair had been singed and fell wildly about his head. His waistcoat and breeches were ruined, the sleeves of his once white shirt were rolled up, exposing his corded forearms. She hadn't made a sound, but, as if sensing her presence, he turned, opening his arms. Jane ran across the carpet and into them, feeling them close around her. Without speaking she held on to him, her cheek burrowed into his chest. The shock of all that had happened had eaten into the deepest cavities of her being and she wanted to remain in the comforting circle of his arms until the memory had gone away. With eyes alive with the fear she still felt, vivid and awash with tears, she raised them to Francis, the sight of them eliciting a wretched groan as he continued to hold her, lowering his head and burying his face in her newly washed, sweet-scented hair.

Unable to pull away from his all-enveloping arms, Jane huddled against him like a child. She tried to speak, but couldn't find the words because of the scalding tears rolling down her cheeks and filling her throat. The pain was so great she was unable to utter a word. Francis felt her body convulse against him and his arms tightened.

'Cry, my love,' Francis whispered. 'You have been

through a terrible ordeal—no one should see what you saw last night. But you are not alone in this. Many Catholic houses in Northumberland have suffered the same fate—and there will be a lot more before this is done. But you are the last person in the world I would wish to see hurting like this.'

'My love?' she whispered, glorying in his close-ness. 'You called me your love.'

'Yes, my love,' he breathed, looking deep into her eyes. 'There you have it, Jane. I love you, which is why I cannot bear to think of you leaving me.'

'You—you are serious?'

'I would not jest on so serious a matter. Do you love me?'

Jane gazed at him. 'Deeply. Mock if you will, but I do love you, so very much.'

'I will not mock, Jane, my love. My darling girl. I think I have loved you from the moment you in-vaded my house when I was entertaining the cream of Northumberland.'

To be told he loved her, that he had loved her from the first, even when they had been at odds with each other, touched the deepest and most sensitive chord within Jane. Savouring the exquisite happiness, the only thing she was aware of was Francis holding her, his hand gently stroking her hair.

'What is between us is too strong to deny. Can you tell me you don't feel what I feel when I hold you in my arms?'

She tilted her head and looked at him, drowning in his blue-eyed gaze. 'That is exactly how I feel. But

I have to fight it. I am so afraid that I will be unable to leave you when the time comes.'

He sighed, placing a kiss on the top of her head and holding her at arm's length. 'We will not speak of that now. I'm a mess, Jane, and I smell of smoke.'

She smiled up at him. 'It doesn't matter. To me you have never looked more handsome.'

'Have you slept?' He brushed a wet strand of hair from her face.

'No, not really. I couldn't stop thinking about everything that has happened. I was also concerned about you.'

'You shouldn't worry about me.'

'How can I help it?'

Francis continued to hold her. 'I thank God you are safe.'

'And I thank God for you, Francis. I really don't know what I would have done these past weeks without you—and last night... It was my worst nightmare.'

Francis looked at the young woman in his arms, at the tears that swam in her wonderful green eyes, and in the midst of one of the most achingly poignant moments of his life, he felt a strange sense of resolve. As he crushed her to him, he thought that he had never loved her more.

The following days were harrowing for Jane as she tried to come to terms with the loss of her home. Captain Walton's body was taken to his family, while houses continued to be searched for fugitives. James

Stuart landed at Peterhead in the hope that his presence would boost the morale of the Jacobites, but they were already deserting in great numbers.

Jane's father was deeply saddened by what had happened. There were no words anyone could say that would lessen his distress. All he wanted now was to leave for France and for Jane to go with him. The day after the fire Bessie left to go and stay with her sister in Corbridge and Sam and his son along with labourers Francis sent to Beckwith Manor, were doing everything they could to bring some semblance of order out of the devastation the fire had caused. Helpful and sensitive to Jane's loss, Francis supervised the work himself.

Jane's primary concern was not so much for the loss of the house as for the few tenants they had left. It was her responsibility to ensure they were taken care of. So far they had succeeded in that end, but at a cost to the estate. Jane's father had decided that the stock must be sold—Francis had assured him he would take care of that side of things. The greatest joy for Jane was when Francis returned one day from Beckwith Manor accompanied by Spike, overjoyed and with tail-wagging excitement on being reunited with his beloved mistress.

Everyone was very kind to Jane, but at first they hadn't known how to treat her. The servants were loyal to the Randolph family and Jane found it hard to believe they didn't know about the fugitive in the tower. It was miraculous how quickly clothes were found for her to wear—Lady Randolph, despite the surplus of gowns discarded in trunks in her London house, had left a fair amount at Redmires, too. Francis assured Jane his mother would never wear them again.

Francis didn't mention marriage again. In his voice Jane heard a special quality which was always there when he spoke to her. There was, she thought, a communication between them, a feeling so exclusive and so special that it moved her deeply.

It was just before Christmas when Lady Randolph arrived, having taken it into her head to travel north at the worst time of year when the roads were precarious. Francis was delighted that she had made the journey. She had left Redmires shortly after the death of her husband and had not returned since then.

Jane watched mother and son embrace in the middle of the hall. She already knew that Lady Randolph was a handsome woman, but there was more than that—there was the easy, sure carriage, the confident, direct gaze. She looked as if she really belonged to Redmires and had the breeding of generations to prove it. When Francis released her he held her at arm's length, surveying her with pleasure and pride.

'I am surprised to see you. You are the last person I expected to come calling.'

She laughed. 'It is not just a call, Francis. I wanted to give the newlyweds a little space and time to themselves—so I thought I would come to Redmires. I hope you are pleased to see me.'

'Of course I am—although I didn't expect to see

you in Northumberland for some considerable time—knowing how you abhor the country and that you are much more comfortable in town.'

'It will be worth it to spend some time with my elder son.' She lanced behind him and her smile broadened when she saw Jane standing in the doorway to the drawing room. Before Jane could speak, Lady Randolph had crossed the floor and embraced her. 'I'm so pleased to see you, Jane. My visit will be all the more pleasurable with you for company.'

She released Jane, who, unbalanced by the effusive welcome, took a step back to recover her composure.

Lady Randolph opened her mouth to say something else, but, seeing Jane's grave expression, a look of concern creased her brow. Glancing from one to the other, she said, 'I trust everything is all right. Has something happened?'

Francis nodded. 'It has, but we will put you in the picture when you've refreshed yourself from the journey.'

Enjoying a warming drink of hot chocolate, Jane and Lady Randolph were seated in a window embrasure in the library, looking out over the bleak Northumbrian landscape. Francis had a business appointment in Newcastle and wasn't expected back until later. Lady Randolph had been deeply distressed on being told of the recent events that had befallen Jane when she had returned from London. Her reaction on being told that Edward Deighton was a fugitive and hiding in the tower was received with subdued silence. After a few tears were shed and a little time had passed for her to compose herself, she had disappeared to the tower to visit Edward.

'Francis tells me you intend to leave for France with your father, Jane—when it is safe to get him out of the country.'

'My home has gone. There is nothing to keep me here—and my father needs me. I will have to plan for our departure.'

Lady Randolph put down her cup. 'Let me worry about that, Jane.'

'No—I—I couldn't…'

'Jane, your father and I have talked long and hard about the past. We have made our own plans. I have decided to go with him when the time comes for him to leave. It is what we both want.'

'But he is weakened from his wound…'

'I doubt it's life threatening. Edward is a strong man, Jane. He has survived so far and he will continue to do so. Besides, you cannot believe that Francis will simply allow you to disappear off to France, do you?'

'Why would he not?' Jane said, refusing to acknowledge the sharp pain that stabbed through her heart.

Lady Randolph smiled when Jane flushed and averted her eyes. 'He loves you, Jane. It will break his heart if you go.'

Jane's eyes became misty and she lowered her head. 'I know.'

'I have never claimed to be a wise woman, but over

the years life has taught me some hard lessons—most of them at the hands of my husband,' Lady Randolph said in a soft, haunted voice. 'The most important lesson I learned when I met your father was that love is a rare and wonderful gift—a gift you should never take for granted. I think you love Francis, Jane. Am I right?'

'Yes—with my whole heart.'

'Then you must stay. When I left, in my fear—and shame—I closed my feelings for a good man who had offered me nothing but unwavering loyalty. Do not make my mistake, Jane. Do not deny the emotions that fill your heart. To do that will only lead to regret.'

Jane looked at her, seeing a woman who clearly still mourned her past. 'I think you are speaking of my father.'

A wistful smile touched Lady Randolph's lips. 'I do—and I am happy to say it is not too late for us.'

Jane looked at her questioningly. 'Not too late. Are you sure?'

'Yes, I am sure. I will be going to France with Edward. I hate to think of him as a fugitive in hiding—in that awful tower. It makes me shudder just thinking about it. Andrew and Miriam will live in the house in London. I will not be sorry to leave it behind. I was merely passing time there. I am looking forward to being with Edward—and Paris is such a wonderful place to be. It is what we both want. And where you are concerned, my dear,' she said, reaching out and giving Jane's hand a gentle squeeze, 'Francis loves you beyond measure. He wants nothing more than to have you as his wife.'

Jane lowered her eyes to hide the tears that welled in her eyes. She knew she should be pleased that Lady Randolph would be in France to take care of her father, but Lady Randolph's decision only served to drive home the fact that once he left England's shores, she might never see him again. Lady Randolph had given her father something a daughter could never match and that left an empty hollowness in her heart.

It was late when Francis returned home. Jane was alone seated in a chair by the hearth, her eyes closed in sleep. She stirred and, as if sensing his presence, opened her eyes and looked directly at him. A look of indescribable joy lit up her face. Their eyes met and locked for a moment, each conveying a message of love and hope to the other. Getting to her feet, she walked into his arms.

'You're late tonight, Francis. You missed dinner.'

'And I've missed you. I'll get something to eat later,' he said, burying his face in her tumbling, sweet-scented hair and feeling a deep surge of compassion for the hurt she had suffered of late. 'Where's Mother?'

'Visiting my father at the tower. They spend most of their time together.'

Raising her head, she gazed at him. His eyes were disarmingly tender as they gazed into hers, which made her heart beat wildly and a soft glow spread over her features. His fingers gently brushed away her hair from her cheeks and, bending his head, he began to cover her face with feather-light kisses.

'Has she told you that when he leaves for The Hague and France, she's going with him?'

'Not in so many words, but I suspected she would.'

'Why did you not tell me?'

'I told you. I didn't know for certain. Do you mind?'

'What? That she's going with him? No, of course not. If it's what they want to do, then I wish them all the joy in the world. My only concern is that Father can escape those who are searching for him.'

'You do realise what this means for us, Jane?'

'Tell me.'

'It means that you don't have to go. Instead you can stay here and marry me. I have approached your father earlier for his permission for us to wed.'

'And?'

'He gave his consent—in fact, he was delighted. It's what I want—for you to be my wife.'

To be told this moved her profoundly. Jane savoured the exquisite happiness, the only thing she was aware of was Francis holding her, gently stroking her hair and the comforting, masculine smell of him.

He placed his lips softly against her head, his arms tightening around her. 'What is between us is too strong to deny, Jane. Can you tell me you don't feel what I feel? That you don't tremble when I hold you and kiss you—that you don't want what I want?'

She tilted her head and looked at him, drowning in his dark-eyed stare. 'That is exactly how I feel, Francis. I never wanted to leave you,' she murmured, raising her lips and placing them tenderly on the warm flesh of his neck. 'I want to be your wife more than anything else.

Lady Randolph was positively delighted when they told her they were to be married, yet she was not surprised. 'Then do it before we leave for France. Edward will be happy for you. It will make his leaving easier, knowing you are being taken care of.'

It was impossible to keep the forthcoming wedding secret. It was the most interesting thing that had happened in Northumberland society for a long time. Francis's friends and neighbours came to call. They were all gracious and polite, but their faces told Jane they were anxious to know every small detail of the fire that had destroyed Beckwith Manor. They could barely conceal their curiosity and probed as deeply as politeness allowed into how Jane's marriage to the most eligible bachelor in Northumberland had come about. She could almost feel them wondering why Lord Randolph had chosen to marry a penniless neighbour, whose father was a man being sought for crimes against King George, when a far more advantageous match could have been arranged to one of the county's elite young ladies. The talk of Beckwith Manor, her father's support of James Stuart and the Jacobite cause hurt her. Even to think of his plight hurt her deeply. So the eagerly gossiping callers got little enough information on either subject.

* * *

Jane found it hard to believe the path her life was taking as the full realisation of what she was about to do set in—she would be married to Francis in such a short time and Redmires was to be her home. Just the thought of being his wife warmed her heart, but the sadness that engulfed her whenever she thought of Beckwith Manor was all consuming. There were hard decisions to make. It would not be rebuilt—what was the point when there was no one to live in it and would more than likely have been confiscated anyway because of her father's treasonable actions. The land Francis had promised he would take on—buy it, if necessary, and work it with that at Redmires.

In a gown of pale cream satin, her hair brushed to a gleaming mass, Jane and Francis were married quietly in Corbridge. It was a small wedding party with an air of sadness. Jane would have given anything to have her father and Miriam present, but it was not to be. She had been adamant that their marriage would not be torn asunder by religious differences. Like Miriam before her, she adhered to the law of the established Church of England.

After making their vows, Francis, his tall frame resplendent in claret velvet, looked down at his glorious, lovely bride with gentle pride. 'You are beautiful,' he murmured, for her ears alone. Her happiness showed in the glow of her hair, and in the clear depths of her green eyes. Taking her hand in his strong, assuring grasp, he led her out of the church to the waiting carriage.

At Redmires, she stood beside Francis to receive the handful of guests who had been invited—mainly Francis's friends and a few business associates. Jane was more than happy to welcome her Aunt Emily. She was shocked when told of the recent events involving her father and the fire at Beckwith Manor, but she was so pleased that Jane was to wed the illustrious Lord Randolph. When she enquired about her father, Jane felt it prudent to keep his whereabouts a secret. Noting Jane's quiet and nervousness, Francis took her hand and drew her aside.

'Is something wrong, Jane?' he asked gently. 'You seem nervous. There's no need to be.'

Jane gazed at the tall, daunting man who would do all manner of things to her later and gave him a quivering smile. 'You are very perceptive, Francis, and since you ask, yes, I am nervous.' She stared at him, a soft pink flush mantling her cheeks. 'It stems from what I know will come later,' she confessed quietly, yet she trembled from excitement, impatience and fear before this virile husband of hers as she wondered how he would react when she made her disclosure. 'I cannot for the life of me understand why I should feel this way about something I've done before—and for which I am carrying your child.'

Francis stared down at her, taking a moment for what she had said to sink in. Then, his heart ecstatic in its joy, with a groan he pulled her against his chest with stunning force, crushing her against him. 'My wonderful, darling wife, thank you,' he whispered hoarsely, burying his face in her fragrant hair. His exultation was boundless as she moulded her body to the rigid contours of his. After a moment he held her at arm's length and gazed down into her melting green eyes, seeing they were wet with tears, but a smile was trembling on her rosy lips.

'You are certain?'

Her mouth curved in a sublime smile while her eyes grew dark. 'I am as certain as I can be at this time. I can see the prospect of being a father pleases you.'

'Pleases me? That is an understatement. I've no experience in dealing with babies, but it fills me with happiness—and gratitude, my love. I never imagined that when you gave yourself to me it would be so wonderful and now you are to present me with a child, which is a rare gift indeed.' Placing a kiss on her lips, he touched her cheek with his finger and smiled. 'We must return to our guests—but let this be our secret for now, Jane. We will tell our parents when the time is right.'

Much later, in the cosy intimacy of Jane's canopied bed, with senses soaring, they reacquainted themselves with each other's bodies.

'You are so beautiful,' Francis murmured, the words like a long, drawn-out sigh. For a moment he hesitated, wanting to give her time, but when she looked at him, her pupils dark and full of passion, her lips hungry for his kisses, it was more than any man could resist. She was so heartbreakingly lovely, so young, so eager, so innocent, the most desirable woman he had ever seen. He seemed to have longed for her, needed her, for ever. His hand tenderly caressed the rosy bloom of her skin, his fingers brushing her breasts, small and round and soft. She was like some wild young creature of the forest, a fawn, a creature of sunshine and shadows. She stretched like a kitten beside him and, with her eyes open, placed her hands on either side of his face and drew it down to hers.

And so they loved. There was no holding back, no hesitation, no thought of past or future. Nothing else mattered, only the two of them, for they were committed to each other as only lovers and man and wife could be. The first act of their lovemaking was as frenzied and wild as a starry sky filled with a desperate need, pulsating waves of pleasure and passion as Jane arched to meet her lover's body.

The second act, with the pleasure of that first time still warm within them, was more lingering, when delay is divine sweet torment that must end soon or sanity would flee. It was shared pleasure, leisurely, exquisite sensations, that unhurried exploration of each other, of taste, of touch, of fingertips and caresses, which is only possible when that first hunger is satisfied, and the joy that comes with fulfilment. There was an assuaging of the longing that the days since their first coming together in York had brought.

Jane felt renewed, loved and cherished. From the day she had ridden to Redmires to confront him she had travelled a long way and she felt older and wiser and infinitely happier.

In the pale, watery light of dawn, emerging from heavy slumber, Jane stretched in the huge bed. Nestling close to the man beside her, feeling his warm, firm flesh next to hers, she felt a deep contentment and languorous peace. She had spent the most erotic night of her life as prey of this creature of the darkness—her husband—who had taken her with unbelievable fervour, having his will with her and rousing her to heights she could not have imagined, desire and passion exploding within her with a force that tore a cry from her throat.

Coming awake, Francis kissed her shining head and placed his arm about her, his fingers stroking the smooth velvet flesh and following the curve of her waist and hip. Half opening her eyes, Jane tilted her head and smiled up at him—the happy smile of a sated wife in love with her husband.

'You look disgustingly wide awake, my love,' she murmured sleepily, wriggling against him until she was in a position to place a soft kiss on the mat of dark curls covering his broad chest.

'I am. I have been for a while. What are you thinking?'

'Oh—how happy you have made me.' Her breath trembled. 'I've never felt like this before. In fact, I never knew I could feel this—this wonderful wanting.' Rolling on to her stomach and resting on her elbows so she had a better look at his face, she said, 'How do you feel, Francis? Tell me.'

Slowly Francis ran his finger down her arm, admiring the smooth lines of her slender body. 'I was thinking how very lucky I am—and how lovely you are. You remind me of a dancer—or a fawn—elusive, wary. After all these weeks, with any other woman I would have known virtually everything there is to know about her—her past, her likes and dislikes. With you it is not like that. You are different—enchanting, fascinating. You fit into no category that I can think of. In fact, I know very little about you.'

Snuggling closer to him, she laughed softly. 'Then think how pleasurable it will be finding out,' she whispered, beginning to place tantalising little kisses on his abdomen, her eyes sending him a message that he easily read.'

It was a subdued Jane who began preparing for her father's departure. With the utmost secrecy Francis had arranged passage on a boat that was leaving for the Hague from South Blythe, south of Newcastle, on the first day of the New Year. The Master was a Catholic—a quiet one, who could be trusted.

Francis knew how difficult it would be for Jane to say goodbye to her father. He watched in silence as she slipped on her warm woollen cloak. His heart clenched with a familiar ache at the sight of the morning light glinting off her fair curls and brushing her face with a golden glow.

He could not believe that she was his wife, this beautiful young woman who had stormed into his life and claimed his heart and soul and was to bear his child. Just being near her was enough to lighten his mood and make his day brighter.

They left Redmires after an early breakfast in a spacious conveyance. The air was crisp and thankfully fine. Relieved to be heading for the coast at last, a rather apprehensive Edward sat beside Lady Randolph huddled in a large cloak, his hat pulled well down over his face. Jane settled herself beside Francis. The journey was fraught with tension lest they be stopped and searched. Fortunately Francis's coach was familiar so those who knew him were unlikely to apprehend them. They passed a small troop of soldiers, but thankfully they took little notice of them and the journey passed without incident.

The small town of South Blythe was quiet when they arrived. As they made their way to the harbour, it was clear from the activity around the vessel they would be sailing on they would not be long setting sail for The Hague. Climbing out of the coach, while the driver unfastened the baggage and carried it aboard, they stood and watched in silence. Jane was dreading the moment of parting from her father. When would she see him again? she wondered. If she ever would. The Master told them the tide was on the turn and they would be sailing within the next half-hour.

Edward turned to Francis. 'Thank you,' he said. 'I am much obliged to you for your aid and discretion. I know I can never openly return to England.

Memories are long and my part in the rising will not be forgotten. The debt I owe to you can never be repaid,' he said with genuine feeling.

'I've done what I felt was right—and for Jane,' Francis said, putting his arm about her shoulders and drawing her close. 'It has taken courage to do what you have done and to keep faith in the man you are proud to call King.'

'This is not the end. The fight will go on.' Edward looked at his daughter. 'I am sorry, Jane, but it has to be like this. I have lived for sixty years and my greatest sorrow is that, in following my beliefs, it has cut me off from you and Miriam for so long. I speak in all honesty when I say that if I could, I would make amends for my stupidity and neglect.'

Looking into his faded eyes, Jane saw that he spoke the truth. She kissed him and watched him go. There was nothing more to be said.

Lady Randolph embraced her, before holding her at arm's length and looking into her eyes. 'Don't worry about your father, Jane. I promise you I will take care of him.'

'I know you will,' she whispered.

'For us to be together at this time is what we both want. We have been given a second chance of happiness and I intend for us to make the most of it. When we reach The Hague I will write—and I will write often when we reach France and who knows, you may be able to persuade Francis to visit us.' She smiled and her eyes twinkled. 'We will look forward to being introduced to our grandchild.'

Jane nodded and lowered her eyes, her throat too clogged with tears to speak.

On the return journey to Redmires, they stopped in Corbridge to see Bessie, who had taken up residence with her sister and her husband. The fire had aged Bessie and she had no desire to return to work, even though Jane told her there would always be room for her at Redmires if she changed her mind.

Leaving Corbridge behind, Jane asked to be taken by Beckwith Manor. It was the first time she had been there since the night of the fire. She stood and looked at what was left of her home. Very little had escaped the flames. An eerie, haunting silence reigned among the ruins. Blackened walls and skeletal chimneys reached up to the sky. It was as though something that had once been beautiful had been through the throes of death. It was hard to believe the devastation she now saw was once her home, the place where she had been born and loved. It struck deep into her heart as she remembered that terrible night, when she had left in bare feet with nothing but her nightgown.

She turned away. This was a time to forget the old and seek out the better moments of whatever life had to give. She walked into Francis's arms and her own arms tightened around him, never wanting to let him go. She adored this man, discarding all else. He eclipsed everything that had gone before. The pain of her past and her parting from Miriam and her father he had eradicated, restoring her to the serene contentment she had known for a short time in London.

She had reached a happiness she had never dreamed possible and she was content to leave the unfolding of their future—their lives together—to fate.

Tilting her face to his, he looked searchingly into her eyes, wiping away a tear with his thumb. 'You are weeping. Are you all right, Jane?'

'Happiness makes me weep—and the conviction that everything is going to be perfect for us now the ghosts of the past have been laid to rest.'

Leaning down, Francis placed his lips on hers. 'You are right,' he murmured. 'It is time to forget the past and for us to start savouring the joys of the future.'

'As for the house,' Jane said, looking back at the ruin that had been her home, 'it cannot be rebuilt. It must all be swept away.'

Francis nodded slowly. 'I know you will have given the matter serious thought and that the decision to have it removed has not been taken lightly.'

'I would be grateful if you would take care of the legalities. You know all about these things. All I want is you—to live with you at Redmires.'

'You will not regret it, Jane.'

'I know. I want nothing that can be bought or sold or bartered. The only thing I want cannot be bought. It is you, Francis. Have I told you today that I love you?'

'You have, my love, but I never tire of hearing it. You are my wife and I will love you until my last breath. Always remember it.'

Joy and happiness welled inside Jane, filling her

because this wonderful, vital man belonged to her. His arms encircled her waist and she responded by kissing his lips. She breathed in the warm, masculine smell of him, tasted the warmth of his mouth as it came down on hers. All the love that had been accumulating through the lonely years of her childhood was in that kiss. Francis felt it in her soft lips. With unselfish ardour she offered herself to him and Francis took what she offered hungrily, feeling it flowing through his veins and mingling with his blood until the joy of it was shattering.

During the late summer months, their son, Charles Edward Randolph, was born. Francis leaned over his wife, feeling relief wash over him that it was over at last. Knowing how hazardous childbirth could be, he had lived the horrors of the things that could go wrong.

Jane sat propped up against the pillow, sleepily cradling their son to her chest. Raising him up, she placed the babe in his arms. 'Meet your son, Francis. He's perfect—just as you predicted.'

Taking his son in his arms, Francis kissed the top of his head and settled himself beside his wife. Jane looked on, smiling softly as he looked proudly down into the tiny, wrinkled face.'

'Are you pleased, Francis?'

His eyes glittered with unsuppressed pride and joy, accompanied by a fierce wave of love. Francis smoothed the fair curls off her cheek stained with a pink blush. His lips quirked in a half-smile. 'Pleased is an understatement. He is beautiful—just like his mother,' he said, his voice raw from the emotion of the past hours of waiting for their child to be born.

'He has his father's dark hair,' Jane murmured, looking up into his face, and in her eyes, shining and clear and uncomplicated by the past, was her love for him.

Francis lowered his head so their foreheads touched and, as though bowed in prayer, they gazed at their son, giving thanks for the gift of their love.

* * * * *